A Bridge Across the Arno

Also by Alec Gunn

The World Belongs To Charlie
The Silver Mercedes
The End of Summer Time

A Bridge Across the Arno

Alec Gunn

The Book Guild Ltd.
Sussex, England

This book is a work of fiction. The characters and situations in this story are imaginary. No resemblance is intended between these characters and any real persons, either living or dead.

The Book Guild Ltd.
Temple House
25 High Street
Lewes, Sussex.

First published 1991

Set in Baskerville
Typesetting by Hawks Phototypesetters Ltd.,
Copthorne, West Sussex.

Printed in Great Britain by
Antony Rowe Ltd.,
Chippenham, Wiltshire.

British Library Cataloguing In Publication Data
Gunn, Alec
A bridge across the Arno
I. Title
823.914 [F]

ISBN 0 86332 554 8

For the officers and men of the Surrey and Sussex Yeomanry Queen Mary's Regiment past and present and to the many Italians who risked their lives and those of their families to protect the Allied fugitives of war.

Authors Note

This is a work of fiction. No regiment or character in this book exists or has existed. The general description of the Italian campaign is accurate enough and I have drawn on my own experience here, and, I am in debt to Lt. Col. T. B. Davis M.C. R.A., whose history of the Surrey and Sussex Yeomanry refreshed my memory. Being a novel, however, the minutiae of each individual battle are not necessarily factual.

In the second half of the book, from Chapter VII onwards, all is pure invention. There was indeed an N. Section, but the story here has no reality outside my imagination. I have used real place names, because although the events did not happen, I like to think they could have done.

To - Lt. Colonel A.J.
Gilbert - Nash. D.S.O. M.C. R.A.
O.C. 321 Field Regiment R.A.
The Home Counties Yeomanry.
Italy.

Eagle House,
Chalkley School,
Chalkley, Dorset

16/12/43

My dear Alex,

Thank you very much for your letter, which I was proud to receive. In addition to your command, I must now congratulate you on your D.S.O., splendid! I looked up the records and note you left in 1930, so you must be one of the youngest Colonels in the Army, it demonstrates the calibre of Regular Army training. I always point this out to boys in the house, fortunately we continue to have a solid Army Class contingent from our chaps.

I am glad to hear that Sholto now commands one of your batteries, he ran the Corps here as you know but that must have been after you left. We did not always see eye-to-eye when he was a master here, but he can be a loyal friend, I must say that, and I am sure a pillar of strength in a tight corner.

I was very interested to hear that J. Crabbe is coming to you and that you are posting him to Sholto's battery. You say that S remarked: nice lad, but could never learn to tie his puttees', and that was all. So you want me to elaborate.

He ran away you know, at the beginning of his second year: just took off alone on his bike one Sunday afternoon with ten bob in his pocket to get home to London. He made it too, after climbing down a cliff in Poacher's Wood and chucking his bike into the river, to escape from two house prefects who ran across him on the road. Then he got a lift in a car driven by a drunken pervert who tried to molest him. However he was lucky and managed to reach the Junction in time to catch a train to London. Here he mingled with a lot of soldiers and by hiding in a lavatory reached London without a ticket. All very reprehensible of course, but the boy showed a great deal of initiative; useful

I imagine in a war.

Lewis was headmaster then, never liked the fellow, but that is past history for, as you know, he left in '39. First he wanted to sack the boy, then relented and proposed to flog him and have him back in another house; Soper's if you please, you can imagine how I felt! Soper is still here, he never got the headship at Clifton, a slimy individual but not so cocky these days.

Well, Alex, young Crabbe's escapade really put the cat amongst the pigeons! Mike came down, the elder brother, a damn good sort, a Surgeon Lieutenant in the Navy now, he arrived with the mother in tow and we had a hell of a battle with Lewis. Sholto was a great help, incidentally. To cut a long story short, the father who was a vicar in Bayswater, had a stroke in his study right in front of his son, and died the next day. Lewis could hardly flog the boy now, so he collapsed, thank God! I had young Crabbe back for a week at the end of the Christmas holidays 1938/39, to make up for lost time, and that was that!

There were extenuating circumstances. Crabbe had been subjected to some very nasty bullying. I blame myself of course but you know how difficult it is, the schoolboy code of not sneaking. I fell on the culprits like a load of bricks, and stamped it out for good.

Crabbe settled down in the house. A strange boy, no good at rugger, cricket or gym, but bright enough. The chaps came to respect him, to tell the truth he was treated rather like a hero on his return. I never managed to understand him, but he is a good-natured boy, and I think that counts in the long run. He did rather well as an officer cadet at Catterick, the second-in-command of the unit was an old Chalkleyan, I met him at the Old Boys' Dinner, and he told me that the boy was officer material. I was pleased naturally, but rather surprised. Then I had a letter from Crabbe after he passed out. He told me that the only reason that he got his commission was that he was very good in some stage show that the unit put on, he even enclosed a photograph. I suppose he was joking, but as I said he is a strange boy.

Well, Alex, you asked for my opinion, and I had to be honest. I hope I have not been unfair to the boy.

My warmest wishes, I wish I was out there with you all, but the powers that be have decided that I am more use where I am. I can only do my best to train our chaps to face the challenges of the future.

Yours very sincerely,
Guy.

Guy de Courcy Buller
Eagle House.

PART I

I

There was little wind so the rain was almost vertical, causing rivulets of water to cascade down the side of the tent. John Crabbe looked at his two companions. Taffy, a burly Welshman, had been in the same intake as John, they had arrived together from Taranto, both raw new Second Lieutenants. Nigel had two pips, and was the older. Taffy was lying on his bed cutting his toe nails, while Nigel was reading a novel. John wanted to break the silence but he was too shy, so he closed his eyes and pretended to be asleep. They had only come together an hour previously and exchanged perfunctory introductions, the general gloom seemed to inhibit conversation. The smell of Taffy's feet was overpowering, so John moved on to his side to escape from it and noticed that water was coming through the bottom of the tent. He jumped up. 'I say, we're getting flooded.'

'So?' Nigel looked over the top of his book.

'Water is coming in, shouldn't we try and stop it?'

'No point. It comes up from the ground, that's why they give us duckboards to sleep on. If this rain continues you will have a very wet bottom by the morning. Taffy and I are on higher ground. Bad luck.'

'What a bloody country.' Taffy stopped cutting his nails. 'Come to Sunny Italy, boyo, "See Naples and Die". We might do that you know, only you can't see Naples because of this fucking rain!'

'It's only ten miles up the road, if you want to walk there,' Nigel said.

Taffy started to pull on his socks. 'A transit camp under Vesuvius, sounds bloody marvellous, doesn't it? Wait till I

tell my mum and dad what it's really like.'
'It rains in Wales, you know.'
'Yes, but you expect it there don't you? This is meant to be a bloody holiday resort!'
'How far are the Germans?' John asked suddenly.
'Forty miles to the North at the Garigliano river,' Nigel replied.
'So we are out of range?'
'Not from the bombs, boy,' Taffy said, 'When they hear that John Crabbe and Taffy Williams have landed they'll come and bomb us all to Hades!'
'In this weather?' Nigel asked. 'At any rate we haven't seen much of the Luftwaffe since Salerno.'
'You were there?' Taffy asked.
'Yes.'
'How come you're here then?'
'I collected a piece of Kraut shell on the Volturno river crossing.'
'Where?'
'In my bum, since you ask.'
'No, where is the Volturno?'
'Twenty miles up the coast from Naples, about half way to the present line.'
'Are you going to tell us all about it?'
'No.'
'Why not?'
'Because you two young things will discover the facts of life soon enough. Why spoil your illusions now?'
Taffy stood up. 'You are a mean old bastard, Nigel, do you know that?'
'Yes.'
'Well, I think I can change your mind. I have a bottle of Scotch which I'm prepared to open, if you will give young John and me the benefit of your experience. It's some time before we can get supper in the mess tent, so we can get quietly sozzled while we are waiting.'
'O.K., on one condition.'
'What's that?'
'That you change your bloody socks, and go to the other side of the tent to do it.'
'Done.'

Taffy changed his socks slowly, wriggling his toes in Nigel's direction, and then opened the bottle. They passed it round, John took a sip, while the other two swallowed large gulps. A third of the bottle had disappeared before Nigel lit a cigarette and said quietly, 'All right, I'll keep to my side of the bargain, what do you want to know?'

'Can you give us the whole story from Salerno onwards? It should be jolly interesting.' John said. The Scotch was beginning to work and he felt less shy.

'I don't know about jolly interesting. It was jolly bloody. We were jolly nearly pushed back into the sea at Salerno. Later it was jolly wet and jolly muddy.'

'Come on, Nigel,' Taffy said. 'Stop taking the piss out of young John here, he and I are hanging on your words, boyo, you should be flattered.'

'O.K.' He took another swig at the bottle, 'if you want a history lesson, here goes. We'll start at the beginning. A bloke I met in hospital at Taranto was in the Reggio di Calabria landing with the 8th Army. All the local Ities clapped as our tanks rumbled through the streets; when they stopped in a traffic jam, a group of youths who had been chanting "Inglesi buono, Tedéschi non buono," they bleat this all the time as you will discover, came up and shouted "Americano a Napoli," that was several days before the Salerno landings, so our security was all to cock.'

'So they knew you were coming?'

'Not 'alf. The Krauts threw everything at us. We managed to get a bridgehead, however, it is good tank country, flat though riddled with streams and rivers. The trouble was that we were not getting stuff ashore fast enough, so there were great gaps in our line and the enemy kept popping through, you never knew where the bastards were. We swanned around all over the bloody shop with the Krauts counter-attacking all the time. Things got pretty desperate, there were strong rumours that we were going to re-embark and get the hell out of it. Then the enemy packed it in and buggered off. Don't ask me why! The RAF and the Navy had been pounding the sods for several days and I think they'd had enough. We were damn lucky.'

'Were they mostly Americans?' John asked.

'General Mark Clark was in command of a combined

force. By all accounts he is an Anglophobe, which didn't help. Apparently he hates our guts, and that wasn't helped by a pretty little British mutiny.'

'No!' Taffy sat up.

'Oh yes, old son. About seven hundred infantry reinforcements sat down on the beach with all the shit flying around and refused to budge. I had an eye-witness account from an officer who was there. The Top Brass didn't know what the hell to do, so they got the Corps Commander McCreery himself down there to talk to them. They gave him a rough ride, too, but he's a tough cookie and eventually shouted them down. He told them that the situation was desperate, that many of the regiments were down to half or three quarters of their strength, and did they really want to betray their comrades when they were in mortal danger? He then promised that if they joined the units, the incident would be overlooked. He is a good bloke, McCreery, and after he'd explained the situation most of them responded.'

'Not all?' John asked.

'No. Nearly two hundred refused to budge, so they were disarmed and sent back to Africa for Court Martial.'

'What will happen to them?'

'God knows. They don't shoot people in this war, so I imagine long terms in the glasshouse.'

John felt a sense of shock. It was so different from what he had expected. It was a nerve-wracking experience arriving in a theatre of war for the first time, but he had tried to buoy himself up with the thought that he was about to join a splendid British Army on the way to beating the Nazis.

'I don't understand,' he muttered, 'all those men scared to go into battle.'

'Of course they were scared,' Nigel snapped at him, 'we are all scared all the bloody time. I ride about in a tank, a tin box that can be set alight any moment, so we're all roasted alive inside.'

'But you didn't mutiny, did you boy?' Taffy said, 'So what went wrong then?'

'They did not down tools because they were scared,' Nigel said patiently, 'but because they were not being sent back to their own units. You'll learn this soon enough. Your regiment is your family, you may not like it, but it's all you've got to hold onto in this bloody war. Many of those chaps were veterans of the 8th Army from the desert, Jocks who expected to be returned to Highland regiments, not parcelled off to fight with complete strangers.'

'Young John and I are joining the 8th Army as far as we know,' Taffy said.

'Up on the Adriatic side. You're lucky. Monty knows what he is doing, and at least you won't be buggered about by an English-hating Yank. Oh my God, I'd forgotten. There's a strong rumour that Monty is leaving, going to England to prepare for the second front, so we'll become more of a side show than ever. Tough luck!'

'Nigel,' John asked, 'In view of what you say, might you be posted to a different regiment?'

'No, old son, I won't. I shall bugger off in the morning and cadge a lift to the Garigliano, I'll find my unit easily enough.'

'Surely that's not allowed, is it?' John asked, 'I mean to just walk out of a transit camp?'

'No, young John, of course it isn't allowed. The adjutant here will be hopping mad, they like everything to be neat and tidy, and chaps just buggering off plays havoc with their book-keeping. Stupid sods.'

'The "Scarlet Majors at the Base" will have their noses put out of joint,' John said.

'Who?' Taffy enquired.

'Sassoon, Siegfried Sassoon, a First World War poet. John here is at pains to let us know that he is educated, not like you, you wild Welshman.'

John felt snubbed, and was aware that he was blushing. He had not meant to show off, it was just that the older man seemed so experienced and worldly wise, and John wanted to get on the same wavelength. He was very keen on the war poets and would have liked to discuss them, but Nigel had just put him down. It was very like the first day at school all over again.

Taffy came to the rescue. 'There's no need to talk like that,' he said hotly. 'Nor to be so bloody supercilious. You see I know some long words too. Not bad for an ignorant Welshman! And I will remind you,' he added, 'that it is my bottle of Scotch that you've just been pouring down your throat!'

'All right,' Nigel said with a rather watery smile. 'I will earn my whisky and give you both a very good piece of advice. You'll know your postings in the morning, so if you have any sense you'll get out of this hole with me, and hitch a lift to your regiments. May I remind you that it is Christmas Eve tomorrow. Surely you don't want to spend the festive season in this dump?'

'Oh I'm not sure about that,' Taffy said doubtfully, 'we are very new, you see. It's all right for you to break the rules, you're an old soldier and you know the form, but I think John and I, being rookies you see, should just obey King's Regulations and all that. I see that you want to be sure to get back to your own unit, but we haven't even got regiments yet have we?'

'You will have tomorrow,' Nigel said. 'Don't be so chicken, Taffy. I'll tell you one thing, free, gratis and for nothing. You'll create a bloody good impression arriving at your unit in the line within forty-eight hours of coming to this camp, instead of sitting on your arses here for two or three weeks and then coming up with the rations. I'm giving you bloody good advice, but it's up to you.'

'Well, we'll sleep on it, shall we, Nigel boy? And see what the weather is like?'

'I'll go anyway.' Nigel pulled open the tent flap. 'It has stopped raining, you can actually see the stars. A good omen, perhaps.'

'Well, that means we can go and eat without getting soaked. I think it would be a good thing for us to have a bit of blotting paper. We can finish the bottle after supper.'

☆ ☆ ☆

John had decided to stay put. He wasn't looking for any adventures and was content to let things take their course. After breakfast he discovered that he and Taffy had been posted to the same regiment, the Home Counties Yeomanry.

Taffy stood outside the tent, taking deep breaths. 'It is a lovely day boyos,' he said, 'Italy looks quite different doesn't it, when the sun shines? A blue sea and Vesuvius over there, just like a picture postcard.'

'Well? Are you coming with me, or not?' Nigel asked. 'It's nine o'clock already and we ought not to hang about.'

'I'm game Nigel,' said Taffy. 'I rather fancy a trip and a little bit of excitement, it is a dreary old place this, isn't it?'

'Well come in and have a look at the map.' Nigel spread it out on his bed. 'It's quite easy for me. The British 5th Army is dug in from Cassino here to the mouth of the Garigliano river. I will go to the Town Major's office in Naples, find out where my regiment is, and get a lift. There's plenty of transport going up all the time.'

'But what happens if the Town Major takes a poor view of you just walking out of the camp here?' Taffy asked.

'He won't. They always turn a blind eye, providing you are going in the right direction. That's what makes the camp authorities so mad.'

'What if they stop us leaving?'

'Ah, that can be a problem. The main thing is to act normally. We pack up, walk out of the tent, and make our way to the exit and hand in our blankets.'

'Our blankets?'

'Oh yes. We signed for them on arrival, so we must hand them in. Otherwise you could be accused of stealing Army property. Oh, I'm quite serious. Everything has to be done according to the book. Then we make our way towards the transport pool, but we never get there, instead we turn left on to the main road and hitch a lift. It's just a question of technique. Any regiment worth its salt teaches you this when you join. Your C.O. will be very impressed when you two arrive, he'll think you worked it out all by yourselves.'

'So you think we'll get out all right?'

'With any luck. It is easier for an officer, because you can bark at people. At any rate, there is so much coming and going, we should be O.K.'

'Do we come to Naples with you?'

'No. The 8th Army is the other side of Italy, we'll have to work out a different plan for you.' He looked at the map. 'I believe the 8th Army is somewhere around the Sangro or Moro river up here, so your best bet is to fly to Foggia airport and then hitch up the Adriatic coast. With any luck you could make Termoli by tonight, the Town Major there will help.'

'Where do we fly from?' Taffy began to sound less enthusiastic.

'Naples Airport. It's all right, I'll look after you. I'll see you on a plane to Foggia, then it's up to you. But we had better get cracking right away.'

John hadn't said a word. But now the situation was getting out of hand, the other two were calmly planning the whole thing as though he wasn't there. 'Hang on a minute,' he said, 'nobody asked me my opinion.'

'Sorry, John boy,' Taffy replied. 'We got rather carried away, but we didn't mean to leave you out. Aren't you very happy about the plan, then?'

'No I'm not. It's easy for Nigel, he hasn't far to go. He said so himself. But we have to travel right across Italy, and there are so many imponderables.'

'That means uncertainties, Taffy, young John is a very erudite young man.' Nigel said.

'Oh shut up, Nigel.' John spoke with surprising force. 'Listen Taffy, there is no guarantee we can get a plane to Foggia in the first place, and if we don't, it will be bloody difficult to get back into the camp without showing proper travel documents, so we will be in the doghouse, having broken King's Regulations before we've been in this country for two days.'

'I've told you,' Nigel said wearily, 'I'll stay at the airport until you get on a plane.'

'Thank you, Nigel, but you know as well as I do that the RAF does not have to take us.'

'Nothing venture, nothing win, John,' Taffy remarked.

'With due respect, Taffy, you are being childish.' John was angry, and getting into his stride. 'All right! Assume we get to Foggia, how far is that from the 8th Army line?'

Nigel looked at the map. 'About a hundred miles,' he said.

'A hundred miles, God almighty!'

'Don't panic, my boy. There will be a continuous stream of traffic from Foggia, you'll have no difficulty at all. One of the advantages of being an officer is that you can just stop a truck and demand a lift.'

'Look John,' Taffy said. 'Nigel is being kind, you know,

he doesn't have to help us.'

'Doesn't he? Nigel you stand a far better chance of getting out of here unnoticed if there are three of us, don't you? A single officer would arouse suspicion at the gate, isn't that so?'

'Since you ask, yes.'

'I thought so.'

Nigel smiled at him. 'So our little mouse has brains, he can work things out for himself. No, I am not insulting you, that was intended as a compliment.'

'So you just want to use us.'

'True. But there is something in it for you both. I'm right about the good impression you will make with your regiment if you turn up on Christmas Day.'

'There is another point.' John said.

'Go ahead.'

'Surely most of the supplies will come by sea from Taranto or Termoli; what chance is there that we will get a lift from the airport at Foggia? It looks to me rather off the beaten track.'

'He has got a point, you know, Nigel.' Taffy had become rather impressed by John's careful questioning. 'We don't want to get stuck at the airport, do we, miles from anywhere?'

'Oh for God's sake, it's the same bloody war!' Nigel said impatiently. 'Once you are over on the far side you'll be home and dry.'

'So you say,' John replied doubtfully.

'John has a point, Nigel,' Taffy said again.

'All right,' Nigel snapped at them. 'I'm not going to waste any more time arguing with babes who haven't got their knees brown yet. I'll go on my own.'

He started to pack quickly and methodically while the other two remained silent. John felt guilty that he had been the one to throw a spanner in the works, but he was relieved all the same. He knew Nigel thought he was a drip, but what did it matter? They would probably never meet again and at least he had persuaded Taffy to see sense.

Nigel had finished packing before Taffy broke the silence.

'I've been thinking,' he said slowly.

'Bully for you,' Nigel replied, picking up his bag, 'but it's a bit late for that, I'm off.'

'Just a minute, boy. I have a proposition, you see.'

'No. I don't want to listen to any more of your prattle, it's nearly ten o'clock. I must reach my unit by tonight. Cheerio!'

'But you will stand a better chance at the gate if we come with you, Nigel, won't you?' Taffy said slowly. 'You were not very honest about your motives, as John pointed out. I think it might pay you to hear my proposition.'

'Well for God's sake come out with it, it's getting bloody late.'

'Of course, boy, that's what I am trying to do. Just sit down, Nigel, and hear what I have to say.'

'Well?'

'The way I see it,' Taffy continued, 'is that it might be difficult to get back into the camp if we draw a blank at the airport and have to come sneaking back here. Now, if you can fix the sergeant at the entrance, then that would put a different complexion on things, wouldn't it? We both admire your powers of persuasion, don't we John?'

John said nothing, but he cursed Taffy inwardly, furious that he hadn't let the whole matter rest.

'I'll have a go,' Nigel replied. 'I can't promise anything, but it is worth a try.'

'And I'll come with you,' Taffy said.

'You mean you don't trust me, you Welsh bastard!'

'Let's just say that I think this should be a joint operation.' Taffy grinned at him.

After they had gone John began to sort out his kit. He hoped they would not succeed of course, but he packed all the same, on the basis that if you take an umbrella it doesn't rain. When he had finished he went outside. The sun was up by now and he felt the comforting warmth on his dank battle dress. Taffy was right. The view was fabulous, Naples to the north was shrouded in mist, bordered by a grey sea which changed to vermilion on the edge of the shadows as the rays of the sun played upon it, finally becoming a deep blue throughout the wide sweep of the bay. Then behind him was Vesuvius standing out with remarkable clarity. He could see the tiers of vineyards on the lower slopes, and although there was a cotton wool cloud on the right shoulder, the summit was clear. Out of it a thin wisp of smoke spiralled upwards as though from a giant cigar. He was lost for a moment in the beauty of it all.

'We've done it John my boy, we've done it.' Taffy's voice brought him back to reality.

'What happened?'

'Well, we argued the toss for a long time and then Nigel produced a bottle of gin. I know what you're going to say, John, why didn't the crafty old sod produce it last night? I thought it was a bit mean.'

'It came in useful though, didn't it?' Nigel said casually. 'Never play all your cards at the same time.'

'True, that's true.' Taffy grinned from ear to ear. 'The old Sergeant melted visibly at the prospect of a nice bit of English gin. We'll be all right until he comes off duty at 1600 hours, that will give us plenty of time.'

John felt an ache in the pit of his stomach and it must have showed on his face.

'I fancy John Crabbe is not very happy at our success,' Nigel said with a thin smile.

'No, I'm not.'

'Well you will look rather stupid if Taffy turns up at your regiment two or three weeks before you, won't you?'

'Come on, John,' Taffy cajoled him. 'We've covered our retreat, so to speak, it is a lovely day, let's have a go!'

'You don't leave me much option.'

'Oh yes I do. If you refuse to go I will stay with you, after all, we are mates aren't we?'

John realised he was beaten. It was moral blackmail, but he hadn't the will to argue any more.

'O.K.,' He said wearily, 'I'll go with you.'

'Good man!' Taffy slapped him on the back. 'Italy, here we come!'

☆ ☆ ☆

John and Taffy did catch a plane round about two o'clock. It hadn't been all plain sailing. The young pilot-officer on transport duty did not want to know. He was a thin young man with a wispy moustache which was clearly never going to grow into a full handlebar.

'Not without proper authorisation,' he said petulantly, 'Brown Jobs are becoming a pain in the neck, hanging around airports. At any rate the old man has clamped down on you lot cadging lifts, so I can't help you.'

'I'm not quite sure I heard you correctly,' Nigel said dangerously. 'What did you call us?'

'Well, Brown Jobs.' He sounded a little less self-confident.

'I see.' Nigel looked at him with contempt. 'Listen! We are Army officers, we do the actual fighting, and don't sit on our arses miles from the front in a cosy little haven.'

'It won't help you being offensive.' His cheeks became pink.

'It is you who are being offensive, sonny boy, and bloody offensive too. I notice you don't wear wings.'

'What's that to you? I have an important job here.'

'Well I suppose someone has to be the office boy, but I'm not having a bloody penguin talking to me like that.'

John thought Nigel was going much too far, and cherished the hope that they would be back in the camp in time for tea, but he had underestimated the other man's resolve.

'You have heard of the Eighth Army Commander's Order of the Day I take it?' Nigel persisted.

'No, not yet.' The pilot officer was clearly embarrassed.

'God almighty.' He paused. 'I don't expect you even know who the Army Commander is, do you?'

'Of course, Montgomery.'

'You are out of date, but then no one would bother to tell you anything, would they? Leese, General Oliver Leese, has issued an order that, owing to a big offensive just after Christmas, all Army officers are to return to their units by the quickest possible route, and that they should receive co-operation from all concerned. Now do you want me to go and see your C.O.?'

By this time the young man had visibly paled under Nigel's onslaught. Taffy joined in the fray. 'We could say that co-operation was rather lacking at Naples Airport in the person of the duty officer, in fact that he was being downright obstructive. It wouldn't look very good for you, would it, in view of the Eighth Army Commander's order?'

'Is there a plane leaving for Foggia or not?' Nigel

demanded.

'As a matter of fact there is,' the pilot-officer said sulkily.

'Where is it?'

'On the tarmac, a DC6 carrying blood plasma. But I must check with the Squadron-Leader.'

'You do that, old son,' Nigel said, 'in the meantime we're off, we don't want to miss it, do we?'

As they ran out of the office John said, 'You were bluffing. There's no such order from the General, is there?'

'Of course not. But he didn't know that, the stupid twit.'

'And when he gets through to his superior officer, what then?'

'His C.O. will be in the mess having lunch. I don't think the silly sod will want to disturb him. By the time they make contact you should be airborne. All that remains now is to square the skipper.'

The Captain was standing by the aircraft watching the crates being loaded, whilst his crew were in the cockpit. He looked tired and bad-tempered.

'Have you authorisation from that pipsqueak in the office?' he asked.

'No,' Nigel replied, deciding not to try any bluff with this taciturn man.

'No go, then!'

'He pointed you out to us though, and said you would have room, so he turned a blind eye. Come on, skipper, just two of them. I'm off to the 5th Army, these are 8th Army bods who only want to get to their regiments.'

'Oh don't come all that flannel with me about dying to get back and fight the Hun.' He looked at John and Taffy. 'God Almighty, you both look as though you're only just out of your nappies.'

'Quite right,' Nigel said cheerfully, 'Eager cannon fodder who have just walked out of a nice safe transit camp, we're all in the same boat, skipper.'

'I don't know why the hell I should.'

'But you will, won't you?'

'Christ!' He stared at them. 'All right, get in, and get out at Foggia. As far as I'm concerned you are not there.'

'We who are about to die salute you.' Nigel said, arm raised.

'Oh, piss off!'

As they clambered into the plane Taffy looked at Nigel with spaniel's eyes. 'You were smashing, we could never have managed on our own, could we, John?'

'No,' Crabbe replied without enthusiasm.

'I said I would see you on the plane,' Nigel said shortly. 'One last piece of advice. That blood plasma is going somewhere, my guess is that it will be up forward, so stick with it and you should get to Termoli by tonight. Good luck.'

'And you, boy.' Taffy waved goodbye.

'We might meet again, you know, it's a funny old war.' Nigel strode off across the tarmac.

☆ ☆ ☆

John had never flown before and felt apprehensive. The events of the last twenty-four hours had persuaded him of one thing, that he was not cut out to be a soldier, let alone an officer. Taffy was naive but full of guts and had a taste for adventure, while Nigel was efficient and self-assured, a born leader. He reminded John of Thomas at his school, an arrogant bully who had been the principal cause of his running away one Sunday in September 1938. Nigel wasn't exactly a bully, but he had the same capacity for making John feel inferior.

And yet during the escape from school, John had met some soldiers on the train, and a tough Glaswegian private said that he had guts. A prostitute, who befriended him, had used the same words. All the memories of that time came flooding back as he waited for the plane to take off. He clung to the opinions of those two unlikely champions, a soldier and a tart, who had done so much to restore his belief in himself.

But that was long ago. The rest of his school days had been uneventful. On his return some of the boys regarded him as a hero, one of their own who had defied the system, but the sudden death of his father while he was at home had changed him, he had grown up over those days. He no longer courted popularity, but withdrew into himself. He was still hopeless at games but his schoolwork flourished, and he gained a respectable Matric. He and Thomas kept each other at arm's-length, and there was no more bullying.

John became an actor on leaving school, much to his mother's disgust. He worked in repertory all over the country, and then came the audition for the Old Vic. He had a love of Shakespeare and a feeling for the poetry. He would like to have chosen *Hamlet*, his abiding passion, as he knew most of the play by heart. But sensibly, not being slim and handsome but short and fat, he chose the comics: Bottom in *The Dream*, and Caliban in *The Tempest*, and for good measure to show his prowess in speaking verse, 'All The World's A Stage' from *As You Like It*. The disembodied voice from the stalls, shrouded in darkness, was encouraging.

'Stay behind my boy,' it said, 'I want to see you at the end.'

John hung around in the wings and nothing happened. Then the auditions finished and they switched off the working lights on the stage. He couldn't see a thing, and finally decided to grope his way to the Pass Door. He tripped over a step and fell into the arms of a dapper little man in a blue suit.

'Who the hell are you?' the man said. 'Oh, you must be the boy Bottom?'

'Yes,' John replied eagerly.

'House Lights, Roger, we can't see a bloody thing.'

The auditorium suddenly came alight and John could see the whole of the famous theatre.

'You were the best of a bad bunch,' the producer said, leading him to the front stalls. 'We can't be choosy anyway, there are so few actors around. When will you get your call up papers?'

'In about a year,' John replied.

'Good! We must have actors, in spite of this war. If you join my company, you might be able to postpone the evil day. Go up to the office, see Rachel and leave your address, I will be in touch.'

The next day the theatre was bombed, so John went back to the real world, and it was during a tour of *George and Margaret* that he received his papers.

He did well as an officer cadet, which surprised him no end. He came top of his squad in written work, and also excelled on the indoor range. This was a large relief map on a table, beautifully made with hills, valleys, and little villages complete with churches, houses and pubs. It was like an elaborate children's toy. You had to work out ranges and then shout orders to imaginary guns. Little puffs of smoke came up all over the map. It was fascinating. John never knew quite how the instructors positioned the smoke in accordance with his orders, but he seemed to win every time. All his targets were hit with monotonous regularity.

The great bugbear was the gym. When John left school he heaved a sigh of relief that never again would he have to risk castration vaulting a horse; but now he had to face this particular horror all over again. He was saved by the Warrant Officer instructor, who liked John mainly for his entertainment value. He would address the squad of nine collectively as sir.

'Now sir,' he pronounced at the start of a session, 'Let us all 'ave a good laugh to get us in the right mood. Mr Crabbe, sir, you will start off on the 'orse.'

Most of his squad got in the habit of drinking in the local village pub of an evening, when the Warrant Officer would regale them with stories of army life. At the half-way mark of the course, the W.O. awarded John ninety per cent marks for physical training.

The final element that helped John was the fact that the Colonel was a supreme snob. Cadets who had not been to a public school were apt to disappear, the fatal R.T.U., Return To Unit. On his first interview with the Colonel, John was asked:

'It says on your report that you were an actor. West End?'

'Oh yes, sir.' John had replied, lying through his teeth.

'Good show! Why not organise an entertainment? Splendid for morale.'

John did just that, a revue. He didn't think it was very good but he was able to do a sketch himself about a raw recruit doing everything wrong. This wasn't difficult, he even incorporated a gym horse. He could hear the Colonel guffawing from the stalls. His future was thus assured.

The plane took off, and John came back to the present with a bump. Taffy was looking out of the window, his nose pressed to the glass. 'We are on our way, John, it's exciting isn't it? Look, there's Naples getting smaller and smaller. I wonder if we fly over Vesuvius, perhaps we will see the crater. I must get a picture of this.' He knelt on the seat and aimed his camera at the window. At that moment the aircraft banked, and the terrace of vineyards on the mountain side suddenly appeared above their heads. John began to feel sick.

'Damn,' Taffy said. 'I think all I got was sky. I'll try again.' But they were gaining height fast, and Vesuvius slid off to their left. Taffy clicked again. 'I don't think that will be much good, too far away.' He put the camera down and continued to look out of the window.

They were not alone. An RAF medical Orderly was sitting at the other end of the cabin reading a book. John, who felt better if he didn't look out of the window, decided to engage him in conversation.

'How long does it take to Foggia, Corporal?' he asked pleasantly.

'Under the hour,' the orderly replied, pulling the book up so that it covered his face, showing the title *No Orchids For Miss Blandish.*

'Rude bugger.' John thought. But they were flying by courtesy of the RAF so there was no point in disturbing the peace.

'It must have been exciting, John boy, being an actor.' Taffy climbed off his knees and sat with his back to the window.

'Not really. I didn't get very far.' He did not want to pursue the subject in front of the sullen corporal. 'You are probably much more use to the community, being a schoolmaster.'

'Well my father was a teacher, see, in Cardiff, and as I did quite well at the Grammar, it was the natural thing to follow in his footsteps.'

'Weren't you in a reserved occupation?'

'I could have been, seeing that I'm a scientist, but I wanted some excitement. It seemed rather boring staying at home with all this going on. So I persuaded my Head to say that I could be spared, and here I am.'

John felt guilty again, knowing full well that he would

have jumped at the opportunity to stay at home. The producer at the Old Vic audition had said, 'Join my company and we might postpone the evil day.' But then the theatre had been bombed.

The plane lurched suddenly and dropped a few hundred feet, as they hit a cloud bank which was clinging to the range of hills ahead. Taffy looked out of the window again.

'Air pockets,' he cried. 'Oh John boy, do come and see, we are right over the mountains, they have snow on the top, it's beautiful.'

John gripped the front of his seat tightly as the aircraft began to bounce up and down like a cork in the sea. Taffy, quite unconcerned, continued to chatter away happily. 'There is a village down there, right on the peak, with a little church covered in snow, just like a Christmas card.'

John did not reply but sat frozen to the metal bench. They had no seat belts so he braced himself against the window at his back. Then he looked at the Orderly who had dropped the book and was clutching his knees, his face the colour of chalk.

'Are you all right, Corporal?' he asked.

The other man ignored him, but seeing someone even more frightened than he was himself made John feel better. Once the plane had crossed the hills it became steady once more, and John relaxed. Taffy had stopped looking out and gone to sleep. The Corporal still looked green.

When they landed at Foggia the Captain came into the cabin.

'Enjoy yourselves?' he asked.

'Not much,' John replied, 'but we are very grateful, thank you.'

'At least you weren't sick all over my aeroplane. Corporal!'

'Yes, Sir?' The Orderly stood up.

'Where is the plasma going?'

'The C.C.S. at Termoli, sir.'

'Right. Now listen. If you can help these officers to get on the truck, you will be making a contribution to the war effort. But unofficially, mind. I don't know anything about it. Understand?'

'Yes, sir.'

John thanked the Captain again, but he said nothing and went back to the cockpit.

'Wakey, wakey.' John shook Taffy hard. 'We are here. Get a move on, if we follow the blood we should make Termoli tonight.'

'We've landed?'

'Yes, you Welsh dormouse. It beats me how you managed to sleep through all that. Come on, get cracking, or we'll miss the boat.'

They stood around while the crates were unloaded.

'Well, Corporal,' John said, 'what do we do now?'

'The truck will be here in a minute, so you had better make yourselves scarce,' he said sourly. 'I will meet you at the main gate.'

They both set off across the tarmac. 'He was quite friendly, the Corporal,' Taffy said, 'it looks as though we are in luck.'

'No thanks to you. The Captain and I fixed it all up while you were sleeping.'

'Good show, boy.' He grinned at John sleepily. 'You know something? My tummy is rumbling away, we haven't eaten since breakfast.'

'Don't remind me. I'm dreaming about the dinner we'll get at Termoli.'

Taffy stopped in his tracks. 'John man, I've left the camera behind.'

'Well leave it, for God's sake, we are meant to keep out of the light. The Captain said so.'

'But it's a good camera, and there are all those pictures I took of the mountains.'

'Mostly of the sky! Taffy, leave it. If you go back we might spoil everything.'

'I won't be a minute. Just stay there, don't move, I'll be back in a jiffy.'

Before John could stop him he was off, running back towards the plane. It all happened so suddenly. There was no warning. The whine of the bomb and the flash by the plane were simultaneous. John threw himself on the ground and felt the blast over his head. He flattened himself against the hard concrete as the ground around him seemed to bounce under the explosions. He could hear the Stukas now screaming like demented cats above his head. He lay there for what seemed an eternity, but it was only a few minutes, about half a dozen dive-bombers making a sneak raid out of the low cloud. John stayed motionless until the wail of the all-clear sounded. He climbed unsteadily to his feet. There was smoke everywhere, an ambulance raced past a few yards from him. He looked at the plane which had just carried him careering over the mountains, and saw a raging inferno. He ran towards the fire shouting at the top of his voice.

'Taffy, I'm coming, I'm coming, Taffy!'

2

'Mr Vice, The King.'

The door was ajar, and John could just see the far end of the table.

'The King!' the chorus of unseen voices responded immediately. But the Colonel, raising his glass, was clearly visible. He was a giant of a man, dressed in a blue uniform with chain armour on the epaulettes which flashed under the lights. The Mess Sergeant in a white coat who had met John at the front door whispered, 'couldn't interrupt the Loyal Toast, sir. But now I will go and fetch the Adjutant, he won't be too happy in the middle of his Christmas dinner.'

John waited. He had travelled from Termoli in the back of a Jeep where there was little protection against the weather, and it had rained incessantly throughout the journey. He had wrapped a ground-sheet over his Army greatcoat and this had kept him comparatively dry, but as he got out all the water had run on to his knees and down his neck.

'Who are you?' A dandified captain, also in the blue uniform, stood in the doorway.

'Crabbe, sir. I am posted to the Home Counties Yeomanry.' John saluted, and the raising of his arm sent a further trickle of water down his neck.

'The hell you are.' The Adjutant looked at him without much enthusiasm. 'Well, you had better come into the office.'

They went to a room at the far end of a corridor, and the Captain leafed through some papers. John was not asked to sit down, which was just as well, as his legs felt clammy and it was easier standing up.

'You are not expected for about two weeks. We have had no notification of an early arrival,' the Adjutant said crossly. 'How did you get here?'

John told the story in a low voice. He felt utterly miserable. Nigel had said he would get a great welcome at his unit, but it was not turning out like that at all. When he started on the air raid at Foggia, the door was flung open and the Colonel strode into the room.

'What the hell is going on, Giles? We are meant to be having our Christmas dinner,' he boomed. 'And who is this?'

John was tongue-tied, so the Adjutant brought the C.O. up to date.

'So where is Williams?' the Colonel asked, his cold blue eyes unblinking.

'He was wounded in the raid on Foggia, sir,' John stammered.

'And where is he now?'

'In the C.C.S. at Termoli, sir.'

'Go on. I want the whole story. Take your time.'

John looked at the supercilious Adjutant and suddenly the adrenalin began to flow. It all reminded him of a ticking-off from his mother when he was little. Usually he looked at the floor, but one day after he had slapped his sister's face for baiting him, he forced himself to square up to her. He did the same now to the Colonel, with new-found resolution.

'Our aircraft was on fire,' he said, 'I ran towards it to find Williams. An ambulance passed me to pick up the crew. I heard one man screaming, just one man. I think the others were probably dead, the plane was completely gutted. I almost tripped over Williams, he was on the ground, about fifty yards from the fire, luckily he had not got any further when the bomb fell. He was sitting up swaying from side to side and moaning, he was covered in blood. Another ambulance came and picked him up. I persuaded them to take me as well.'

'They took you along although you were not hurt?' the Adjutant asked suspiciously.

'Yes, sir. I insisted. You see, Taffy, I mean Williams, was my friend.'

'You were damn lucky.'

John ignored him, and continued to talk directly to the Colonel.

'I saw him into the Casualty Clearing Station, but they would not let me stay. The Town Major in Termoli found me a bed and some food, he was very kind, and I went back to the C.C.S. this morning.'

There was no comment from the others, so John went on with the story.

'Williams was rather dopey, sir, I mean drugged, his face was white and he was still swaying from side to side, but he knew me.' John felt tears coming into his eyes, but he fought to keep control. 'Before I left I spoke to an M.O., a major. Apparently Williams had been hit in the shoulder and lost a lot of blood, but it's not very serious, that's what the Major said.'

'How did you and Williams get separated in the first place?' the Colonel asked.

'He went back for his camera, he had left it on the plane.'

'Bloody fool! How did you find your way here?'

'I went to the docks, sir. There was a supply convoy, R.A.S.C. going forward, the Captain in charge knew where you were. I came in his Jeep and walked from the main road.'

There was a long silence, the Colonel was the first to speak.

'So, Crabbe,' he said quietly, 'You walk out of a Transit Camp, contrary to King's Regulations, before you have been in the country for two minutes, get a fellow officer half-killed on the way, and then arrive two weeks early looking like a drowned rat and disturb my Christmas dinner. Apparently you have a taste for adventure.'

'Sir.'

'Well, I understand that you ran away from Chalkley, my old school as well as yours, but at least this time you were going in the right direction.'

Oh God, thought John. Would he never live down that episode in his life! He had often been bullied at school, but now he was so wet and hungry he didn't care any more. He held the Colonel's gaze.

'That was a long time ago, sir, and it is not fair to hold it against me.'

The Adjutant looked up sharply, and John, conscious that he had gone too far, dropped his eyes. The Colonel still spoke quietly, but his words were measured and calculated.

'No officer in my regiment speaks to me like that.' He paused to let the message sink in. 'And particularly not a very young officer who is still wet behind the ears. However, I will bear in mind that you have had a shock, and it is Christmas Day, so I will be charitable. What I was going to say before you were impertinent enough to interrupt me, is that you did well. You showed resource and courage, particularly in the way you looked after your friend. If Sholto — he is 622 battery commander and you know him well — boots you up the arse hard and often to show you a little discipline, you will make a good officer. Now I am going back to my Christmas dinner which was so rudely interrupted. Giles.'

'Sir?'

'Get a batman to run a bath, and see that the boy is well scrubbed. Ring Sholto and arrange transport to the battery in half an hour, and order the Mess Sergeant to take up a glass of brandy to the bathroom, a large one.' Before John had time to thank him he went out, slamming the door behind him.

☆ ☆ ☆

The driver of the Daimler Dingo which had come to collect John was still in a state of euphoria after his Christmas lunch. He gripped the steering wheel as though his life depended on it, leaning forward with his face a few inches from the windsceen. The wipers were going full blast, fighting a losing battle against the rain. He prattled away non-stop.

'The officers are in the middle of their dinner, we must get a move on or you'll miss your plum pud. You have come to 622, the best battery, sir. Major Sholto is one of the lads, he's all for a party, the Major. We liberated a crate of Asti Spumanti on the way up, I prefer bitter myself, but Itie beer is piss. This Asti has a kick, I'll say that.'

At that moment the vehicle hit a bump and John struck his head on the roof. 'Driver' he cried, aware for the first time of the black void ahead, 'you haven't got your lights on.'

'Oh no, sir. No lights. Jerry is only a few miles away, don't you worry sir, I'll get you there in one piece.'

John thought this observation was a trifle optimistic, particularly when a moment later the near side wheels of the Dingo began to mount a bank by the side of the track.

'Sorry about that, sir,' the driver said cheerfully as the steering wheel began to spin, 'must be a landslide. Just like the dodgems, isn't it?'

John knew he ought to take charge and make the driver slow down. But he was such a friendly little man, and John did not want to appear afraid. So he held his breath and said nothing.

'My name is Fish, sir,' the driver continued once the vehicle was upright again. 'They all call me Haddock, even the Major. I am to be your batman. I share you with Mr Pilling. He is a clever one, went to Oxford or Cambridge, we call him the professor. Actually I'm a Charlie Troop driver, and I help out in the officers' mess when we are out of the line, better grub and I learn what's going on.' He jammed on the brakes and the vehicle came to a stop. 'I think this is where we turn left.' He shone a torch through the windscreen, and John could see a stone wall a few feet ahead. 'Better not have an argument with that,' he chuckled, 'now off to the left, and we are nearly there.'

John heaved a sigh of relief.

'You are lucky coming to us, you know, sir,' Fish was off again. '647 Battery is on the river knocking shit out of the Jerries, while 622, that's us and 621 are having Christmas in this village. You see our guns are worn out, we're getting new ones, but they found four that worked so 647, the poor sods, copped it.'

Fish slowed down at last. John was conscious of houses on each side of the road, his eyes had become accustomed to the darkness. There was not a sign of life anywhere.

'It looks like a ghost town, doesn't it, sir?' Fish said, 'but all the chaps are billeted here. Good black-out, isn't it?

'Yes it is,' John replied, 'most of the houses seem to have been bombed.'

'Oh yes, sir, stonked to buggery. But it is surprising what you can do with a few tarpaulins to keep out the rain. Better than sleeping in trucks or bivvies.'

They turned off the road and after a few minutes on a bumpy track, they arrived at a large house.

'Here we are sir,' Fish said, 'home at last!'

The long journey was over and John should have been excited and relieved. Instead, he felt a moment of panic. He was tired and hungry and as he climbed out of the truck, he was conscious of his hand trembling as he opened the door. The last forty-eight hours had seemed like a nightmare, and he was unable to put out of his mind the sight of Taffy lying on the tarmac covered in blood, and also of the supercilious Adjutant who clearly thought that his irregular arrival was showing off and bad form. Perhaps Sholto and the battery officers would think the same. Not for the first time, he cursed Nigel for landing him in this silly little adventure. It would have been so much easier to have joined his unit in the orthodox way, and Taffy would not have been hurt. John had always hated that phrase, "showing off." His mother had used it often, and his sister Felicity, but not his father, they had always understood each other. He felt himself blushing at the memory.

When they reached the door there was a long, low whistle overhead, and seconds later a dull crump. John instinctively ducked.

'It's all right sir,' Fish said 'It's only the Jerry heavies, harassing fire on the main road, they've been doing it all day, the bastards. Every hour like clockwork. You would think they would let up on Christmas Day, wouldn't you?'

John felt ashamed. Now he was letting himself down in front of his batman.

Fish took him down a long corridor, some of which was open to the sky. There was a light showing below a door and the sound of shouting and singing coming from inside. When his batman opened the door there was a sudden silence, and John was conscious of a sea of faces looking at him. Sholto was sitting at the head of the table. Instead of formal uniform he was dressed in a bush jacket with a multi-coloured scarf knotted round his throat. A roaring log fire at his side cast a flickering light over his face and enormous black moustache, so that he looked like a benevolent Mephistopheles. He strode across the room and put his arm on John's shoulder.

'Young John Crabbe, come and join the party,' he shouted, 'the C.O. has been on the blower, told me you ticked him off!'

'Oh no, sir,' John mumbled.

'Damn good show. Old Alex appreciated it, and your little adventure. When did you leave Naples?'

'Yesterday morning, sir.'

'Sholto, John, Sholto. Only sir in front of the chaps. Bloody marvellous! The Bosche tried to Stuka you too, I gather.'

'Yes, Sholto.'

'Don't worry about the Welsh boy, he'll be O.K; coming to us in a week or two. Now, here is your place next to me, you must be starving.'

John was so overwhelmed that he found himself unable to speak.

'I taught him, you know,' Sholto grinned at his officers, 'didn't I do a good job? Pass the brandy, he's got a hell of a lot of drinking time to make up.'

☆ ☆ ☆

John awoke the next morning to the sound of a high-pitched whine and a flash of light drilling his eyeballs. 'We are being bombed,' he thought to himself. 'Never mind, I will just let myself sink into a peaceful oblivion and the hammer blows in my head will stop.'

'Sir, sir.' The blinding light was obscured for a moment and slowly he became conscious of a figure standing between him and the window. 'It's Haddock, sir. I've brought you a cup of tea.'

John sat up putting his arm over his eyes. 'Is it an air raid?' he asked, too sleepy to care.

'No, dear boy,' Charles Pilling replied. 'A hangover, the symptoms are not dissimilar.' He was lying on his back using a small dynamo razor which he operated by squeezing two short handles. The shrill wail seemed to penetrate John's skull.

'That contraption of yours sounds like a Stuka,' he said, gulping his tea.

'Sorry,' Charles replied, 'I've finished now, anyway. You can borrow it if you like.'

'Thanks.'

'If I can give you a word of advice, I would drag yourself into the land of the living. A hungover Boxing Day is just the time for Colonel Alex to play one of his little tricks. It's called keeping us on our toes.'

'What do you mean?'

'I fancy we'll find out soon enough.'

And they did. John had just finished dressing when the Battery Captain, Max Gregory, put his head round the door.

'Orders in the Mess now, boys, and I am afraid you are going to miss your breakfast this morning.'

'What did I tell you?' Charles said with a grin. 'When the colonel says jump, we all jump.'

John looked around in panic. It was just like being back at school, getting ready for an inspection before the Head Prefect in the house yard.

'What do we take with us?' he asked, looking in dismay at the pile of equipment which he had thrown into a corner the previous night.

'Keep calm, old boy, keep calm. Haddock will sort it all out for you while we are getting orders, he is well trained.' Sholto was the only one fully dressed. 'Fred Karno's Officer Corps,' he said cheerfully. 'Colonel Alex has had a nasty gleam in his eye over the past few days, I thought he might decide to have a little fun in the early hours of Boxing Day.'

All the other officers were in various forms of disarray, the Battery Captain had shaving soap all over his face. The door opened and the Sergeant-Major entered in his shirt sleeves and saluted smartly.

'Hello, Ernest,' Sholto grinned at him. 'Glad to see you have got your trousers on!'

'Sir!'

'The Colonel's little exercise. Get 622 Battery lined up on the road outside Don Troop's billets, Charlie Troop leading, in half an hour.'

'Yes, sir.'

'Correction. Make it twenty minutes. We don't want 621 Battery to get there first, do we?'

'We'll be there, Major Sholto.'

'Good, Sergeant-Major.'

After he had gone Sholto rapped out his orders.

'Information. Enemy counter attack with tanks north-west of village.

Intention. To knock them to buggery.

Method. Deploy our guns in and around the village with observation posts to cover all the area to the north. Any questions?'

'Who are we supporting, Sholto?' Max Gregory asked.

'A phantom brigade of armour which have materialised by magic. Oh, and one important point. The C.O. says that all seconds-in-command must take over, which means that I stay here and have my breakfast, Gun Position Officers man the observation posts, the Troop Leaders the gun positions.'

'Sholto,' Pilling said, 'John Crabbe only arrived last night, he hasn't even met the troop yet. He can't be asked to take over the gun position.'

'Good point,' Sholto replied. 'Well, how do you feel, Johnnie? You know the form, you've been trained, and you gave us a very spirited rendering of Henry V last night standing on the table.'

'Did I, sir?'

'Yes, you did. Very good experience for you, the G.P.O. is in full command, not like the troop leader who has to wander around like a spare prick at a wedding.'

'Say no,' Pilling whispered.

'I'll have a go, Sholto,' John said tentatively.

'Idiot,' Pilling hissed.

'Good. Well that's it, gentlemen. Good hunting!'

'Are you sure you wouldn't rather change your mind?' Max asked. 'No one will think any worse of you.'

'No, I think I can manage,' John replied.

'Don't say I didn't warn you,' Pilling muttered.

Charles took John to the starting postion in a Jeep and

then drove off. 'It's all yours now, you will learn one day when to volunteer and when to keep your trap shut. Good luck, you are going to need it,' was his parting remark.

The two troops of four guns were lined up on the road, each led by a half-tracked vehicle. The guns were Priests, 105 mm guns mounted on Grant armoured chassis, they looked rather like large open tanks, the crew riding inside. John felt at one remove from reality. The fresh air and the persistent rain beating against his face had eased the pain in his head, but he had the curious sensation of floating on air. He decided that the leading half-track was his truck, so he strode towards it in what he hoped was a purposeful fashion. But when he was half-way there, the whole convoy began to move. None of his training had taught him what to do if your own troop takes off without you, and although he felt it was hardly in keeping with his dignity he began to run after it. But it was a losing battle, and soon the last gun had overtaken him and Don Troop was a few hundred yards behind, so, panting for breath, John stopped and waited for the others to catch up. At that moment a motor cycle drew up beside him.

'Who the hell are you?' It was a troop Sergeant-Major. 'sir,' he added, as he noticed John's one pip.

'Mr Crabbe, Troop Leader, Charlie Troop.' John managed between gasps for breath.

'Good God, where did you pop in from, sir?'

'I arrived last night, Sergeant-Major.'

'Did you, now. And where is Mr Pilling?'

'At the O.P. in the church, I think.'

'You don't know, sir?'

'No, he didn't say.'

'I see. Well, we had better get you up to your truck, sir. We can't have a Troop Leader bringing up the rear, can we? Hop on!'

John climbed on the pillion and gripped the S.M. round the waist. It was hardly a propitious introduction to his troop.

'My name is Cobber, S.M. Cobber, Charlie Troop. So we are going to see quite a lot of each other, sir,' he said as he stopped the convoy. 'By the way, do you know where you are leading us?'

'I thought a gun position in the football field.' He had looked at his map while he was dressing.

'If you are lucky, sir. 621 battery is billeted near there, I reckon they may well have bagged it by now. Anyway climb up, sir, and we will see.'

Haddock was at the wheel. 'Hullo, sir. Sorry we started without you, I thought Mr Pilling would catch us up in his Jeep. Where is he?'

'In the O.P.'

'So you are acting G.P.O., are you sir?'

'Yes.' John stood up and clutched his map. 'We are going to the football field about five hundred yards ahead.'

'O.K. sir.'

They nearly made it, but as they rounded a bend in the road John's heart sank. Four Priests were lumbering into the field, their tracks churning up the pitch. Cheerful badinage was exchanged between the rival crews and V signs from the 621 Battery.

John halted the convoy and peered at his map. The Sergeant-Major drew alongside on his bike.

'I told you so, sir. Where now?'

'We passed an olive grove on the right, I reckon we could get the guns in there,' John said, trying to sound efficient.

'Don Troop are already there sir, and if we go any further the ground slopes down, so we would be in full view of the enemy. This is the last place with any cover.'

At that moment John wished he was back in bed nursing his hangover. He also wished he had never left the transit camp, above all he wished he had taken Pilling's advice and not volunteered.

Cobber took pity on him. 'We passed a cemetery, sir, I suggest we go there. It won't be easy, but it's the only place left.'

'We will have to turn in the football field.'

'That's right, sir.'

John gave the signal, and C Troop swung off the road and onto the pitch.

'Not in front of the guns, sir!' the S.M. bellowed. 'If this was for real they would blow our arses off!'

It was not easy manoeuvring round the back of the Battery and C Troop had to suffer the further indignity of cheerful catcalls while they did it.

It was well over half an hour before the troop was safely positioned between the tombs and wireless contact had been made with Charles, who was indeed in the church. John had got something right.

'You've taken your time, old boy,' Charles' voice came clearly on the R.T., 'the bloody war is nearly over.'

Normally the signallers would lay telephone lines from John's truck to the four guns so that he could transmit firing orders from the O.P., but to save time, as his troop had entered the battle so late, John decided to use a loud-hailer instead. It worked quite well and John at last began to feel on top of the situation. He had been trained in gun drill for a long time now, and almost began to enjoy himself. He was so absorbed playing soldiers that he failed to notice a staff car draw up on the edge of the cemetery. He jumped when a hand tapped his shoulder.

'Why are you using that thing?' Colonel Alex asked quietly. 'You're not a bloody crooner.'

'Sir.' John stood to attention.

'The loud hailer, young Crabbe, is only used as a last resort when enemy action has cut your lines, weren't you taught that?'

'Yes, sir.' John thought quickly and unwisely decided to push his luck. 'Lines have been cut, sir, so I am using alternative means to relay orders.'

The Colonel nodded. 'I see. By the way, how long have your guns been in position?'

John knew he was trapped and decided to tell the truth.

'About fifteen minutes sir.'

'And I gave the original orders nearly two hours ago, what the hell have you been playing at?'

John thought it prudent to remain silent.

'In a real battle your fart-arsing about all over the village could have cost vital time in holding the counter attack, couldn't it Crabbe?'

'Yes, sir.'

'And where is your camouflage? This may be an exercise, but we are within range of real Hun aircraft, the guns are standing out like sore thumbs, so do something about that anyway and be quick about it.'

He was gone, and a deflated John Crabbe began to organise nets over the guns.

'They should never have let you become a soldier,' Pilling said as they drove back to the mess for lunch.

'I agree,' John replied miserably.

'Never mind, you will get one out of ten for trying. What did the Colonel say to you?'

'I was using the loud-hailer to save time and he said I wasn't a crooner, he also ticked me off rotten about camouflage.'

'That's a bee in his bonnet, but he is right and you have learnt something.'

'I suppose so.'

'Were you a good actor? Your drunken "Once more unto the breach" had a certain panache.'

'I think I'm quite good.'

'Well, there is a Sergeants' Mess party tonight, so you can do an act for them. But I fancy *Eskimo Nell* is more in their line than Shakespeare.'

'Oh my God, do we have to go?'

'Yes, old son, we do. It will be a very good opportunity to meet them after all.' Charles grinned at him. 'Cheer up! They won't hold this morning against you, they are used to nurse-maiding raw young subalterns. But no *Henry V*, O.K?'

'Of course not. I'll just crawl into a corner and keep out of the way.'

'They won't let you do that. Just relax and enjoy yourself, the Sergeants' Mess parties are quite an education. I should go and have a kip after lunch and you'll feel fine by this evening.'

'I'll go now,' John replied. 'I could sleep for two days.' He went straight up to his room, and in a few minutes was snoring his way into total insensibility.

☆ ☆ ☆

The Sergeant's Mess party was an ordeal. Sholto personally introduced John to all and sundry. The Battery S.M. Ernest Sprott, a huge man known to the troops as Bolster Belly, was very much on his dignity, he made no reference to the events of the morning, but John felt that he was sizing him up and deciding that this little pipsqueak of an officer was not much of an addition to the Battery. The others were polite enough, but after the initial meeting wandered off at the first opportunity.

These parties, which are held regularly when out of the line, are probably unique to the British Army. They are a safety valve and an opportunity to let the hair down. As drink flows inhibitions vanish, home truths are told, and it soon becomes clear which officers are respected and which are found wanting. But the distinction is subtle. Army discipline in a good regiment is paramount, so no one goes too far, the delicate balance is maintained, however much drink is consumed. It is on these occasions that the English penchant for being facetious becomes apparent.

In other words, you are rude to those whom you like, and polite to those whom you view less favourably. Sholto, for instance, who was loved by all, came in for the most vigorous teasing.

'Did you have a good breakfast, Major Sholto?' one Sergeant shouted above the din. 'While we were all sweating our guts out!'

Sholto beamed at him. 'Scrambled eggs, toast and marmalade and four cups of coffee.'

'And I bet you had a cigar after.'

'I did, and then went back to bed.'

Pilling also was teased, he was known as The Vicar because of the precise way he spoke, and Max Gregory was Humpty because of his figure. It is difficult to imagine this particular scene in the German army or even the American, it is a British phenomenon.

John felt right out of it all. These men had been fighting together for several years, some of them had even been at Dunkirk, and as the temperature of the party rose, old battles were fought again, and the close comradeship, only to be found among fighting men, inevitably excluded an outsider. John could not even find solace in drink, he still had a hangover from the previous night, and the rough vino felt like acid in his mouth.

Then the singing started.

'Three German officers crossed the Rhine,

To fuck the women and drink the wine,
Inky-Pinky, parlez-vous.'

John looked round the room to make sure no one was looking in his direction, and then went outside into the cool air. It had stopped raining, so he walked along the road to the place where he had found his troop moving off without him. He welcomed the cold for it cleared his head, but standing at the bend on the track the memory of his humiliation of the morning came flooding back to him. He suddenly felt an agonising home-sickness. He didn't really miss his mother or his sister Felicity, the mail had not caught up yet, so he had not heard from them since he landed in Italy, and events had moved so rapidly during the last few weeks that he had not had time to miss his old life. But now his plight hit him right in the pit of his stomach.

'They should never have let you become a soldier,' Pilling had said to him. Tears of self-pity welled into his eyes. There were lots of actors of his age still working at home, why wasn't he one of them? He had managed his life so badly and instead of working in the theatre in England, he was now standing dressed up as an officer in a remote part of Italy in the freezing cold, and it was Boxing Day.

Wearily he walked back towards the Sergeants' Mess, and then he began to panic, perhaps he had been missed. He had blotted his copy book enough today without being accused of walking out of the party. He need not have worried, he slipped quietly into the room and stood at the back, no one noticed him at all.

'I don't want to join the Army,
I don't want to go to war,
I'd rather hang around
Piccadilly Underground,
Living on the earnings of a high-born Lady'

The raucous singing was deafening after the quiet outside, and John was just thinking that he might disappear again when he felt a hand touch his arm. It was S.M. Cobber.

'Cheer up, Mr Crabbe,' he said, 'you look down in the dumps. Let me get you a drink.'

John hesitated. 'O.K., thank you, Sergeant-Major.' He watched the other man as he filled his glass, he was a square, stocky little chap with a red face and eyes that laughed.

'Not worrying about this morning, are you, sir?'

John was surprised at the direct question but he decided to be honest.

'Yes, I am actually.'

'No need, sir. The Major should not have landed you in it on your first day. I told him so, but he said you volunteered. Did you?'

'Well I suppose I did in a way.'

'They will think better of you for doing that.' He paused and looked at John with a fatherly smile. 'And I understand you had a ripe bollocking from Colonel Alex.'

'Yes,' John replied, and felt himself blushing.

'You don't want to worry about that either, sir. We all get it from time to time, officers and NCOs, it's his way of keeping us up to the mark.'

John felt grateful to this little man and the black shadow began to lift.

'You have cheered me up, Sergeant-Major, thank you.'

'Good. And I'll tell you something else, sir. Playing at being soldiers is the very devil. Everyone runs around shouting and finding faults. That is the object of the exercise, really, you must have found it the same at training camp. But once you are in action it's quite different, you are all on the same side, see? Everyone helps everyone else, and this is a bloody fine unit, though I say so myself."

'Have you been with the Regiment a long time Sergeant-Major?' John asked.

'I was a driver in France, made up to a Bombardier after Dunkirk, a Sergeant just before El Alamein, and B.S.M. in Sicily.'

'Gosh, that's jolly quick promotion.'

'Dead men's shoes, I'm afraid, sir. It was the invasion of Sicily when we caught it. Bloody stupid, really, there was hardly any opposition from the "Ities", then the Stukas came over and hit three of our landing craft, and a lot of good chaps were lost that day.' He paused and his eyes changed to hard steel, all the laughter had left them. 'The Stukas attacked one of our hospital ships that night, Mr Crabbe, all the lights were on and the Red Cross could be seen for miles. They set it on fire from bow to stern, the filthy fucking bastards.'

John remained silent.

'Just remember that, sir. Just remember what they did in Avola Bay in Sicily when we next get to meet the bloody Krauts.'

Cobbers's whole personality had changed in those few moments, and John felt a measure of the other man's anger pass to him.

'I will, Sergeant-Major, don't you worry.'

Cobber said nothing for a while but stood quite still looking at the glass in his hand. John sensed that he was embarrassed by the outburst.

'You'll be all right sir,' he said, 'You'll be all right.' He turned on his heel abruptly, and rejoined the party.

3

Today the pundits would probably say that the end of 1943 in central Italy was the wettest since records began. The fact is that it rained continuously and it was raw and cold at the same time. The Colonel did not order any more regimental exercises, but Sholto kept 622 Battery busy. There were football matches in the rain, lectures by officers and NCOs, and stringent maintenance on all vehicles and equipment. John was given the job of inspecting the 3 ton and 15 cwt trucks, a sort of MOT Test, and had to sign a form at the end certifying their roadworthiness. He had a complete block as regards anything mechanical, and when he pulled up the bonnet of the lorry and looked at the engine his eyes misted over, it was like asking a monkey to mend a watch. However the NCO with him was indulgent and told him what to say. John felt woefully inadequate, but everyone was friendly and he began to warm towards his new Battery.

He received his first mail from home on New Year's Eve, two letters, one from his mother and the other from Felicity. His mother wrote:-

> Dearest John,
>
> We were so pleased to get your letter saying that you had arrived in Italy, but of course we have no idea where you are. We read the papers and wonder if you have been involved in any fighting yet.
>
> You did well to get your commission, your father would have been proud of you.

Not much news our end. I am busy with the WVS, and we are hoping to put on a good show at the hospital over Christmas.

The weather is miserable, dark and gloomy, I gather you are having rain in Italy, one paper referred to mud like Flanders, but at least I expect it is warmer than here. Cheltenham is rather a backwater and the war seems a long way away, I suppose we should consider ourselves fortunate.

Felicity is enclosing a letter so she will give you all her news.

Take care of yourself,

Love

Mother.

Agnes Crabbe had never been one to show her emotions, it had been the same when she wrote to him at school. In a way he was grateful to her, a more affectionate letter would only have accentuated his homesickness. They had always held each other at arm's-length, particularly since his father died.

Felicity's letter was brief and it took him some time to decipher her childish scrawl.

Dear Johnnie,

So you have arrived in Italy. Have you seen a battle yet? All the talk here is of a second front in Europe next year, so your war is rather a sideline I suppose. I am going to be Captain of house hockey next year and I want to join the ATS before it is all over. Funny both of us being in the army, I am determined to be an officer too.

Love,

Felicity.

'The little cow,' John thought. 'She could never resist a dig at me.'

He screwed up her letter and threw it away. He looked at his mother's again. Reading between the lines he recognised that she was worrying about him and this gave him a momentary pang, then he threw hers away as well.

Later in the day he went down to the Battery position with Charles Pilling to hold a pay parade. As they sat at a trestle table in the front room of one of the houses, they heard the sound of armoured vehicles coming up the hill beyond the playing fields. It was the third Battery 647 coming out of the line. Pilling halted proceedings so that the Troop could go outside and give them a welcome.

The Battery commander led in a Jeep followed by two O.P. Sherman tanks, and then the guns. An assortment of supply vehicles brought up the rear. These men had not had a cushy billet over Christmas, but with five guns from the regiment which were still serviceable, had fought a bitter action across the Moro river west of the town of Ortona. The rain had turned the whole area into a morass of mud over which the tanks and guns had squelched until, at times, many became bogged down as their tracks dug deeper into the mire. The Germans were in the same position of course, but were determined, in persistent counter-attacks, to drive the Allied forces back across the Moro river.

It was a war of attrition. 647 Battery was in support of the tanks of the Cumbrian Yeomanry and to their left was the Duke of Newcastle's Light Infantry, the DNLI, all fighting bitterly in the swamp to keep their bridgehead over the Moro. It was fire-power which was the vital factor, and there were many acts of heroism during that week, not least among 647 Battery who managed to keep the shells pounding the enemy in near-impossible conditions.

It was the weather that finally ended the battle, in fact both sides ground to a halt. But the 8th Army had held their foothold over the river. 647 Battery and the Cumbrian Yeomanry were relieved, but the new regiments were only in a holding position, any mobility was out of the question.

A cheer went up from the troop as the Battery rolled past along the village street. John watched them, fascinated. These were battle-weary men. They were caked with mud and grime. Their eyes were glassy through lack of sleep, a few of the lightly wounded had bandages wrapped around heads or arms. Some would be sent down to the Casualty

Clearing Station at Termoli, but most would have attention by the M.O. at the Regiment Aid Station. A few of the brighter sparks shouted casual insults.

'All right for some!'

'Had a good Christmas did you?'

But most were silent, they were like automata, too tired to take in the scene.

There was a New Year's Eve party that night for the officers at Regimental H.Q. John had been give a T.A.B. innoculation by the M.O., this is the worst of the jabs and often gives the semblance of forty-eight hour 'flu, he felt hot and feverish and left the party early and went to bed. But he stayed long enough to hear stories of the action across the river. The 647 officers were the centre of attention, all of them clean and scrubbed and in their smart service dress, giving little indication of the exhausted men that he had seen in the morning riding through the village.

The Colonel greeted each officer as he entered the room. He looked resplendent in "Blues", a dark uniform with chain armour on the epaulettes.

'Settling in, John?' he asked.

Crabbe was so surprised at the use of his Christian name that he stood tongue-tied for a moment before blurting out 'Yes sir, absolutely sir.'

'Good. You are lucky, it is always difficult for a young subaltern to join in the middle of a battle. You have had a period of preparation and an opportunity to get to know everybody first.' He paused and gave him a friendly smile. 'And you have learned a number of lessons, haven't you, young man?'

'Yes sir, I have indeed.'

The Colonel nodded and turned to the next officer. The brief exchange was at an end.

All the talk was of the exploits of a troop commander who found himself on his own north of the river. The other O.P. Sherman tanks had been unable to join him, either stuck in the mud or put out of action. He left his tank and found an observation post, a wattle hut, and directed the Battery guns against the enemy, although under severe shell and mortar fire. His O.P. assistant, a lance-bombardier, was hit in the foot and was sent back to the tank. He himself was wounded in both the shoulder and the leg. But he continued directing the firing, and after shelling had destroyed his wireless, continued to give fire orders by voice over 140 yards. He stayed, bringing devastating fire against the enemy, until the light faded. His wounds were fortunately slight and although evacuated to the C.C.S. he was expected to rejoin the regiment in a few days.

The Colonel told the assembled officers that the Brigadier of the Cumbrian Yeomanry had been in touch with him and recommended a medal. There was even talk of a V.C.

John collapsed into bed shortly after midnight. He had remained to drink to 1944 and then left unnoticed. He felt feverish and light-headed. He had learnt a great deal of what war was like at the party. The story of the troop commander had opened his eyes. He buried his head in the pillow and tried to visualise himself in that situation. He was quite sure that his first instinct would be to run like hell. Then he thought of the Colonel calling him by his Christian name, of Sholto, Pilling and Cobber, and of all the friendly men of his Battery. He was aware of the disgrace if he let them all down; for better or worse he was an officer with people depending upon him. He was terrified of going into action, but also afraid of being afraid. He did not know, as he drifted off to sleep, whether terror or duty to his friends would prevail when it came to the test. He was soon to find out.

☆ ☆ ☆

All the regimental guns were now clapped out. Early in January 1944 the regiment moved to a depot near Naples to receive new equipment. There was a great deal of work to do, checking that the twenty-four new guns and ten Sherman O.P. tanks were correctly fitted out, modified and loaded with kit. John stood around trying to look useful, but all the activity really passed him by. He did escape for one day, though, with Charles Pilling, and they went to Naples.

The city had not suffered very much from the war which had largely passed it by. But ever since it was the capital of the Kingdom of Naples it had developed into a cesspit, personifying the poor south of the country. Rich villas existed cheek by jowl with appalling slums and dereliction. It had been bad enough before the war, neglected by Mussolini and the Fascists in favour of Rome and the cities of the North. Now with the Allied Administration trying to restore some sort of order, it had sunk even further into chaos and despair.

Hordes of dark-skinned ragamuffins, some as young as five or six, followed Charles and John as they made their way to the Officers' Club, pulling at their sleeves, and chattering like a wagon-load of monkeys.

'You fuck my sister, very clean, very cheap, she twelve years.'

'You like me, nice bum, you fuck me.' This was from the leader of the gang, a boy of about ten with a roguish little face and mischievous eyes.

They were in a narrow street off one of the main throughfares, and soon they were surrounded by a solid mass of shouting children and unable to move. John tried to read his map, and this lead to a further cry from the leader.

'I show you way, girls, nice girls, cheap, clean.'

'Put that map away,' Charles said sharply. 'Guard your wallet or these little bastards will fleece you. We have got to get out of this. Punch and kick, come on, charge them. I don't want to end up as a corpse in a back street of Naples.'

The sudden onrush of the two officers cleared a corridor between the children and Charles and John ran full tilt, but the leader was very agile, he leapt ahead and stood blocking their path holding a long kitchen knife. The rest of the kids, like a well-trained army, closed ranks and once more they were surrounded.

The leader stood looking at them. He was still smiling, but the eyes were no longer mischievous but hard and unblinking.

'Da' me soldi, subito.'

At the same time a small girl started to pull at the watch on John's wrist. The leader lunged the knife forward towards John's stomach.

'Give it to her,' Pilling muttered.

They were both fully aware of the situation. It was

ridiculous, really. A main road was only about 400 yards away, they could see the traffic on it, but they were in this dark alley and hemmed in by the children. They knew that the kids could at any moment pull them to the ground and then the leader could slit their throats and strip them of all their valuables.

As John handed over his watch, Pilling shouted suddenly, 'John, pull your gun and shoot!'

It was fairly obvious that they were not armed, but the leader hesitated for a moment, and Charles kicked out catching the child on the knees, and as he fell to the ground, they ran. There was a concerted howl of rage from the kids, two of them leapt on John, he managed to shake one of them off but the other tightened his grip on his neck and he fell to his knees. Charles turned round, caught the child by the hair and pulled him off, then he seized John by the arm and dragged him to his feet.

'Back!' Pilling cried. 'Backwards!'

It was a wise move. Most of the children were in front with the leader, behind they were thin on the ground. It was not difficult to break out of the pack and then they had the narrow lane to themselves. The trouble was that they were going in the wrong direction, getting further away from the main road into the maze of fetid passageways. Also, the kids quickly regrouped and were in hot pursuit.

They both saw it at the same time. A *salita* of stone steps climbing between two blocks of dingy apartments. They went up two steps at a time and when they reached an intersecting path they were several stairs above the children. Here they stopped, panting for breath. Being above the miniature army gave them a tactical advantage. Charles held his foot out in what he hoped was a menacing fashion, and John prized a loose piece of concrete out of the side wall and held it above his head ready to throw.

The kids stopped in their tracks, about ten feet below them uncertain of what to do next. It was a stalemate, for the moment anyway.

The liquid hit the space between them with surprising force, splashing both sides, and there was a shout and a roar of laughter from above. A very fat man with a bucket in his hand was leaning on a balcony. Faces began appearing from other windows on both sides. Almost at once a woman followed suit and a pail emptied this time mostly on the kids, seconds later a third came splashing down. They were being bombarded with foul smelling slops. The two officers did not know whether they or the children were the target, nor did they stop to find out. Seeing the opposition in some disarray, they took the lane to the left and did not stop running until they came to the top of another flight of steps, at the bottom was the main road.

☆ ☆ ☆

'Vermouth tastes quite different in Italy,' Charles observed as they propped up the bar in the Officers' Club. 'Not at all like the bottled stuff you buy at home. You can get it from the wood, dry like a good sherry.'

'I'm still shaking like a leaf,' John said. 'I will have a large brandy.'

'As you wish. But don't get drunk too early, we have the whole day in front of us.'

'You are jolly cool, you realize that those bloody urchins could have murdered us?'

'Yes, but they didn't.' Charles smiled at him. 'I don't want to appear pompous, but when you have been in action for a while you will learn to forget danger that has passed. If you continue to look back on every nasty moment and think what might have been you will end up a nervous wreck.'

'I'll try.' John gulped his brandy. 'But you said yourself I would never make a soldier.'

'Did I? Well, I should not have been so presumptuous. Life is full of surprises. You will probably end up as a hero. But as I am being paternal, here is another piece of advice. Live for the day in this stupid war. And at this particular moment of time, we are alive and kicking, drinking in a pleasant bar, and after lunch we will sample the delights of Naples.'

'Charles,' John said as they ordered a second round of drinks, 'it is a bloody good thing that those kids understand English.'

'Do they? Apart from "fuck my sister, very clean, or fuck me" I don't think they have a comprehensive command of our mother tongue.'

'They knew the word "shoot".'

'Yes, you are right, that was lucky. Maybe it was just my magnificent tone of command, like saying "sit" to a dog.'

'John Crabbe!' A young tank officer was pushing his way towards them from the other end of the bar.

'Good God! Nigel!' John exclaimed.

'Yes, Good God Nigel it is, and Taffy's here, just gone for a pee, he had a week's convalescence in Sorrento, lucky sod. Quite a reunion. I'll go and steer him in this direction.'

John had hardly finished putting Charles in the picture before there was a shout from outside the Gents.

'Johnnie Boyo!' Taffy came up. 'This is bloody marvellous. I just came in for a drink before going to the Town Major to get transport to your unit and there was Nigel, we met in the doorway.'

'Did you walk out of the same transit camp?'

'No need, boy, this time. The Regiment worked wonders. I was picked up at the hotel in Sorrento and told they would arrange a lift from here. No red tape, I feel like a VIP.'

'You can come back with John and me,' Charles said after they had been introduced.

'Good! How about another round, pronto. What is it to be?'

John and Taffy chattered together non-stop, exchanging all their news. Eventually Nigel broke into their conversation.

'You will have to start where I left off,' he said to Pilling. 'I did my best to try and initiate young Crabbe into the facts of life.'

'Come off it, Nigel,' Taffy said hotly. 'Don't you look down your nose at Johnnie here. He came back for me, didn't he? The bloody plane was exploding like it was Guy Fawkes night. And he stayed with me all the way to the C.C.S. He was a bloody good friend was Johnnie, so don't you run him down, see!'

John blushed. 'It was nothing, Taffy, I couldn't just leave you, could I? Anyone would have done the same.'

'Modesty will get you nowhere,' Charles observed. 'Actually, Nigel, our madcap Colonel was quite impressed.'

'Of course!' Nigel replied triumphantly. 'I told these two that if they hived off from the camp they would get a hero's welcome, and I managed, over the head of a prissy little

Penguin, to get them on a plane.'

'Which was blown up.'

'Well that added lustre to Crabbe's adventure. All due to me!'

'You are an arrogant old sod you know, Nigel.' Taffy grinned at him. 'But we are all together now in one piece, so what is the programme for today?'

'After lunch,' Charles said 'the Opera.'

'Oh no,' John replied.

'Why not? I thought you would jump at the chance.'

'I don't like opera, I'm afraid. All those fat ladies with tiny frozen hands.'

'Nonsense, Johnnie,' Taffy cried. 'It's the singing, all that glorious singing. What's the programme?'

'A double bill. Cavalleria Rusticana and a ballet of Ravel's Bolero.'

'Is the opera Puccini?' Nigel asked.

'No, Mascagni.'

'Never heard of him.'

'I am surrounded by Philistines, except for you, Taffy. Well! We will go. There's a matinee at three, you two can please yourselves.'

They all went together by taxi. Over lunch, Nigel had made no secret of the fact that he thought John and Charles had been incredibly stupid getting mixed up with a mob of *ragazzaglia*. Pilling was piqued but said nothing; he decided he did not like Nigel.

John enjoyed the show all the same. The opera was short and colourful and the Bolero exciting. Ravel's pulsating rhythms stayed in his head as they settled down to dinner in a black market restaurant, in the centre of the city.

'It is not their fault, you know,' John said suddenly as they started their meal.

'Whose fault? What are you talking about?' Nigel enquired.

'Those kids. They are so poor, probably starving, they have to steal to survive.'

'They tried to knife you, didn't they? And you start getting sentimental about them?'

'He is not being sentimental, he said it is not their fault and he is right,' Charles said sharply.

'Christ,' Nigel replied, 'we have enough on our plate without feeling sorry for a lot of murderous guttersnipes. Are you two socialists, or something?'

'What if we are?' Charles was getting angry.

'Now we have taken over things will be better for them,' Taffy said soothingly.

'I doubt it very much,' Pilling rejoined.

There was a pause in the conversation. Taffy broke the silence.

'Well I wonder what life has in store for us? I would like to have a crystal ball and see what we will all be doing in two weeks' time.'

'I can tell you, having the shit knocked out of you on the Garigliano,' Nigel replied.

'But we are 8th Army,' John said.

'You were, but having brought you right across Italy, they are hardly likely to send you back again. I don't think even our High Command is as stupid as that. No, you will join us in the 5th just in time for the big offensive.'

'I think it extremely unlikely that there will be a push before the spring,' Charles remarked, looking at Nigel with distaste.

'Balls. Yankee Clark sees himself in Rome wrapped in the Stars and Stripes as a toga before the winter's out, and he doesn't care how many of us poor bastards get blown to buggery on the way.'

'You are only guessing though, Nigel boy, aren't you? I mean you are not in the confidence of General Alexander,' Taffy said.

'No, but I keep my ears to the ground, and remember this is where it is all happening, I haven't been wintering on the Adriatic like you.'

Pilling wanted to deliver some stinging riposte, but couldn't think of one, so bit his lip and remained silent.

'And another thing,' Nigel lowered his voice, 'there is a loud buzz on the bush telegraph of a seaborne landing further up the coast to coincide with our offensive. With any luck we have both missed the boat on that one, just as well because if it is under the command of Mark bloody Clark it is certain to be a monumental cock-up.'

'Bumptious little sod,' Charles said as they drove back to

the camp.

'Oh Nigel is not so bad, really,' Taffy replied. 'Just a little self-opinionated, that's all.'

'You don't think there will be an attack soon, then, Charles?' John asked.

'No I do not. Your friend was just showing off, that's all.'

☆ ☆ ☆

John stood at the edge of the sea. The mist sat lightly on the water some fifty yards from the shore, the tiny waves sliding out from under it exploding with a gentle plop upon the white sand. Behind, a plantation of Christmas trees screened the guns and as the dawn light topped the highest branches it touched the specks of foam, making them sparkle.

He felt an urge to go for a walk along the beach. He used to do this on holiday at Pevensey Bay when he was a child, striding away over the pebbles with the rising sun in his eyes before the world was awake. But it was different now, he was not on holiday, the shore might well be mined and he could not stray too far from his truck where Haddock was manning the wireless. 622 Battery had moved in at around midnight. Charlie Troop was by the sea, and Don Troop, which Taffy had joined, inland on their right. 621 Battery was deployed by the road and 647 in reserve.

'Admiring the view, sir?' It was Cobber.

'Hullo Sergeant-Major,' John replied.

'Those trees come to an end just ahead of No. 1 gun, it should be possible to see the Garigliano from there. Coming sir?'

John hesitated.

'It's all right, Mr Pilling is awake, I have just been having a chat with him.'

They skirted the wood walking along the edge of the beach, and in a few moments came to a shallow brook which marked the end of the plantation. A mile of water meadows stretched out ahead, much of it under floodwater. It was not possible to see the river, but the line of it was evident under a shroud of mist, billowing in off the sea. Above this the foothills stood out in the early sun, appearing disembodied like a Chinese painting.

'The enemy must be up there,' John observed.

'A complete army of them, I reckon,' Cobber replied.

'So we are overlooked.'

'That's right sir. Lots of nasty Krauts are squinting at us with their binoculars.' He looked at John with a wry smile. 'I bet they told you, sir, during training, that you should always choose a gun position behind a hill, or at any rate in a hollow, so that you have flash cover.'

'Yes they did.'

'What they didn't tell you is that half the time it isn't possible, like here for instance, this position is a bastard.'

'But there are the trees, and we are using flashless propellant,' John ventured.

'That helps, sir, yes. The trouble is, the trees aren't tall enough. Still, to look on the bright side,' he continued, 'at least we are dry, there is a regiment of infantry dug in on those mud flats, Ross and Cromarty Highlanders, poor sods.'

'Do you think there will be an offensive?' John asked as they walked back to the gun position.

'You tell me, sir! Mr Pilling thinks we will hold this position till the spring. I only hope he is wrong. The sooner we get out of this death-trap the better as far as I am concerned.'

John's first day in action was uneventful. The guns fired from time to time; Max Gregory the troop commander, who was forward with the infantry, registered targets such as enemy batteries and forward positions. John, supervised by Pilling, was allowed to take over, relaying orders from the wireless in his truck to the guns. It was some time before he realised that Sholto was sitting behind him.

'Good boy, Johnnie,' he said 'you know your stuff.'

John felt himself blushing and mumbled something in reply.

'Charles.' Sholto climbed out of the truck. 'Orders at Battery Command Post at 1800 hours. You stay here, John, I don't want all the officers in one place in case the Krauts get nasty. Charles will put you in the picture.'

After he had gone, John looked at Pilling.

'What does all that mean?' he asked. 'Is something going

to happen?'

'I think it means that I was wrong,' Charles replied. 'I know that look in Sholto's eye. They won't be routine orders, I fancy, so take a deep breath, young John. It looks as though tomorrow we will be going into battle.'

4

GUSTAV LINE.	
17 JANUARY 1944	OFFENSIVE BEGINS. BRITISH TROOPS ESTABLISH A BRIDGEHEAD OVER THE GARIGLIANO
19 JANUARY	BRITISH FORCES FAIL TO CAPTURE S. AMBROGIO NORTH OF RIVER.
20 JANUARY	U.S. DIVISION FAIL TO REACH S. ANGELO OVER RIVER
22 JANUARY	U.S. AND BRITISH TROOPS LAND AT ANZIO JUST SOUTH OF ROME.
24 JANUARY	U.S. AND FREE FRENCH FORCES BEGIN FIRST BATTLE OF CASSINO.

'This is the form,' Charles Pilling said as he and John sat in the truck eating M. & V. stew out of their mess tins. The rest of the crew had gone for supper at the cookhouse, and they were alone. It was curiously quiet, so they could hear the waves gently lapping the beach. It had been like that all day, apart from occasional fire from their own guns. There had been little evidence of enemy activity, only the intermittent crump of enemy shells on the infantry positions a mile or so away.

'I will be giving orders,' Charles continued, 'to the NCOs at 2100 hours, meanwhile this is the picture. At first light we fire a barrage to support the infantry who will secure a bridgehead over the river. The immediate objective is two villages, Minturno and Trimonsuoli, both on high ground. Now here is the fancy bit. "A" Troop of 621

Battery is on a seaborne landing just north of the river, so if, and it is a bloody big if, all goes well, we will have guns and an O.P. on the far side, together with a battalion of infantry. We can consider ourselves extremely lucky, young John, that we are not in that little party.'

'I do see your point,' John said, with relief, 'so we have the easier job.'

'Yes, at the moment. But you can never tell in war, things have a nasty habit of suddenly catching up with you when you least expect it.' He paused. 'Now for the general picture, which for security reasons will not be given out at the NCOs' briefing. Over the next few days there will be attacks by our troops and further inland by the Yanks all the way along the river, culminating in a major push at a place called Cassino on the old Appian Way to Rome. Apparently there is a monastery there on a tall hill which, if the Krauts occupy it, gives them a commanding view of the whole valley. Cassino is the crunch point.'

'Is that the Yanks'?'

'Yes, with the Free French Forces, whom I gather are fairly good. They had better be. One other point,' he hesitated, 'U.S. and British forces are on their way to Anzio, just south of Rome, for a beach landing, the idea being that they will strike inland and link up with us.'

'So Nigel was right,' John cried tactlessly.

'Either your friend was just guessing,' Charles said testily, 'or he had prior knowledge. In which case he should have kept his bloody trap shut, and not gone shouting about it in a restaurant in Naples. His little exercise in showing off could cost lives.'

'Is that the lot?' John asked.

'Yes. Isn't it enough?'

John felt duly chastised. 'I am sorry Charles,' he said, 'actually I don't like Nigel much either, he is such a know-all.' There was no response, so he rummaged in his bag and pulled out a bottle of whisky.

'A peace offering, Charles?'

'You are appealing to my baser nature.'

'It is, after all, the eve of battle.'

'All right, I am placated by your Scotch. Incidentally, we won't get the fire plan until round about midnight, and the fun starts at 0500, so neither of us will get much sleep tonight.'

John would not have slept anyway. He never did on the night before his return to boarding school, dread at the prospect of the coming day kept him fitfully awake. It was the same now. He recalled the pre-battle atmosphere so perfectly realised in Shakespeare's *Henry V*, but he could not identify with the warrior king, more with the soldier, Williams.

'We died at such a place; some swearing; some crying for a surgeon; some upon their wives left poor behind them; some upon the debts they owe; some upon their children rawly left.'

The cry of the common soldier through all history.

When the barrage actually started, it was almost a relief.

The sudden noise rending the morning stillness, the flashes highlighting the silhouette of the guns against the fir trees like a Christmas party, the whiff of cordite wafting across the position, and above all the pulsating power of the guns firing non-stop, then pausing for only a few seconds before they were off again on a higher trajectory as the barrage moved inexorably forward. It was impossible not to be caught up in the excitement of it all.

Charles was in control in the truck, while John walked between the four guns. He did not know exactly what he was meant to do, keep an eye on everything presumably, but they were managing very well without him.

Eventually the guns stopped firing. But the noise of battle continued ahead. The crump of shells falling and the almost simultaneous sharp whistle, denoting the deadly German 88mm guns. Nothing landed near the position and they felt almost cocooned from the battle amidst their Christmas trees.

News started to filter through during the first day. The seaborne landing just over the river had been a fiasco. The first wave of infantry, together with 621 "A" Troop commander O.P., landed too far to the north, and the enemy attacked them in strength. Also the beach where they landed was strewn with mines. Their casualties were heavy but the O.P. managed to establish itself, the only wireless link with the forces south of the river. "A" Troop, due to a navigational error by the Navy, were landed south of the Garigliano, not far from John's gun position, which probably saved them from destruction. So all the regimental artillery were together on the same side of the river.

The battle raged during the next few days. A bridgehead was established on the far side at heavy cost in dead and wounded. Cheerful news came through that the Allied forces had made a successful landing at Anzio. But still the guns of Charlie Troop continued to fire, without any unwelcome attention by the enemy.

It was on the morning of the sixth day that Sholto came up to Charlie Troop in his Jeep. He spent half an hour with the guns talking to all and sundry, and then arrived at the truck.

'Any coffee?' he asked, climbing inside.

'Tea, Sholto. Just brewed.'

'O.K. Thanks. Haddock!'

'Yes sir?'

'I have been asked by Bombardier King at Command Post to tell you that your supply of vino has dried up.'

'Oh really, sir?'

'Yes. The C.P. staff discovered your hiding place and drank the lot.'

'Oh, that's a pity Sir.'

'For you, but not for them. When this little party's over I will give you a Jeep to liberate some more, but this time you won't keep it to yourself, will you?'

'Of course not, sir.'

'Good! Now let's get down to business.' He looked at Charles and John for a moment before continuing. 'Max has had nearly a week at the O.P., and he needs a rest. I am going up there myself, but I shall be swanning around to keep an eye on things. I need an officer to man Max's O.P.'

'Of course, Sholto.' Pilling said.

'No not you, Charles. I must have an experienced officer at the gun position. The battle is pretty fluid and the Krauts are counter-attacking like hell, I don't think it will happen, but this position could be overrun.' He gave John a smile. 'I'll look after you, Johnnie, and it will only be for a couple of days at the most. O.K.?'

☆ ☆ ☆

A cigar glowed in the darkness as John reported to the Battery H.Q. truck.

'My last,' Major Sholto said, 'Until we get back to civilisation, so I am not going to waste it. There is time enough.'

'If that is the case I'll have a cigarette.' John pulled a dog-eared packet out of his pack.

'Got all your gear, Johnnie, map, compass, etc?'

'Yes, Sholto. Charles fitted me out.'

'Good.' He paused for a moment. 'I am sorry to land you in this, but I will be near at hand to see the mad Jocks don't bugger you about. Max will have registered all the necessary targets, and the Jocks will tell you where they want the fire. It is just a question of holding the fort for a couple of days to give Max a rest. If there is any movement, I will take over and send you back. O.K.?'

'Yes Sholto.'

'It will be bloody good experience, and don't worry. You will cope O.K., otherwise I would not be taking you with me.'

John did not answer. He felt a sudden sickness in the pit of his stomach and pulled furiously on his cigarette.

'You are frightened,' Sholto said. 'Of course you are, so am I. But it is always worse the first time. We all have to have our baptism of fire, and you will feel better afterwards. It must be rather like your first night in the theatre, sick with nerves at the time and feeling bloody marvellous when it is all over, isn't that so?'

'I will do my best,' John replied.

'Of course you will. Incidentally,' Sholto's manner changed abruptly, his voice becoming quite sharp, 'you underestimate yourself, you always have, and that is bloody silly. Now go and call Bombardier King and Mason. We must be off.'

The Major drove the Jeep himself with John next to him. King the driver and Mason the signaller were in the back. They edged forward slowly in the pitch darkness, the road was pitted with shell holes, so the Jeep pitched and tossed, but Sholto drove with calm assurance. Shapes of vehicles came at them out of the dark going in the opposite direction, mostly three-ton lorries which had just delivered supplies, they could only travel at night, and John noticed an ambulance. Otherwise there was an eerie silence, all the guns on both sides seemed to be asleep. They did not stop until they reached the Bailey bridge over the river, here there was a jam of vehicles waiting to cross.

'Bugger,' Sholto whispered.

John had never been in a battle before, but it was obvious even to him that the enemy shelled bridges, and that the longer the delay the more chance there was of trouble. Progress was appallingly slow as they inched forward.

'Is there someone controlling the traffic?' John asked, his voice shaky.

'Yes,' Sholto replied. 'Military Police. You might think that we are sitting ducks here, but they have to stay at their post the whole bloody time, poor sods.'

The previous silence was now shattered by the engines of the queue of vehicles stopping and starting, it seemed incredible that the Germans were not taking any action. John tried to think of other things. Christmas in the Mess, the day in Naples at the Opera, but it didn't work, he just sat and gripped his knees.

It probably only took ten minutes to cross the bridge, but it seemed a lifetime. Once over they were able to move more quickly and John noticed that the line of vehicles was far longer on this side. Three-ton lorries, Scout cars, Bren Gun carriers and ambulances. Sholto knew the way and after about half a mile they turned off the main road and took a track to the left down a sunken lane.

'Nearly there,' he whispered.

Then suddenly the silence was rent by an appalling noise. It sounded like the screaming of animals in pain, or a demented air-raid siren.

'Moaning Minnies,' said King from the back.

'That's it.' The Major stopped the Jeep. '*Nebelwerfers*, a multiple Kraut mortar. You will hear that noise, Johnnie, often enough whenever we get close to the enemy.'

A sheet of flame shot up into the air behind them.

'Poor buggers on the bridge are getting it,' Mason

observed with surprising calm.

'We were bloody lucky, sir,' King said.

'Yes,' Sholto replied. 'They are cunning bastards. They must have heard the trucks leaving and held their fire until they were sure that there was a major build-up by the bridge. Meanwhile we had better stay put, the shelling is too near for comfort.'

As if in confirmation there was a loud crump on the top of the bank, sending a shower of earth all over them.

'You managed that very well, sir,' Mason said, shaking the dirt off his helmet. 'A nice sunken road just when the stonking started.'

The Major grinned at him. 'All the same I don't think we will tempt providence by moving on until this little party is over.'

But the party continued. As soon as the mortars stopped the shelling started, most of them fell behind by the river but the occasional one exploded in front and on both sides of their narrow haven.

'How about a hot drink, sir?' Bombardier King produced a thermos of coffee.

'Good idea, and I think we might lace it with a little brandy.' Sholto emptied the contents of his hip flask into the four cups.

John had started to shiver in the cold night air and the warm liquid was a comfort. The shelling stopped eventually, and the complete silence that followed was uncanny.

'Can I take a look-see, sir?' Mason said.

'Yes O.K.,' Sholto said, 'you might like to go too, Johnnie, but keep your heads down. They will start harassing fire soon, the odd one all over the shop until first light; very predictable, the Krauts.'

John was glad to be able to stretch his legs, he had begun to feel claustrophobic down below, so he followed Mason and climbed on to the top of the bank. They could see the bridge quite clearly, several fires had lit the scene like a spotlight, traffic was still moving and the burning vehicles had been pushed off the road. It all seemed quite unreal, like watching a war film. There was a vestige of light on the horizon to the east, so they could just make out the outline of the sunken road which was only about two hundred yards long. Their Jeep was the only truck on it.

Ahead it was still pitch-dark. A whine just above their heads caught John unawares, he was just about to leap down the bank when Mason held his arm.

'Ours, sir. Charlie Troop.' He grinned at him. 'Our guns are giving the fuckers a return match. Didn't Mr Pilling tell you that they were going to give us a bit of moral support?'

When they got back to the Jeep Major Sholto started the engine.

'The village of Trimonsuoli is about a quarter of a mile ahead. Take over, Bombardier, and drive slowly in high gear, we don't want to announce our arrival. If we wait much longer it will be getting light.'

But it was still dark when they reached the village. King parked the Jeep behind a stone wall and they groped along the little street, picking their feet over the rubble, and found R.H.Q. of the Ross and Cromarty Highlanders. The black-out was complete, but Sholto knew the way and they came into a room at the back of a house lit by one paraffin lamp.

The Colonel was sitting behind a desk. The lamp lit his face from below, giving the impression of a large disembodied head.

'Hullo Sholto, you old sod,' he said cheerfully. 'I wondered if you would make it. The Hun has been busy at the bridge.'

'So we noticed, sir, but we were ahead of the party, as luck would have it.'

'Bully for you. Glad to see you, anyway. I am afraid we have only tea to offer.' A sergeant appeared out of the gloom with four mugs. 'Max has done a bloody good job, I told Colonel Alex as much on the blower, he needs a rest though. Is this boy the relief?'

'Yes sir.' John saluted smartly.

'What is your name, young man?'

'Crabbe, sir, John Crabbe.'

'Welcome, John Crabbe. We have woken Max, he is next door getting ready. The O.P. is on the floor above. A bit draughty as there is only half a roof, but not a bad view.'

'Go and see him, Johnnie,' the Major said. 'He will show you the ropes. There is half an hour before it gets light.'

The room upstairs was really quite comfortable. There

was an armchair by the window with a table by the side, and on it a map covered with cellophane and a row of coloured chinagraph pencils. Mason took over the radio by the door.

Max Gregory put his hand on John's shoulder.

'Bloody good of you to give me a break,' he said. 'Don't worry, I will be back tomorrow night and if the Krauts counter-attack Sholto will take over. I don't think they will, though, it is stalemate at the moment. The Colonel puts a brave face on it, but he is sick as a dog at the pasting his Jocks are getting. They are bloody marvellous in attack, but here they have to sit, bogged down, with the Krauts stonking them rotten.'

'The enemy holds all the high ground?' John asked.

'Yes, and watches our every move. But if they try and attack the Jocks will give them a very bloody nose indeed.'

John looked at the map. Each target was marked from A to K, covering most of the area.

'Charlie Troop has registered all of them,' Max continued, 'just bellow out the letter and you will get the fire. The Colonel downstairs has his map marked up too. So it is all quite simple. O.K.?'

'Yes, Max.'

'Oh, one thing before I go. Target F is the remains of a barn about five hundred yards away. I don't know what it is, could be Battalion H.Q. At all events, at first light, as soon as they can see what they are doing, the little grey men are apt to venture out with a spade to crap. They have the cover of the olive grove, but if you watch through glasses you can often spot them. Stand Charlie Troop by, and as soon as they have got their trousers down, let them have it. If you sit forward in the chair the barn is just visible on the right side of the window. Good hunting.'

'Well, we are on our own now, sir.' Mason said, after Max had gone.

'Yes,' John replied.

☆ ☆ ☆

John never saw any Germans with their trousers down, but he was kept busy. Guns fired from both sides and several shells landed in the village on the first day, but nothing very near their house. Most of the fire was directed behind them onto the main road and on the undulating country ahead where the Jock infantry were dug in. A runner came up from R.H.Q. below at regular intervals and gave orders from the Colonel, while John watched the puffs of smoke billow up over the target, just like on the model used during his training.

It was so fascinating that for the most part he forgot to be afraid. There were times, however, when a shell landed close, that he felt an urge to run down the stairs, but Mason's seeming indifference to everything that was going on outside steadied him.

The signaller had been quiet all day, concentrating on his radio set and transmitting John's orders to the guns. Then, during a lull in the late afternoon, he said suddenly, 'Enjoying yourself, sir?'

'Yes, yes I am in a way,' John replied, grateful that the silence between them had been broken.

'O.P.s are the best, you can see everything happening. Though this is a cushy one, nice and comfortable, not like being in a bloody O.P. tank expecting to be brewed up any moment.' He paused. 'Can I give you a tip, sir?'

'Of course, please do.'

'Well don't look through the glasses all the time. Your eyes get blurred and you can't see anything. Captain Gregory never uses them, until he spots something, then he focuses on the target, just for a moment, and Bob's your uncle, one Jerry tank knocked out.'

'Thank you, I'll remember that.'

'That's O.K. sir. Oh, and another thing —'

'Yes?'

'We've got thick walls round us. A shell will have to come through that window or the hole in the roof to do us any harm. I should think the law of averages are against that sir. As I said, this is a cushy billet.'

John did not reply. He wasn't quite sure whether there was implied criticism in the signaller's remark, or whether he was just trying to be helpful. At all events he felt a flush coming to his cheeks.

It was the next day about eleven in the morning when

John actually saw something. There was a stretch of road visible just to the left of the olive groves, it was only about a hundred yards long before it disappeared behind a fold in the ground. John had been watching it continuously until his eyes ached. Suddenly, he spotted a motorcycle combination caught by the rays of a wintry sun. It looked like a child's toy and he could see the rider and passenger sitting bolt upright like tin soldiers. He seized the map and identified the road immediately. The contours showed that it was concealed for about a quarter of a mile before it came to a T-junction which could be seen by the naked eye. This point was target C on his map.

'Target C fire by order,' he shouted to Mason. Now he had to work out how long the vehicle would take to reach it. 'Thirty miles per hour,' he thought, 'it won't go faster on the shell-pitted road.' He clicked his stop watch. Half a mile a minute, so a quarter of a mile in thirty seconds. At twenty-seven seconds on his stop watch he bellowed 'Fire!'

The screech of four shells overhead made him duck. The tableau on the hillside only lasted for a few seconds, but was embedded on his mind. The motor-cycle appeared and ran straight into an orange flash, debris shot into the air and then seemed to hover like a slow motion film. He could see one wheel, apparently undamaged, descend vertically until it vanished in the smoke.

'Good shooting, sir,' Mason said appreciatively.

'Rather a fluke I am afraid.' John could not hide the pleasure in his voice.

'Not a fluke sir, because you worked it all out. But lucky, dead lucky. And there are now two less bloody Jerries in this world.'

John caught his breath, and his feeling of exhilaration vanished abruptly. It had all been a game, a very exciting game. But he had not just scored a try at rugger, he had killed two men.

☆ ☆ ☆

Sholto dropped John at the gun position before midnight. It was good to be back in the little fir forest again, he had felt vulnerable and out on a limb at the O.P. Also the news that he had actually hit something preceded him.

'You jammy bastard,' Charles said when John arrived at the truck. 'It can take months of slogging it out in an O.P. before you get a chance like that.'

'Do I detect a note of envy in your voice Mr Pilling?' S.M. Cobber appeared out of the darkness.

'Absolutely right, Sergeant-Major. I am green with jealousy. Talk about beginner's luck!'

'Luck, sir? I imagine Mr Crabbe must have made some contribution to hitting the target smack on.'

'All right. Although I don't think the destruction of one Kraut motorcycle will have a very significant effect on our war effort, I had better join in the general congratulations. Mr Crabbe I salute you, in that on your first visit to an O.P. you actually succeeded in doing something.'

'I join in that, sir,' Cobber remarked.

'Give me a call at first light, Sergeant-Major. Meanwhile we will both get some kip. I shouldn't worry about any enemy action, Mr Crabbe here will have already pounded them into submission.'

The two officers went to their slit trenches covered by bivvy tents at the back of the truck.

'Charles.' John turned to the other man before he began to prepare for bed.

'Yes?'

'How did you feel when you first killed someone?'

'Oh no!' Pilling groaned. 'We're not going to have a guilt complex now, are we?'

'I only asked a simple question,' John replied angrily.

'All right, calm down.' Charles smiled at him. 'That is what we are here for, John, to kill Germans. If it makes you feel any better, think of Hitler, already responsible for the deaths of millions of innocent people. He has to be stopped and you are playing a tiny part in the process. Even an old cynic like me will admit that we are on the right side. And another thing. Every time you order our guns to fire from here in our little seaside riviera, you are trying to kill or maim human beings. It is just that you saw what happens on the receiving end for once, and that has made you get all sentimental. Forget it and go to sleep.'

But John could not forget it. He had seen the two

German soldiers quite clearly. He wondered what they were like, possibly married with children, and he had blown them up, and what's more, thoroughly enjoyed it. All his life he had never been able to understand how people could shoot birds or animals for sport, the whole idea was repugnant to him, yet earlier that day he had tracked two men and killed them.

He thought of his father, a gentle parson, who had died of a heart attack while John watched as a helpless spectator. He had loved him dearly, and since his death neither his mother nor sister meant much to him and his brother Mike was away at sea. They would not understand what he was feeling at this moment, but his father would. He wished that he could talk to him about it. He would understand the necessity, perhaps, but not the relish in the hunt and the killing. John still had the cross round his neck that his father had given him on his birthday a week or so before he died, Charles had teased him about it, but he didn't care. It was his most precious possession.

As he lay on his back, he tried to pray, hoping that he would have some sign. Of course it never came. Was there a God at all? Would he ever see his father again in some cosy heaven? It seemed unlikely. His faith had always meant a great deal to him, he now felt it ebbing away in the middle of a battlefield in Italy.

'Wake up!' Pilling was shouting through the tent flap.

'Your chance to be a film star at last, the newsreel cameras are here.'

John looked at his watch. It was nearly eight o'clock, Charles had let him sleep on. After he had climbed out of the slit trench he saw the film crew getting ready behind the guns. An hour later, after shaving and breakfast, they were still there.

Suddenly all the guns started firing. Pilling put his head out of the truck.

'Go on John, get into the limelight. Think of all your fans at home seeing you on British Movietone News.'

John took up his position behind No. 1 gun and was aware of the cameras of the Army film unit going into action. He felt rather self-conscious, yet at the same time excited that he might actually be in shot and be seen at home. He had never been in a film, his short theatrical career being confined to rep theatres in the provinces. Now he wasn't acting but taking part in a real life drama. He moved around trying to look important, but realising that the most anyone would see would be the back of his neck.

When the firing stopped, he decided that his big moment had come and that he would turn round and walk towards the cameras, like Gary Cooper appearing out of the smoke of battle. He held his head high with an expression of nobility on his face until he noticed that the whole unit had finished and were hurriedly packing up their equipment and preparing to leave.

'Bravo!' Pilling was standing outside the truck. 'I liked the cowboy walk, pity no one will see it.'

'Oh, shut up.' John turned on his heel and walked away.

'Mr Crabbe.' Cobber appeared, running up. 'Ammo trucks on the way.'

'Right Sergeant-Major, I'll organise things this end.'

'You will make sure all the ammunition is dug in, sir?'

'Yes of course I will,' John replied angrily, and immediately regretted his display of irritation. Cobber was a friend. Damn Charles Pilling for making him lose his temper.

Burying the ammunition below ground was easier said than done. The guns were in action non-stop, so there were few gunners available to help with the unloading and packing the shells down into the trenches. John took off his jacket and worked away with a handful of men. It was a slow, laborious business and he watched with dismay as the pile of ammunition increased. Then the firing stopped suddenly, and he shouted for help from the men manning the guns.

'John, come here!' Pilling shouted from the truck.

'I am busy, can't you see?' he replied testily, still angry with Charles for his teasing.

'Leave whatever you are doing, and come here, now.' Pilling's voice was sharp and John ran up to the truck.

'Right, now listen. Max has been killed and the Krauts are attacking. Sholto is up in Trimonsuoli taking control, you are in charge here and Taffy is coming over from Don Troop as your troop leader. I am off to the O.P. so put your jacket on and get cracking.'

Charles left without another word. John briefed the Sergeants from each gun with Sergeant-Major Cobber present, and then settled down in the command truck. The guns were silent for a while as the O.P. was unmanned, and it was only then that John was able to take in the fact that Max Gregory had been killed. He had not known his Troop Commander well, but vignettes over the past few weeks came into his mind. The jollity at Christmas, and Max saying kindly on Boxing Day, 'No one will think badly of you if you don't take part in the exercise.' He had always seemed so calm and capable, so reassuring. Now he was dead.

'Johnnie, Johnnie, boy.' Taffy's red face appeared over the driver's seat.

'My God Taffy, am I pleased to see you.' John seized his hand.

'Bad business about Captain Gregory.' He climbed into the seat next to John. 'We had all the gen from Don Troop. He was in a slit trench and a mortar landed on it. He and the signaller were killed outright. They wouldn't have stood a chance, would they?'

'Mason too?'

'Was that the name of the signaller? I didn't know.'

Mason. 'Oh my God,' John thought, 'it was only yesterday that he was with me in the upstairs room in Trimonsuoli.' He could hear his voice saying 'Can I give you a bit of advice, sir?' John had though at the time that the signaller had been getting at him, being almost impertinent, now he realised that the man had been bolstering him up, giving him confidence. He and Max had obviously left the cushy billet and dug in on the slope ahead to get a better view of the enemy, and that had killed them. He had never thanked Mason for helping a raw and frightened officer and now it was too late.

'Was the signaller with you at the O.P., Johnnie?' Taffy asked.

'Yes.' John turned away, caught up in an emotion of profound self-disgust. He had been playing to the cameras, pretending to be a film star, when Max and Mason had been killed.

'Major Sholto is coming through sir,' the wireless operator shouted.

'Listen John.' His voice sounded loud and clear. 'Charles will be in position in the house before long. The Jocks are about to counter attack, you will get details of a barrage within the next hour. We must give continuous fire power. Brief the guns, O.K.?'

'Yes Sholto, of course.'

'Good man.'

John jumped out of the truck, glad of something to do. He walked round and spoke to all the gunners, explaining the situation, then returned to the truck and awaited orders.

The barrage actually started in under an hour. John could not help being relieved that the ammunition had arrived in time, though any thought of burying it had long since been abandoned. Soon Charles took over at the O.P., sounding very calm and businesslike on the radio, and John felt that he must do the job properly and not let him down.

It was just after one o'clock when the first enemy shell fell on the position. It landed on the beach sending a shower of sand over No. 1 gun. Nothing happened for a time, and then another exploded in the trees just behind the truck. The enemy were getting the correct range, that was quite obvious, and the pause that followed gave John no reassurance. It must have been at least two minutes before the real stonking started. They seemed to be exploding everywhere. The terrifying whistle of the German 88mm guns coincided with the crumps and flashes of orange light. Soon the whole area was enveloped in smoke, the shelling was so intense now that the noise of the explosions and the whine of the shells all merged together making a thunderous cacophony. A shrill scream topped the din, crying out in short bursts like a dog in pain.

Taffy shouted 'Someone has been hit, boy, I'll go and see if I can help.'

He leapt out of the truck and vanished into the fog. John and the wireless operator lay on the floor of the truck, glad of the armour plate of the half-track vehicle. Pilling's voice came through on the radio.

'I can see what is happening, John,' the voice crackled, disappeared for a time and then came back '— must keep firing, even if there is only one gun left, we must finish the barrage.'

'I've got the mail, Mr Crabbe.'

Haddock climbed in over the tailpiece, seemingly oblivious of all that was happening around them.

'Get your head down for God's sake,' John shouted at him.

'I think you are right, sir. I'll go round the guns when this little party is over. There is a letter for you, sir. Do you want it now?'

At that moment something struck the side of the truck, there was a metallic twang echoing along the whole side of the armour plate like the plucking of a giant guitar.

'Fuck,' Haddock said. 'If that has hit the track we are grounded sir. I had better have a look.'

His face reappeared in the window. 'That was one of our own shells, it hit us sideways-on so of course it didn't explode — two of our ammo dumps are on fire, sir, and they are ricochetting all over the place. Tracks not damaged though, we must be thankful for small mercies.'

John climbed up and looked over the side. Not only the shells, piled high above the ground, were on fire, but the trees at the back of the position had caught alight and were burning furiously. The smoke was so dense that he couldn't see the guns, shadowy figures came into view running, and John saw that they were stretcher-bearers. Siezed with panic, he gripped the side of the truck and it was some time before he heard Haddock's voice.

'Mr Pilling on the blower, sir, wants to know the position?'

'I'll take it.' Cobber was by his side. 'No. 3 and 4 guns out of action, sir, a number of casualties but at any rate they are out of ammo. No. 1 and 2 are still in action.' John couldn't hear the response, but then Cobber replied:

'O.K. sir, I'll tell him.' He caught hold of John by the arm.

'The barrage is over but fire is urgently needed on Target A. All the telephone lines are cut so you will have to get close to 1 and 2 and use the loud hailer.'

Haddock started up and they lumbered forwards until they were a few yards behind the guns. John leaning over the bonnet shouted the orders.

'John.' Taffy came running to the truck, he had lost his steel helmet his face was black and there was a streak of blood across his forehead. 'We must get 3 and 4 out. The fire is closing in on them, see, soon they will be cut off.'

John knew he had to make a decision, he wondered in passing if he would be court-martialled.

'Can you get them to the beach?'

Only in front of the other guns.'

'Right, I will stop them firing.'

'How far down the beach?'

'As far as you like, Taffy. Get them out of this bloody place.'

Now that he had decided on a course of action he felt better. He was shaking like a leaf, but at least he had taken control.

When No. 1 and 2 ceased firing Pilling came on the radio in a flash.

'Why have they stopped? What is going on?'

'They will start again in a moment,' John yelled down the blower. 'I can't explain at the moment.'

'I hope you know what the hell you are doing.'

John hoped so too. Then things happened quick and fast.

Cobber came running up. 'Did you order 3 and 4 out in front of the guns?' he yelled.

'Yes, but I stopped them firing first, there was no danger.'

'Where the hell have they gone?'

'Mr Williams is taking them down the beach.'

'It is probably mined, Mr Crabbe.'

John shut his eyes. He hadn't thought of that. All the same, the only other avenue of escape was through the water meadows in front of the position and that would have put them even more in sight of the enemy. He dropped the loud-hailer on the floor, there were no orders to give at the moment anyway, as the guns had their target and were still in action.

He stood still in an agony of indecision, his steel helmet was biting into his forehead and the sweat was streaming down his face so that he could hardly see. He took it off and rubbed a hand across his eyes. If only somebody could give him some advice, tell him what to do. He looked around for Cobber, but he had left the truck and was helping heave ammunition by No. 2 gun. He felt helpless and entirely alone.

Haddock's voice made him jump.

'Major Sholto is coming through on the blower, sir.'

Feeling a tremendous surge of relief, John crouched down by the wireless.

'He has gone, sir,' the operator muttered. 'It was his voice alright, but now nothing. Just crackling.'

'Try, try again.' John was aware of hysteria creeping into his voice.

'It is no use sir. The R/T has gone silent, not a dicky bird.'

John shot his head up again like a Jack-in-a-box and looked round wildly. At that moment a sheet of flame careered across the trees in front of the position, the heat was so intense that he could feel it on his face. Now the only escape route was the sea shore. He shouted to Haddock.

'Drive for the beach!' At the same time he picked up the megaphone and yelled:

'Cease firing, cease firing and follow me!'

Cobber jumped on the running board.

'Keep on the tracks of the others and take it slowly, we don't want a shower of fucking sand to tell the Krauts what we are doing.' He then went back to the guns.

Progress was agonisingly slow. No. 2 had to thread its way between burning trees and exploding ammunition, and the rest of them had to wait on the shore for several minutes. John noticed that there was no longer any enemy fire, only the raging furnace of the plantation to contend with. He could see the sand stretching ahead, a highway to safety, but he was aware that the enemy could start shelling again at any moment.

But they didn't, presumably because they reckoned, quite rightly, that they had knocked out the position and were short of ammunition. Eventually the slow convoy set off, lumbering along the tracks left by the other half of the troop in case of mines. John began to take stock as the blazing inferno that used to be their cosy little haven among the Christmas trees receded behind them.

He realised at once how lucky he was, in that all the guns were mobile, the tracks on the Priests could so easily have been damaged. At least, he thought, we are a complete troop. The euphoria was short lived. He had on his own initiative ordered a retreat, a very young second-lieutenant in his first battle had pulled his guns out of action. He hoped he could justify this, but the other thing that really upset him was that throughout the whole time he had never left the safety of his armoured truck. Taffy and Cobber had been out in the open, looking after the wounded, helping to keep contact with the guns, even shifting ammunition, while all hell was let loose around them. It was this, above all other considerations, that made him feel a coward.

They must have travelled about two miles before Taffy appeared and waved them down.

'I'll take you to the rendezvous, boy, not very far along this track.'

John could not even reply, he just sat next to Haddock in silence.

They came out of the wood to a clearing by the shore, it was now almost dark and S.M. Cobber was parking the guns by a lane running inland from the sea.

'Major Sholto wants you at Battery H.Q. right away, John,' Taffy said. 'I'll show you the way.'

☆ ☆ ☆

Battery H.Q. was in a stone barn which had miraculously suffered only minor damage. The officers and NCOs were assembling when John arrived. He stood on the fringe of the crowd making himself as inconspicuous as possible, however the Battery Sergeant-Major saw them and boomed out 'What has happened to Cobber, Mr Crabbe?'

Heads turned and John felt as though a spotlight had been focused on him.

'He is parking the guns, I'll go and find him.' But at that moment Cobber and the sergeants arrived and John moved in behind them.

Sholto looked exhausted, his eyes were red and bloated through lack of sleep, and his voice hoarse.

'The enemy attack, which was carried out with some force, has petered out.' He paused for a moment to allow a few latecomers to join the gathering. 'The Jocks are back in control of all the important features. Intelligence sources are of the opinion that the German offensive has now ground to a halt. The rest of the regiment is still in action, but will be relieved within the next forty-eight hours. The Battery and the battalion that we were supporting bore the main brunt of the attack. We suffered casualties.' He picked up a piece of paper. 'Captain Gregory and Bombardier Mason were killed near Trimonsuoli. Charlie Troop had two killed and eight wounded, Don Troop one killed and eight wounded, these figures are provisional. I will read out the names.'

There was a silence after Sholto had finished, in a few moments he continued. 'You all did well, as I would have expected. In spite of continuous enemy fire the barrage was completed and subsequent targets engaged. When the gun position became untenable there was an organised withdrawal. Unfortunately as much damage was done by our own ammunition exploding as by enemy action.'

John felt a cold sweat breaking out on his forehead.

'Let me make it quite clear, however,' Sholto went on, 'that I do not attach blame to anybody for the fact that the ammo was not below ground. I fancy that the Krauts saw the supply trucks arriving and took advantage of the fact. I have explained the situation to Colonel Alex who accepts my view. Ernest.'

'Yes, Major Sholto.' The Battery S.M. came to attention.

'I imagine that most of the personal kits on the gun position have gone up in smoke, do what you can to organise whatever blankets are available.'

As they all began to disperse, Pilling found John on his own walking back towards his truck.

'Cheer up,' Charles said. 'You managed quite well. You now know what war is all about. As I said before, forget the past, live for the moment; it is the only way to keep one's sanity.'

Cobber met them on the track. He had a habit of turning up out of the blue.

'Mr Crabbe suggested to me, sir, that we both go back to the position and try and lay our hands on some blankets and any kit that has survived, otherwise we are in for a cold night.'

'Oh.' Pilling looked surprised. 'I suppose it's all right. But don't take any risks, for God's sake. We don't want any more casualties. If our ammo is still catapulting about, give up the idea. O.K.?'

'Yes we will be careful,' John replied.

'Well good luck, I am going to get some sleep.'

'As they walked back to the gun position, John did not know what to say. He had never made any such suggestion to Cobber, but he realised instinctively that the Sergeant-Major was trying to help him.

'I reckon Haddock might like to come along sir, he can drive the truck. Just the three of us,' Cobber said.

John stopped before the clearing in the wood where the troop were bedding down for the night.

'I never suggested this expedition, did I Sergeant-Major?'

'No sir.'

'Then why did you tell Mr Pilling that I did?'

'Well I thought you were rather down in the dumps, sir. You have no reason to be, but it did occur to me that you might like to do something before you went to bed. A little walk in the open air clears the head, sir. You will sleep better for it.'

'And you thought Mr Pilling would be impressed?'

'Well, it is a tough life in an O.P. Maybe he didn't realise quite what it was like by the guns, just to let him know that we are pulling our weight too.'

'Thank you, thank you very much Sergeant-Major.'

'Don't thank me, Mr Crabbe. I am no bloody hero, if the shit is still flying around, we will scarper. But we do need blankets. I'll go and find Haddock.'

They took the three-ton lorry up the beach, there were so many tracks in the sand that it was apparent that the sea-shore was not mined. They could see the fires ahead, and after about a mile the trees on the right were burning furiously. Haddock pulled the lorry to the water's edge so that the wheels were splashing in the sea. Showers of sparks were shooting up in the sky above them and the waves were tinged with golden light. But as they neared their old position the furnace abated, and it was obvious that the flames had spread southwards and their own part of the fir forest had burnt itself out.

Haddock turned the truck and parked it in the small clearing whence earlier that day they had made their escape. The fires behind lit up the position so they could see quite clearly as they picked their way across the area. The whole place was strewn with unfired shells. The vast majority of them had not exploded but landed either on their base or on their sides. Some had nosed into the ground but the impact had not been of sufficient force to set them off. John had been too busy and too scared to notice at the time exactly what was happening, but now it was plain enough. Their own ammunition, ignited by the cordite charges, had travelled all over the shop, carpeting the ground around them.

Haddock put his foot on a shell. 'Fucking hell, they're hot,' he said.

'Then don't tread on them, you silly sod,' Cobber shouted. 'Look for kit, anything that has survived, even half-charred blankets will be a help.'

It took John some time to find his old slit trench. The sleeping bag had been neatly bisected by the fire, but his personal belongings in the pillow were intact. There were several letters, a photograph of his mother, his copy of Shakespeare's plays, and an old programme signed by all the members of the cast when he finally had to leave the company. They were part of another world, he did not want to be reminded of the past, so without a moment's hesitation he took the Shakespeare copy and his mother's photo and pushed the rest back into the charred remains of his bedding.

It took them the best part of half an hour to collect the kit, personal effects were packed into one of the dozen or so blankets that they were able to recover.

'Right,' Cobber said. 'That's it. We don't want to hang about. Start up, Haddock.'

'Just a mo', Sergeant-Major,' Fish pleaded. 'There is a bottle of Itie brandy somewhere. Give me a couple of minutes and I think I can lay my hands on it.'

'No,' John said firmly, impatient to get back to the relative security of the new battery position.

'Run for it to the truck!' Cobber shouted.

John saw the next shell quite plainly silhouetted against the flames to the rear, it wasn't moving all that fast, and looked like a baby airship homing towards their three-ton lorry. It hit the roof a glancing blow and then buried its nose in the sand just behind the tailpiece.

John had never run so fast in his life but Haddock beat him to the truck, Cobber was close behind and the three landed in a heap on the front seat. Fish started the engine, but the heavy tracks of the guns had churned up the sand so much that they felt the rear axle sinking.

'Try reverse,' Cobber cried.

The vehicle then moved a little, but slewed round forty-five degrees before it settled even deeper in the sand. The ammo dump which had been smouldering for some time then let off a shower of sparks like a firework display and shells started thudding all over them.

'The blankets,' John cried, and jumped out of the lorry. Strangely he did not feel afraid, the ammo was not exploding, it was still dangerous but this caused the adrenalin to flow and he felt a curious elation, at last he had a chance to prove himself.

They packed the blankets in front of the rear wheels and after two tantalising lurches the lorry started to move, and Haddock drove hell-for-leather back along the sea-shore.

'Sorry about that, sir,' Cobber said. 'That dump being nearest to the beach escaped the fire, and then decided to take off while we were there.'

'It was just bad luck,' John replied.

'No sir, not bad luck. We should have taken a good look first before we decided to look for kit.'

'But we made it, that's all that matters. Pity about the brandy, though,' Haddock said cheerfully.

It was probably the relief, but John suddenly felt light-headed.

'You know what, Sergeant-Major?' He chuckled.

'What, sir?'

'I think we used all the blankets.'

John's laugh was infectious and they all three began to giggle.

'We mount an expedition to collect the bedding, get

divebombed by our own shells for our pains, and then use all the blankets to get us out of the shit.'

'And come back without the brandy,' Haddock chortled.

'That's war, sir.' Cobber grinned at John. 'That is fucking war.'

When they rejoined the new Battery area they discovered that there were two blankets left, together with a pile of personal effects.

'We will have one each,' Cobber decided. 'I think that we have earned them. Oh I know we should look after the chaps first, but two are not going to go very far.'

John and Haddock dossed down with one slightly charred blanket. It was becoming very cold and the ground was soggy. They both hugged each other to try to keep warm. John had never slept with anyone before, often he had dreamed of melting into the arms of a beautiful woman; all he had now was Haddock, with elbows like knuckle-dusters and a snore like a pneumatic drill.

PART II

5

Taffy was asleep in the back of the Jeep and Charles was driving. John was excited and wide awake as they sped along the coast road of the Bay of Naples. Pilling was concentrating on the road ahead and not inclined to talk. John, grateful for the quiet, was able to indulge in his own thoughts. He allowed himself to relive the last few months as he watched the sea sparkling in the sun and the rocky coastline sliding past below them.

After the Garigliano the regiment had moved to the central part of the Gustav line, behind a little hillock called Monte Trocchio a few miles south of the town of Cassino. To their right was the main road that ran through the town and on to Rome, and on the left a railway track now used as a route for vehicles. Towering above them and dominating the whole area was Monte Cassino with the famous monastery on its peak.

The weather had been worse than ever. The rain and sleet continued day after day unabated, and it was bitterly cold. The ground soon became a morass of mud, the slit trenches filled with water and the fragile canvas of the bivvy tents were no match for the relentless downpour. It was soon apparent that the battle was bogged down also. The projected break through the town of Cassino into the Liri Valley and along the road to Rome became impossible, so there was no relief for the Allied forces at Anzio who were just managing to retain a fragile bridgehead.

The Rapido River which ran just in front of Monte Trocchio was mined on both sides, and New Zealand and Indian troops fought courageously in the mire to no avail.

To make matters worse, the enemy held all the high ground to the north, and although the town of Cassino was flattened by allied shelling and air attacks, the Germans had an intricate system of tunnels and after the bombardment was over emerged to defend every inch of the ground. The destruction of the town was in fact counter-productive, because the rubble was piled high on the streets and when the Allied tanks managed to gain a foothold they came across an impenetrable barrier.

Charles Pilling had been promoted to captain and troop commander. He had a bad time by the river and later was holed up unable to move in the railway station in the town. He kept continuous fire on the enemy and was later awarded an M.C. On the gun position the main enemy was the weather. John and all the others were permanently wet and cold, and there was no way to keep spare clothes dry. There were long periods of frozen boredom, punctuated by brief moments of action as the enemy shells found their mark. One night they were stonked for two hours, after it was over John climbed out of his armoured truck and walked round the position. There had been no casualties. He learned one of the lessons of war, that if you are well dug in or have armour plate around you, it takes many shells to kill a man.

He came nearest to death in one of those stupid accidents which occur so often in war. Sholto, aware that his men were soaked to the skin and very miserable, decided that a little liquid refreshment would help. He had a friend, the C.O. of a medium artillery battery about four miles behind them, who had told him on the blower that they had "liberated" several crates of Asti Spumante and would he like some?

'Not as good as champagne, Johnnie' he had said. 'Too sweet, but I reckon it would cheer the chaps up a bit don't you?'

'Yes Sholto,' John said happily.

'Well pop down and fetch a few crates. Lionel says their chaps are getting sick of it. While you are there the Yanks are going to bomb the monastery, Flying Fortresses, a thousand bomber raid. You should get a good view.'

'Do we know that the Germans are in the monastery?'

John asked.

'No, we don't. I agree it seems a bloody shame. An act of desperation because our lords and masters don't know what the hell to do. But ours not to reason why; Tennyson would have changed his mind if he had seen this bloody lot.'

John drove south along the main road, each side was parked with all the troops and impedimenta needed to maintain an army in battle. Guns, casualty clearing stations with red crosses on their tents, rear echelon supply dumps of the R.A.S.C., R.E.M.E. workshops to carry out repairs on tanks and vehicles; being near the front line he had not realised the density of the support groups behind him. He found the turning on his right quite easily with the regimental sign pointing the way. The narrow track wound northwards bringing him nearer to his own battery position, he could see Monte Trocchio quite plainly and his own guns nestling in the valley behind. After about a mile he stopped in a ruined village on the top of a hill and there behind him was the medium battery with their long barrels pointing up into the sky.

The air-raid on the monastery had already started and John paused for a moment to watch. Squadrons of Flying Fortresses of the US Air Force passed overhead at about ten minute intervals. White dust, billowing high above the Monastery, could be seen over the black smoke of the exploding bombs which swirled around the peak of Monte Cassino. It was quite a spectacle, but John suddenly felt rather sick. It was a sacred building full of monks presumably at this moment praying for survival.

He drove down the hairpin bends from the village and stopped on the road that came to an end by the remains of a small farm. The guns were a few hundred yards away on the far side of an olive grove. He could see what was probably the battery command post, a collection of trucks to the rear, and decided to make his way there. Everyone on the position seemed to be out in the open watching the raid, as the monastery could be clearly seen above the ruined village.

John could not remember hearing the first whine of the bombs, but he must have done. He could only recall the stark horror as he watched the group of vehicles in the rear go up in the air. The men who had been standing there literally disappeared. He flung himself onto the ground amidst the trees, but could not resist looking up into the sky for a moment, the American bombers had started to wheel round southwards. It couldn't be true, the US Air Force were bombing them, the monastery was over five miles away, how could they miss it?

The bombs landed all over the area, through the smoke he saw men running everywhere for cover. Just the other side of the grove about 200 yards away a man came towards him with his hair on fire, he was shrieking at the top of his voice and trying to beat out the flames with his fists, then another bomb fell and he vanished. John hugged the ground as a shower of hot twigs fell over him.

After it was over John climbed slowly to his feet, he took off his cap and knocked the burning embers off his clothing. As the smoke cleared he could see the exact pattern of the bombing run. They had straddled the village and landed in a straight line across the gun position to the area behind which was blazing furiously. If he had arrived a few minutes earlier he would have been in the thick of it. As it was, the narrow grove of olives had acted as a shield against the blast and saved his life.

'John, John,' Pilling shouted. 'My God, you two are a dozy lot. Taffy snoring in the back, and you are miles away reliving tales of derring-do no doubt. Wake up this is Sorrento. Remember the song? We are stopping here for a pee, drinks and some lunch in that order.'

John jerked himself into the present.

'Oh. Jolly good,' he murmured.

'No it is not jolly good, we have been passing some of the greatest scenery in Italy and neither of you have seen any of it!'

They stopped in a little square in the centre of town and over lunch John retreated again into his reverie, Taffy, now wide awake, prattled away happily.

After nine weeks at the Cassino front the regiment had been relieved. The weather had finally improved in the wake of an Italian spring. There had been three separate battles of Cassino and in spite of dogged and courageous fighting spirit by the British, New Zealand and Indian troops, the main German line remained unbroken. For John, a tiny cog in the military machine, grand strategy was a closed book. But it was perfectly obvious that the High Command had grossly underestimated the strength of the German defences and put far too small a force into battle to crack the redoubt. Three lost battles were enough to give all of them cause to doubt the efficiency of the conduct of the war.

It was at the beginning of April that the regiment assembled on the disused railway track at two o'clock in the morning to start the journey south. The position by Monte Trocchio had been shelled heavily earlier in the evening, fortunately before the battery had started to pack up. They all knew that the Germans brought harassing fire on to the track at regular intervals, keeping to a rigid timetable, and judging by past experience, the next shelling was due at 3 am. The regiment was packed nose-to-tail along the railway and by 2.45 had not started to move.

Tempers were getting frayed, after over two months of slogging it out in the mud, no one wanted any trouble now that rest and leave were in the offing. Even the ever cheerful Haddock was feeling the strain. 'What a fucking shambles Mr Crabbe,' he muttered, gripping the wheel of the truck and beating his foot on the floor. 'Fred Karno's Army, the Generals are all in some palace or other, aren't they? They couldn't organise a piss-up in a brewery.'

It was after 3 a.m. before the convoy began to move, and then at an agonisingly slow pace. But no shells came and after about half an hour they began to relax.

'Jerry missed an opportunity there sir.' Haddock was happy now. 'Must have changed their fire plan, stupid fuckers, they could have stonked us to buggery.'

'What is Positano like?' Taffy asked as the three of them climbed back into the Jeep after lunch.

'It will be bloody marvellous,' John replied. 'Seven days at the seaside and the sun is out.'

☆ ☆ ☆

As they drove round the bend on the coast road several hundred feet above the sea, the village of Positano came into view, bathed in evening sunlight. John thought it was the most beautiful place he had ever seen. Myriads of brightly coloured villas tumbled down the hillside, many perched on the top of precipices, others seemed to be suspended in mid-air. Wild flowers clung to the rocks in a blaze of colour, while bushes and trees of many shades of green carpeted the area between the houses. Mountains towered above with pinnacles etched against a bright blue sky, and below the sea sparkled like diamonds. Pilling stopped the truck at a small *albergo*.

'This is where we get out I think,' he said, 'the road continues to climb away at this point.'

'How do we find the Pensione Roma?' Taffy asked.

'We walk, old son. Down the hillside, should be someone to meet us.'

John jumped out and looked over a small stone wall. It was quite clear that they could go no further by road. A network of *salitas* with stone steps branched out at this point down towards the sea. By this time a crowd of locals had clustered around them. They were extremely friendly and chatted away, each jostling for position.

'Pensione Roma,' Taffy shouted above the din.

'Si, si.' One old man with a grey beard started to pull the luggage out of the truck.

'No,' Pilling snapped. 'Niente, niente. We had better wait for the chap from the hotel.'

At this moment a small round man in a striped apron pushed his way through the throng.

'Pensione Roma? Buono, benvenuto! Parca la màcchina. Vieni with me, pronto!' he yelled at the crowd in voluble Italian, and they scattered. Pilling parked the Jeep by the *albergo*, being careful to remove the rotor-arm.

'Me Giovanni,' the man beamed at them, as he picked up all the baggage. 'Positano bella, molto romantica, benvenuto!'

Festooned with the luggage, he led the way down the steps, at a brisk pace, the others had difficulty keeping up with him. The *salita* threaded its way between the villas, at times they had to duck under trellises of purple bougainvillea, and as the stairway twisted and turned they could see the sea appearing at intervals, a sheer drop below them.

'Too bad, boy, if you suffer from vertigo,' Taffy remarked.

About half-way down they came to the Pensione Roma. It fitted snugly against a rock face, and they entered on the top floor. Each had a separate bedroom and as John looked out of the window, all the weariness after the long journey vanished. He could see the sandy beach, now quite deserted, with the little church just above it. On either side of the bay a promontory edged out into the sea. On the right one a small tower was couched on the rocky headland.

He unpacked quickly and went to explore. Throughout, the floors were tiled with bold colours and the walls a brilliant white. Everything was spotlessly clean and smelt of the sea. He found a small staircase with a wrought iron rail and descended to the floor below. Pilling emerged from a bedroom.

'Hullo, Johnnie,' he said cheerfully. 'Taffy and I are going for a stroll, care to come?'

'No I don't think so, I'd rather stay here for a while if you don't mind.'

'And make straight for the bar no doubt, you boozy old sod, O.K. see you later.'

John found another staircase which led to the ground floor. Here was a spacious dining room with a bar at one end. A man was standing looking out of the window. He turned round as John entered.

'Good evening,' he said in perfect English. 'My name is Mr Angellini, I am the manager here, would you care for a drink?'

He was a tall thin man, smartly dressed in an open-necked shirt and well-creased pale grey trousers.

'Oh yes, thank you,' John replied.

'We have most things, due to the courtesy of the British Army, but if you wish to drink Italian I suggest either a Campari-Soda or a Vermouth.'

'A Campari-soda thank you,' he paused. 'You speak jolly good English.'

'I had an English governess, and I spent a year at Oxford on a course before the war. But that was a long time ago, a great deal has happened since then.'

Something in his manner seemed to inhibit further

conversation, so John took the drink and walked out on the patio. This ran the full length of the dining room, wisteria provided a canopy and pots of geraniums hung from the trellis. The view across the bay was breathtaking.

'Hullo.'

John swung round. A girl was sitting at the far end with a glass of white wine in her hand. She was probably only in her early twenties, but there was an air of casual elegance about her. She wore a white sleeveless blouse and a tight-fitting blue skirt. Her arms and legs were bronzed by the sun and her brown hair bleached to the colour of pale honey. John wished he had gone out with the others. Ever since leaving school he had been frightened of girls, not the actresses in his rep companies, they had been young and bouncy just out of RADA, he had accepted them easily enough, but this young woman looked so cool that he found her intimidating.

'Well, aren't you going to join me?'

'Yes, of course.'

He sat down, conscious that his knees were almost touching her legs.

'Just arrived?' she asked.

'Yes.'

'From Cassino?'

John hesitated.

She smiled at him, 'This fleshspot by the sea is reserved for officers from the 8th Army or Caserta. You don't look like a G.H.Q. type to me.'

'No, I'm not.' He felt tongue-tied and furious with himself for being so gauche. 'Caserta is a palace isn't it?' Luckily he had heard the name, so he was able to show off his knowledge.

'A very large one actually, it also happens to be General Alexander's H.Q. By the way my name is Lynne Gardener. And yours?'

'John Crabbe.' He stood up expecting to shake hands, but she remained seated. He felt himself blushing. 'Oh, can I get you a drink?' he asked with an air of desperation.

'Thank you, a glass of Vino Di Capri, it is better than the local brew.'

He went to the bar, ordered a double Campari for

himself and drank half of it before he took the drinks outside.

She was leaning over the metal railing looking out over the bay.

'It is pretty, isn't it? You get the most wonderful sunsets here.'

'Are you from Caserta?' John asked.

'Yes, on and off. Nothing very grand, it is just that I speak fluent Italian.'

She returned to her seat. 'Tell me about yourself.'

'There is nothing much to tell.'

'Rubbish!' She looked at him sharply and he noticed that her eyes were bright blue. 'You have been at the sharp end of this war and I'm interested.'

After three Camparis on an empty stomach, John relaxed. He gave her a resume of his adventures since landing in Italy. At first he was guarded, but then suddenly he decided to unburden himself to this beautiful young woman, partly because he had never had an opportunity before to talk about his experiences, but also because he realised that she would see through an edited version. After John had finished she stood up.

'I must go,' she said briefly.

'I arrived yesterday with a staff captain from Caserta, he is in a hotel further up the hill, we became separated because there was a muddle over the booking. I am having dinner with him at the restaurant on the beach.'

She took John's arm and led him to the edge of the balcony.

'You see the church? Well just below it there is a bar cut into the rock, you can't miss it. Join us for a drink at about ten o'clock if you would like to.'

'Oh yes I would, thank you,' John stammered.

'Bring your friends too.'

After she had gone John had another Campari and sat looking out to sea. He felt peaceful and happy. It was rather like a Noel Coward play, standing on a terrace drinking with a pretty girl with the blue Mediterranean below, very different from Pevensey Bay where he had usually spent his summer holidays. The sun had started to set, and above the pink glow, fingers of purple reached up into the sky. A long shadow had begun to creep over the sands, but there was still a golden patch to the right and the little tower on the rocks was turning blue in the evening light. He thought about Lynne. Strange that he had been able to talk to her so frankly. It wasn't only the effect of the Camparis, she seemed sympathetic and genuinely interested. Her departure had been rather abrupt after he had finished his story and she had made no comment, but they had arranged to meet after supper.

John began to daydream. On his first evening on leave in Positano he had met a lovely girl who appeared to like him, and she was actually staying in the same pensione.

He allowed himself to become really excited. But then he remembered that she had not come here alone, there was the Staff Captain from G.H.Q., probably smooth and supercilious, he realised he was no match for types like that. John knew that he was not handsome or sophisticated, and he was also aware of the fact that all through his life when everything seemed to be going well, fate had so often dealt him a nasty blow and brought him back to reality.

'Hullo Johnnie boy, are you sloshed?'

Taffy and Charles came on to the balcony.

'We have been for a long walk,' Pilling said, 'and we are ready for dinner. Old Angelo, or whatever his name is, has announced that it is ready. We met a couple of blokes from the Jocks on our travels, and they say that there is a cabaret at the *albergo* on the beach later on, so we thought we might all go on there afterwards.'

'I can't, I am afraid,' John said shyly.

'Oh really. So what have you been up to, Johnnie boy, while we have been away?' Taffy asked.

'I've met a girl, she's staying here.'

'My God!' Charles looked at him in admiration. 'You haven't been here five minutes and you have found some bint already. It's more than we have done, you sly old bastard. Who is she?'

'She is from Caserta and arrived yesterday.'

'G.H.Q. type. Is she pretty?'

'Yes.'

'Well, well. Talk about dark horses!'

'She did say bring your friends. We are meeting in a bar

near the church.'

'Wouldn't dream of it. You have staked your claim, John Crabbe, and good luck to you. We will presumably meet her over breakfast tomorrow. I can't wait.'

'You go ahead, Johnnie, you are coming out of your shell, boy,' Taffy grinned at him. 'Good hunting.'

After dinner when the others had gone, John finished unpacking. He put on a clean bush shirt and changed from shorts into a pair of slacks. He looked at himself in the mirror. The shirt wasn't too bad, but the trousers were creased. Some people could wear clothes with an air, but John never could, he always looked awkward. Charles, for instance, could climb into anything, and still appear neat. John ran a comb under the tap and worked on his hair, but it still stood on end. He shrugged his shoulders, he had done his best and it would have to do.

He felt nervous as he walked down the narrow steps towards the sea. It was dark now and all the lights twinkled like stars. There was no black-out here. The night was balmy and there was a sweet scent of spring flowers.

He found the bar easily enough, it was, as Lynne had said, cut into the rock. It was quite large with lights spread along each side. He saw her immediately and she rose to greet him. The officer who had his back to the entrance turned round, he had a small clipped moustache but John recognised him at once.

'No . It can't be.' He stood up and peered at John near to one of the lights. 'It is. It is the crab. It is the bloody crab.'

☆ ☆ ☆

John froze in his tracks. Lynne's companion was Thomas, the leader of the gang who had made his life such a misery at school, and caused him in desperation to run away. The years slipped past and John was back in the Day Room in September 1938. Thomas had sat next to him at prep, and just after the supervising prefect had called for silence he had sunk the two points of a geometry compass into his backside. Involuntarily John had cried out, and the prefect had threatened him with a beating. After prep was over a boy called out to Thomas.

'What did you do to the crab? He squealed like a little pig.'

'He is a little pig,' Thomas replied, 'but no good for bacon, too fat.'

'Oh, I don't know.' Another boy joined the group. 'He might do for the cheaper rashers.' He picked up a large ruler from his desk. 'Let's de-bag him, give him a bacon slicer, and find out.'

'Good idea.' Thomas slammed the door and leaned against it.

There was no escape. John fought like a demon, his fists flying out in all directions, but the boys were like a pack of hounds, determined to have their bit of fun. They bent him over a desk and pulled his trousers down; he wasn't even conscious of the pain as they whacked him, but only of the laughter which rang in his ears.

'So you two know each other,' Lynne said.

'Oh yes indeed,' Thomas replied. 'We were school chums, weren't we Crabbe? This calls for a celebration. I will recharge our glasses, what's your poison Crabbe?'

'I will get them,' Lynne said.

'Ladies don't buy rounds.'

'I am not a lady and I do. John?'

'A brandy, thank you.'

'Tommy?'

'The same if you insist.'

When they were alone, John was conscious of breaking into a cold sweat. Thomas looked at him straight in the eyes. John tried to hold his gaze but rather like a rabbit with a snake, he faltered and looked down. There were a couple of Jock officers at the bar ordering drinks so Lynne had to wait. Thomas said nothing. He was savouring the situation and enjoying John's obvious discomfort. He timed it perfectly, he didn't speak until Lynne had left the bar then he said softly, 'One drink and bugger off. Otherwise I will give Lynne an account of John Crabbe's schooldays. Savvy?'

When Lynne had returned Thomas turned his back on John and spoke as though he wasn't there.

'How about Capri tomorrow, Lynne dear? I've found out

where we can get a boat, or would you prefer a day of beach-combing? And then there is Pompei, but I thought we might save that for later.'

'You have changed your tune, Tommy, haven't you?' Lynne observed. 'You told me that you intended to spend all your time on the beach. Why this sudden desire for activity?'

'Well you are the intellectual one. I thought you might educate me. All those Roman remains at Pompei and what is the other place?'

'Herculaneum.'

'That's it, and isn't there some house on Capri you wanted to see?'

'Axel Munthe's, yes.'

"Good. Say the word and I will organise it.'

'I haven't made up my mind yet Tommy, so don't rush me.'

John stood up. 'My round, what are you both having?' He tried to make his voice sound casual.

'Oh are you still here, Crabbe?' Thomas said, looking over his shoulder. 'I thought you said that you were going off to join your friends?'

'No. I never said any such thing,' John replied. He felt a tight feeling across his forehead as anger began to take hold of him. At moments like this he was apt to stammer, but he was determined this time to keep calm.

Lynne looked at them both curiously before replying. 'I am rather thirsty actually, John. I would love an acqua minerale.'

'Right.' He went to the bar, ignoring Thomas, and when he returned the other man was lounging in his chair smoking a cigar.

'Lynne my dear,' he said slowly, blowing smoke rings and watching them billow upwards. 'A trick I learned at Sandhurst, anyone can do it with a cigarette, but it takes practice to achieve it with a cigar. Where were we? Oh yes, strange that you should end up at the same hotel as my old school chum Crabbe. He is quite a fellow, has he told you about all his adventures at school?'

'No,' Lynne replied. 'Why should he?'

'Well, the escapade created quite a stir at the time. You

see, he ran away because he was terrified of a beating. He took a train to London without paying his fare, thus bilking the railway company, and ran crying to mummy. There was quite a scandal. First the Head proposed expulsion and then a birching, but our hero managed to wriggle out of paying for his crimes altogether.'

'Quite a resourceful chap, Crabbe, isn't he? Conscripted into the Army, he has even managed to wangle himself a commission, one only hopes that his running away has not become a habit.'

Lynne finished her drink without saying a word. Then she stood up and took John by the arm.

'It is stifling in here,' she said quietly, 'I'd like a walk to cool down. Anyway as you have just returned from Cassino, I don't expect you have much in common with an office boy from Caserta.'

When they were outside John said miserably, 'Oh my God, I am sorry.'

'What about?'

'Well he is a friend of yours and after what you have just said to him . . .'

'Oh don't be so stupid. Do you think he's my lover or something?' She looked at him angrily.

'I thought . . .'

'Well you thought wrong. We just happened to be on the same leave allocation. I hardly know him. Oh I see.' She smiled at him. 'You were taken in by all that "Lynne dear" stuff. That was for your benefit. the arrogant little public school twit.'

'Gosh, I am relieved.' John could not hide the pleasure in his voice.

'Gosh, so am I,' she mocked him gently. 'As a matter of fact, I have been trying to work out a way of getting him out of my hair, and along comes John Crabbe who does it for me.'

'I didn't do anything,' John muttered. 'I ought to have stood up to him.'

'It is easier for a woman. It was quite simple to smack him down.'

'He will be absolutely furious.'

'So what? He can't do you any harm, you are not still at

school, are you?'

'No, but how about you? You have to work with him at G.H.Q.'

'I am quite capable of looking after myself.'

'I am sure you are.'

'By the way, did you see his face when we flounced out?'

'No, I kept my head down.'

'He was so surprised, he just sat there white about the gills with his mouth open. I don't think he is used to being put in his place.'

'No I am sure he isn't,' John replied. But he felt uneasy. He remembered the boy at school, so self-possessed and sure of himself, he knew that he would not take this humiliation, in front of someone he despised, lying down.

They descended the last few steps to the beach. The evening was mild and there was no wind. The lights from the *albergo* on the shore lit up the whole area, and the sound of music and laughter wafted across the sand. Charles and Taffy were enjoying themselves watching the cabaret, John hoped she would not want to join them, he wanted her to himself, but she showed no inclination to do so and led him to the water's edge.

They stood together looking out to sea, which was a deep velvet blue with ridges of fluorescent white on the crest of the waves.

Lynne broke the silence. 'You are still worrying about Thomas, aren't you?'

'Yes.'

'Well don't. He is just a boring little man, forget him.'

'I can't. I just wish it had never happened.'

'Oh for God's sake don't be such a wet blanket.' She turned to him and seeing the hurt look on his face, relented. 'Cheer up. You are meant to be on holiday enjoying yourself. Tell you what, I am going for a swim, coming?'

'But we haven't got our togs.'

'Togs? You are funny, do you know that? Togs! Well I am going to swim without any togs at all, does that shock you?'

'No, of course not.'

'I bet it does, but we'll dive in off the rock at the far end by the tower, out of sight of prying eyes. Race you!'

John arrived first by a short head.

'I would have beaten you if it hadn't been for my tight skirt, I should have taken it off.' she grinned at him. 'I'll be in first though.'

She undressed in seconds, throwing her clothes back up the beach, ran into the sea until it covered her knees, and then arched her back and plunged. For a split second like the snap of a camera, John saw the smooth curve of her naked buttocks before with a loud splash she disappeared under the waves.

She reappeared some way out to sea. The lights from the village provided an orange glow on the water and he could see her quite plainly.

'Come on,' she cried. 'It is bloody cold but lovely. Hurry up.'

He undressed clumsily. His shoes got caught up in his trousers but he ripped them off as he started to panic. She seemed to be so far from the shore, perhaps there were currents he didn't know, and the jagged rocks were quite near.

'Don't go out too far,' he yelled.

'I'm all right. Come on.'

He ran into the sea as fast as he could, in his haste he had forgotten to take off his underpants and they flapped against his thighs. Soon he was out of his depth and saw with increasing unease that Lynne had drifted about twenty yards to the right nearer to the headland. There he became aware of the cross current, and realised that although the beach was obviously safe, there was a dangerous swirl round the promontory. John was a strong swimmer and reached her in minutes. By now she had realised the situation and began to crawl towards the shore, but she was only standing still.

'There is a current here John,' she said breathlessly, 'be careful.'

'I know, turn on your back.'

'It's all right, I can manage.'

'For God's sake, on your back,' he shouted at her, and then seized her shoulders and pulled her round.

He turned round himself so that his body was underneath hers. He then slid his hands round her breasts cradling her head on his neck, and kicked out his legs using all his strength. He remembered what he had been taught and used his legs in a powerful rhythmic movement, like a breast stroke but on his back.

Slowly they began to make progress. He did not aim for the beach, it was too near the rocks, but kept a straight line until they were well clear of the current. Soon he could feel the sea-bed with his hands and he gently let her go.

It was not until he stood up that John realised how exhausted he was. He swayed and Lynne caught him in her arms. He was panting for breath and they stayed still for a moment with the waves lapping at their feet.

'Thank you.' She continued to hold him tight. 'If this was a novel I would cry out, "My Hero" and faint right away.'

'You would probably have coped on your own.'

'I wouldn't. I'd have ended up on those rocks. I might have climbed ashore but very much the worse for wear. You were very professional, where did you learn all that stuff?'

'At school.'

'Lucky for me.' She was shivering and John hugged her tighter, with her wet hair clinging to the sides of her face she looked like a little girl. He was quite unconscious of her nakedness, his only desire was to comfort her.

'Ouch!' She disengaged herself gently. 'My breasts are a bit sore, you did grab them rather hard.'

'Oh God, I'm sorry.'

'John.' She caught hold of his shoulders and shook him. 'You are a funny boy. I behaved like a complete idiot, and got us both into a nasty situation, you fished me out and you start apologising.'

She started to laugh but tears were not far away. 'You are my hero, but you don't look very romantic with your knickers at half-mast.'

John looked down and saw that his pants had dropped to his knees. Instinctively, he started to pull them up.

Lynne stopped laughing and kissed him again, this time on the lips.

'You know, John Crabbe,' she said, 'there is something very endearing about you. Come on, we had better get dressed and back to the hotel before we both get pneumonia.'

☆ ☆ ☆

'That long building with the pillars was the barracks of the gladiators,' Lynne said.

'Did they feed them to the lions?' Taffy asked cheerfully.

'No they did not, you bloodthirsty tyke,' Charles replied. 'That happened in the big amphitheatres, like the Colosseum in Rome. Here they had plays, and gladiatorial combats as a diversion.'

'Some diversion, boy, but they fought to the death didn't they?'

'Yes, but no lions.'

'We ought to put Thomas up there, and see John run him through with a broad sword, he has a Welsh name too, he lets down the side doesn't he?'

'You know Taffy,' Charles said, 'you are not real. You are exactly like a stage Welshman, I didn't know they existed outside a play by Emlyn Williams.'

'Don't you be so sarcastic, Charles, you know you make me quite angry sometimes.'

'Sorry. I tell you what, if we ever meet up with this Thomas character I will allow you to thump him first.'

'Quite right, boy, we are your bodyguard John, always at the ready.'

They were sitting in the larger of the two theatres at Pompei, eating their packed lunch and drinking wine out of two bottles. It was a beautiful setting. They were high up amongst the Cypress trees, behind them the blue mountains, and below the full sweep of the auditorium.

The first four rows of stone benches were virtually intact, skirting the semi-circular stage, but further up they became fragmented and the long grass had taken over. On each side of the acting area stone arches provided the entrances and the exits for the actors.

Lynne had met the others at breakfast. She wasted no time in recounting the events of the previous evening. John wished she had not told the others about Thomas, but she made light of the situation and both Charles and Taffy were delighted that she had been able to put the smart little Staff Captain in his place.

They decided to go to Pompei for the day in Lynne's staff

car, and John took a great deal of pleasure in the fact that if Thomas had required the car himself, it was just too bad.

The spring sunshine was hot at midday and the effect of the wine began to make John feel drowsy, but at the same time heightened his consciousness. He was in a theatre and could almost sense the ghosts around him, an audience packed on the benches. Young and old, rich and poor, cheering and clapping, perhaps drinking, as he was, the golden wine from the vineyards of Vesuvius, though today it was called Lacrima Christi, "the tears of Christ."

As they toured the city, John became lost in a time-warp. There were the beautiful villas, complete except for their roofs; the pattern was similar throughout, square courtyards, often quite small, with a pond in the centre and rooms leading off on all sides. Here the murals were in striking colour almost as though they had been just crafted, instead of 2000 years ago.

They could see the marks of the chariot wheels that had caught the edges of the stepping stones around the narrow streets, all preserved for posterity under the lava which had engulfed the town with terrifying speed. Only the people able to reach the sea and escape in boats had survived, most had perished in the avalanche.

Then there were the famous brothels. The various positions for successful copulation were depicted on the walls, still in bright colours, rather like a do-it-yourself manual.

'They don't look very happy,' Taffy observed, 'having their bit of fun. Perhaps it is because of the stone beds all over the place. They must have been jolly cold and a bit bumpy too.'

'They had mattresses and cushions under their bottoms,' Lynne said.

'All the same, it is rather chilly in here. I should have thought it would have put them off a bit.'

'You have no imagination, Taffy,' Charles remarked. 'At any rate they were hot-blooded people, Pompei was a seaside resort where all the Romans flocked to enjoy themselves.'

'They did that all right, very different from the Mumbles back home.'

They were tired by the time they reached the main gate and climbed back into the car.

'You have been very quiet, Johnnie,' Taffy said. 'You have enjoyed the day, haven't you?'

'Of course, it was absolutely marvellous,' John replied.

'He was reliving the past,' Lynne said. 'It is easy to become completely absorbed in this place. I felt the same when I came here first.'

'When was that?' Charles asked.

'Just before the war.'

'You lived here?'

'Yes, with my parents in Florence.'

'Where are they now?'

'In Gloucester,' she smiled at him. 'To satisfy your curiosity, my father is English, he is an expert on the restoration of old paintings and had a contract with the Italian Government. He met my mother, a teacher of English, in Florence. I was brought up in the Cotswolds and Tuscany, so I am bilingual. Hence my job as an interpreter. That's all. Nothing very exciting.'

John sat next to Lynne as she drove the big saloon. He watched her hands on the steering wheel and, when he dared, took a peep at her slim legs. He knew that he was falling in love. He had been taken completely by surprise, suddenly meeting this girl in the middle of a war. It was so unexpected. He had had a crush on a boy at school, and also on his sister-in-law, Judy, his elder brother Mike's wife, who was so kind when he ran away. She had not written since he arrived in Italy, and this had hurt him.

But Lynne was different, he was absolutely bowled over. He just could not credit the fact that he had held her naked in his arms the previous night, in retrospect it seemed totally unreal.

They stopped to have dinner in a black market restaurant at Castellammare on the coast road. It was full of rich Neapolitans and the food was excellent. Charles was disgusted that these places could exist with all the food shortages and poverty around.

'We are like that,' Lynne said. 'There is a black market in England of course, but it is under the counter. Here it is quite open. If you have the money or the influence you can survive the shortages of the war. The fascist bureaucracy looks after its own.'

'But surely now all that will change,' John said.

'I doubt it,' she replied. 'You see, we don't play cricket in Italy.'

'You said we,' Charles asked with interest. 'Do you see yourself as an Italian?'

'Half of me.'

'What do you really do at G.H.Q.?' He pressed her.

'I am not a spy if that's what you mean.'

'I didn't think you were, but you are not just an interpreter either, are you?'

'Don't be too clever.' She spoke quite sharply. 'I have told you all you need to know. Let's change the subject, shall we?'

When they got back to the pensione, Charles came into John's room.

'She is quite a girl, the mysterious Lynne,' he said. 'Taffy and I intend to keep out of the light for the rest of our leave, so the field is yours.'

'There is no need.'

'Oh yes there is. You found her, and we don't intend to interfere.' He paused. 'You are in love with her, aren't you?'

'Yes, I think I am,' John replied.

'I am bloody sure you are, looking at her with poached egg eyes all through dinner.'

'Was it that obvious?'

'Since you ask, yes it was.' He paused. 'But be careful.'

'What do you mean?'

'Well she is in Intelligence, that much is for sure. She is also quite senior in spite of her tender years. Otherwise she would not have been in a position to flatten your cocky little Staff Captain.'

'What you are saying is that she is out of my league?'

'Well, you fished her out of the sea which is a good start. Look, I don't want to be patronising, but Taffy and I have grown quite attached to you, you silly old sod, and we don't want to see you get hurt.'

He left without another word and closed the door behind him.

☆ ☆ ☆

John closed his eyes, the light behind his eyelids was golden brown for the sun was bright. He half opened them so that they appeared to be shut, and thus was able to peer at Lynne secretly. She was lying on her back with her knees up, her bare thighs were only a few feet away, it was like looking at one of the coloured photographs in *Picturegoer* which he had pored over when he was at school, a well-thumbed copy that had been passed around among the boys, kept out of sight of the housemaster who strongly disapproved of such magazines. But this time the thighs were real, and Lynne was sunbathing by his side on a beach in Positano.

'Stop squinting at me like that Johnnie,' she said suddenly. 'Haven't you ever seen a girl's legs before?'

'Yes, but they weren't like yours.'

'How about all your actresses in the theatre?'

'Oh none of them were at all glamorous.'

'I am not glamorous.'

'You are to me.'

She turned on her side and looked at him. 'You know something,' she said, 'it is high time you lost your virginity. Then you would stop being a schoolboy and grow up.'

John did not reply.

'And don't look all hurt,' she said to him. 'I am quite right anyway. Someone ought to take you in hand. Oh look!' She sat up. 'There's Thomas over there with a boyfriend.'

John shaded his eyes with his hand.

Two men were coming down the steps onto the beach, one was Thomas and the other a fair-haired youth.

'I bet you didn't know he was queer,' Lynne said.

'Homosexual? Oh no, I am sure he isn't.'

'A woman always knows.'

'But he was so tough at school and good at games and all that.'

'Exactly. He is just the type. Not all queers go flouncing around like pansies, he is a typical public school product, he likes to have a little boy to bully.' She began to giggle. 'Lets go over and annoy him.'

Before John could protest, she took his hand and they ran over the sand to the spot where the two men were just settling down on the beach.

'Hullo Tommy,' Lynne cried. 'Enjoying yourself?' She stood in the shallows and began splashing John, making sure that some of the spray reached Thomas. Then she dived under a wave and reappeared some way out to sea. John swam after her and when he came up, she jumped upon his back and ducked him. He surfaced with his mouth full of salt water and his eyes stinging, she shouted to him. 'Come and get your revenge if you can catch me.'

They played together like kids, whenever John closed in on her she dived under and managed to evade him. When at last they waded ashore, Thomas and his companion were still lying on their backs in the sun.

'I thought you were trying to drown your little friend,' he said without bothering to move, 'pity you didn't make a better job of it.'

'Oh the things you say, Tommy,' she replied sweetly. 'Actually John is a very good swimmer. How about your little friend now? He doesn't look as though he would like to get his feet wet.'

Together they climbed the steps of the pensione, John experiencing a feeling of elation. A ghost had been laid to rest, Thomas did not matter any more.

'Come and dry my hair,' Lynne said when they came to her room on the ground floor. John followed her in shyly. She slipped out of her bathing suit and disappeared into the shower. She squealed like a little girl as the cold water squirted over her body, then she bent over allowing the full force of the shower on her hair. Wrapping a towel over her shoulders, she ran back into the room and sat on a chair by the window with her back to John.

'Get a dry towel and dry my head,' she said breathlessly. 'Rub really hard, I am lucky, as soon as I comb it out, it will look O.K.'

'Harder,' she cried as John started gingerly with the towel,' I am not a china doll.'

When John had finished, she stood up and faced him.

'Now dry me all over,' she said. John took the large towel and began to pat her shoulders, carefully avoiding her breasts.

'Johnnie,' she placed her hands around his neck. 'I am trying to seduce you, but it is bloody hard work. One moment I want to slap your face and the next moment I want to mother you. But I don't intend to throw myself at you.' She pulled the towel away angrily.

'Oh Lynne, I love you,' he pulled her towards him and, smoothing the damp hair away from her face, kissed her on the lips.

'That's better,' she smiled at him, 'and about time too.'

An hour later John met Charles Pilling on the stairs.

'My God,' he said, raising an eyebrow, 'you look like a cat who has just swallowed the cream.'

☆ ☆ ☆

The next day they went to Capri, Angellini had arranged a boat for just the two of them. John had never known such happiness before, he tried hard to forget that it couldn't last, all the same half their leave had already passed and the realisation that there were only three more days gave him an occasional stab of pain in the pit of his stomach.

Capri without hordes of tourists was a paradise. There were a few RAF from a leave hotel, and inevitably some rich Italians, but for the most part it seemed as though they had the island to themselves. They found a trattoria open in the little square and had lunch fussed over by the Padrone who looked like Stalin. They called him Uncle Joe.

'He knows that we have been to bed together,' Lynne remarked, 'that is why he is being so fatherly. Italian men have second sight.'

'Oh Lord, does he really?' John looked embarrassed.

'Yes he does really,' she mocked him gently, 'it is rather sweet, don't you think?'

'Well yes, I suppose it is.'

The previous evening, after dinner with Charles and Taffy, she announced casually, 'I am going to have an early night, are you coming now John? Or do you want to stay up a little longer?' He had followed her sheepishly, not daring to look at the other two.

After lunch Uncle Joe kissed Lynne's hand with a grand

gesture. He didn't actually wink at John, but the expression in his eyes was eloquent.

'I wish he hadn't looked at you like that,' John said.

'Why?'

'Well, he was mentally undressing you.'

'You are not jealous, are you Johnnie?'

'Perhaps I am.'

'He meant it as a compliment. So don't be so stuffy.'

They found that the chair lift on Anacapri was working. John was not fond of heights, but they glided up the hillside never very far off the ground with their feet dangling just above the orange groves. On the top they stood together looking at the view, the rocky coastline from Sorrento to Amalfi.

'Tiberius lived here and must have looked over the sea all those years ago,' Lynne said.

'It is so beautiful,' John sighed. 'If there is a heaven I like to think it looks like this.'

'Not as far as Tiberius was concerned. He was a dirty old man with a penchant for little children.'

'Don't spoil it.'

'Then there was the Duchess of Malfi holding court over there, a very nasty savage lot they were.'

'Amalfi, of course. I hadn't thought of that. All the same, Webster had never been there had he? It was just a place on the map. No more real that Shakespeare's Illyria.'

'What I am trying to say, darling Johnnie, is that you take far too romantic a view of life. People are just as cruel and unpleasant even if they do live in pretty surroundings.'

It was the first time she had called him darling.

They changed the subject and talked about themselves. Lynne was reluctant to talk about her present job, but she painted the picture of an idyllic childhood, spent half in England and half in Italy. She had no brothers or sisters and her parents treated her as an equal from an early age, which accounted for her maturity. The only cloud on her life, as she grew up, was her parents' obvious distress at the growth of Fascism. They both loved Italy and the people, but could not understand how they came to accept the ridiculous bully Mussolini, together with all the corruption and bureaucratic nastiness of the Fascist state.

'I understand, though,' Lynne said, 'most of our friends thought "Musso" absurd, but they always came back to the same conclusion, that Italy was now a power in the world and that the Italians need strong government.'

'He made the trains run on time.'

'Exactly. They could not see where he was leading them. If you chip away at personal freedom, a little at a time, you don't notice. The English would, of course, because they are a bloody-minded race and distrust authority, but the Italians are different. Even if they care, and many of them do, they are either too lazy or too cynical to do anything about it.' She sat up. 'That is enough about my life story, now tell me yours, all of it mind, I want to hear the Crabbe saga from start to finish.'

John was able to talk quite freely without any inhibitions. He told her of his father, a parson in Bayswater who he loved dearly, who had suffered a heart attack in front of his son and died the next day: of his brother Mike and his wife Judy, both much older, his mother, cold and reserved and beyond his reach, and of his young sister Felicity who he frankly hated. He also told of his escape from school and the aftermath.

'You don't much care for you mother or your sister, do you darling?' Lynne said when he had finished. 'By all accounts you ought to have turned out to be a woman hater.'

'Hardly.' John squeezed her hand.

'No, not altogether I agree. But the text books would say that you were bound to end up as a homo.'

'Well, I haven't.'

'Lucky for me!' She rolled over and climbed on top of him. 'If only you realised it, you silly sentimental old thing, you are so much more attractive than the average Philistine young officer I meet at G.H.Q. I bet Thomas has never read the Duchess of Malfi.'

They began to make love lying on the rough grass.

Lynne started to giggle. 'It is so prickly here, much more uncomfortable than Taffy's stone beds in Pompei. Let's save it for tonight. Also the ghost of Tiberius is putting me off.'

The sun was low in the sky as they went down on the chair-lift and by the time they reached the little town the lights were on. The boatman was waiting for them, and they sat together in the stern as they slid gently between the lobster pots over a black calm sea.

'We never saw St Michele, Axel Munthe's house', John said.

'Never mind, we might come back tomorrow or the next day.'

When they reached the little jetty, they were surprised to see Angellini waiting for them on the shore.

He helped Lynne out of the boat and the two of them started to talk urgently in Italian. John knew instinctively that something was wrong, he couldn't wait until they had finished but blurted out, 'Lynne, what is it? What has happened?'

'Just a minute John.' She spoke quite sharply. After Angellini had gone she took John's arm.

'We must hurry,' she said. 'There was a phone call this morning, I have been recalled off leave.'

'Oh God, no!'

'I am afraid so. They are sending a car for me at nine.'

'In the morning?'

'No, tonight.'

'But it is half past seven now.'

'Yes, I know. Angellini is bringing us both a meal in my room. So we can have a little time together.'

'Oh Lynne, why?' John's voice faltered.

'They have got a job for me to do.'

'Couldn't it have waited? You only had four days' leave.'

'No, it couldn't. Johnnie, I don't like it any more than you do. It is just the bloody war, isn't it?'

He watched her pack in the little bedroom. It was now dark outside and the lights of Praiano twinkled from the other side of the bay. He had always taken a last look at this view before going to bed each night, now it just served to mock him.

They ate their meal in silence. There was so much to say and so little time to say it in, but neither of them could find the words. At last John spoke.

'What time will you get back to Caserta? I could phone you.'

'I am not going back to G.H.Q. for the moment. I don't

know where I am going, the driver will bring me my orders.'

'I see.'

'Darling Johnnie, it had to end eventually, either now or in a few days time. We will try and meet after the war, or maybe sooner, who knows? Just look upon our time together as a rather sweet interlude. I have loved being with you, I really have.'

John took her and hugged her hard, unwilling to let her go. He noticed that she had tears in her eyes.

Gently she took his hands and squeezed them.

'Just one thing. Angellini works for us, so you could write to me through him.'

'That's wonderful, so we can have some contact.'

'Yes.' She let him go. 'I must be off. No. Don't come to the car, I'd rather you didn't. Cheer up, my darling, it's not the end of the world.'

It was only a few minutes later that he heard the sound of a car from the hillside above, soon to fade away into the silence of the night.

6

MAY 11.1944	BRITISH, POLISH, CANADIAN, & FREE FRENCH FORCES BREAK THROUGH ON CASSINO FRONT.
JUNE 4	FALL OF ROME.
AUGUST 13	GERMANS WITHDRAW FROM CENTRE OF FLORENCE

After Lynne's departure, Charles and Taffy took John to Amalfi and then up the zig-zag road to Ravello above the town, which commanded one of the best views on the Sorrento Peninsula. Charles wanted to see the Greek temples at Paestum near Salerno, and they arrived there in time to catch the setting sun bathing the columns in a deep orange glow. John tried not to be a wet blanket, but his heart ached.

On their last night, the two men decided to get John drunk. They were all feeling melancholy at the end of the holiday, so they sat on the terrace of the Pensione with two bottles of Vecchio Romagna brandy on the table.

'I was wrong,' Pilling said suddenly. 'I will confess,' he helped himself to another glass, 'that I am sometimes a self-opinionated bastard.'

'That's right boy,' Taffy said cheerfully.

'Shut up you Welsh git. I am talking to our lovesick friend here. As I was saying, I was wrong on this single occasion. Lynne, the mysterious and beautiful Lynne, is keen on you John Crabbe, otherwise she would not have taken you into her bed, to coin a phrase. God know's why, but it is a fact, so I was wrong.'

'That's true you know, after all, Lynne is not a loose woman, is she?'

'Taffy!' Charles leaned across the table. 'You are an anachronism, do you know that?'

'A what?'

'An anachronism.' He spoke the word slowly, stressing each syllable. 'Loose women went out with the Queen Victoria.'

'Well, I mean she isn't fast or anything like that.'

'Oh God, I give up. No Taffy, Lynne is not a fast, loose woman, so she must be partial to our friend here. Agreed?'

'Agreed.'

'So John, my boy, you are bloody lucky. You come here on leave with two friends, you steal, from under our eyes, the only woman around, and a very beautiful one to boot, and you go to bed with her. In the meantime Taffy and I, being perfect gentlemen . . .'

'Agreed.'

'Get out of your way and leave you alone to . . .'

'Cherchez la femme.'

'Exactly. Taffy, you know three French words.'

'I also know vive l'amour,' he chuckled.

'Correction. Six French words. Now alcohol is the great healer, so come on John "we'll teach you to drink deep ere you depart".'

'Hamlet,' said Taffy.

'Good god! He speaks French and knows his Shakespeare, such erudition.'

'We do have schools in Wales you know boy, so don't be so toffee-nosed. He is a stuck up old sod, isn't he Johnnie?'

John had only had two brandies, but he did not want to get drunk, it would not solve anything, just give him a hangover for the long journey the next day. Suddenly he felt terribly tired.

'You have both been awfully nice to me these last few days,' he said, 'I must have been an absolute pain in the arse. I'll cheer up once we get away from this place. I'd really rather go to bed now if you don't mind. I'm sorry to break up the party.'

'Heel-tapper,' Charles said.

'You leave him alone,' Taffy replied. 'You always want to

boss people around, you know Charles. At any rate it will be a good thing, if you ask me, to have at least one of us with a clear head in the morning.'

As soon as John was undressing there was a tap on the door and Angellini came in. He looked as immaculate as ever with a silk scarf neatly knotted around his neck, and carefully pressed trousers.

'Mr Crabbe, forgive the intrusion,' he said in his precise accentuated English, 'but I have a message from Miss Gardener. She is based at Bari, and can be contacted at this address.' He handed John a piece of paper.

'Oh, thank you.' John felt a mounting excitement. 'She 'phoned you?'

'She made contact, yes.'

'What did she say? Had she any message for me?'

'Yes. She thinks it might be better if you kept this information to yourself. I am sure you will do as she asks, Mr Crabbe. Goodnight.'

John read the address, memorised it, and then put the paper away in his wallet.

The black cloud of depression, which had hung over him since Lynne had gone, suddenly lifted. He knew where she was and he could write to her. He wanted to go downstairs and tell the others but he knew it wasn't possible. All the same, he was able to look out of the window again across the bay without pain, feeling at peace once more.

The regiment moved again up to the Cassino front towards the end of April. As soon as they rejoined the regiment it seemed as though the holiday had never happened. The days with Lynne belonged to another life, a four day suspension of time. Soon, John had difficulty remembering her face. Every night in bed, he tried desperately to conjure up her smile, slightly mocking, but softened by the warmth in her eyes. It was no good, he couldn't do it. He felt as though she was slipping away from him. John had never realised that such happiness was possible, but they had only spent one night in bed together, one precious night, before she had been abruptly recalled. Now, even the memory of that was fading.

War has a habit of pulling one back to reality. As the convoy of guns moved slowly towards the front, notices appeared by the side of the road.

THIS AREA IS SUBJECT TO SHELLING. A grim reminder that life was not normal anymore. John was now back again in the war zone with his ears always cocked to hear the whine and crump of enemy firing. In a way, the leave in Positano had unsettled him, and he was as nervous as a kitten. Haddock prattled away happily describing his amorous adventures in Sorrento, and how he had traded a crate of wine for some cigarettes, the bottles were bouncing about together in the back of the truck. John envied him for his lack of imagination, he remembered how he had delivered the mail cheerfully when all hell had let loose on the Garigliano — he never seemed to be aware of what might happen.

John had seen enough of war already to be conscious of the effect of shelling on frail human flesh. Blindness was his own particular nightmare. A sudden flash and darkness for the rest of his life. He was very young with a long future in front of him, and now he was in love so the terror was even more acute.

But the journey was uneventful. The gun positions were further back than on the previous time on the Cassino front, and as far as the Battery was concerned they were not unduly harassed, while one of the major battles of the Italian campaign raged ahead.

Charles Pilling in his O.P. tank was in the thick of it, while John and Taffy worked away and the troop guns belched forth fire from dawn to dusk without much unwelcome attention from the enemy. One day before the offensive started, Sholto came on to the troop position and took a stroll with John in the cool of the evening, as the sun set below the hills to the west.

'Charles tells me that you made a conquest, Johnnie, in Positano.' He slapped him on the back, 'Good for you.'

'Oh Lord, what did he say?'

'That she was an extremely pretty Intelligence officer and that you saved her from drowning.'

'Oh no, that is an exaggeration I am afraid.'

'Don't be so modest! You want to blow your own trumpet sometimes, if you don't, no one else will.'

'She is lovely,' John said quietly.

'So I understand.' Sholto changed the subject suddenly. 'Have you looked at a map of Italy recently?'

'No.'

'Well if you had you will notice that we are barely half way up the mainland. There is a hell of a long way to go yet. For the umpteenth time we are about to try and break the Cassino front, it may succeed or it may not, I hope to God it does. At any rate the Krauts have a number of fortified lines to retire to. It is going to be a long haul John, you realise that?'

'Yes Sholto I do.'

'So don't let your leave unsettle you. It is easy for anyone to be blown off course even by letters from home. I'll tell you something, I dread receiving letters from my wife Sheila, because they make me brood. I sometimes think that mail from home is one of the most difficult things that a soldier has to suffer.' He was silent for a moment and then he turned to John and put a hand on his shoulder.

'I hope you see your girl again, and if you marry her I shall demand to be asked to the wedding. But the future for all of us is uncertain. So for the time being you must forget her, put the whole episode behind you, you must do this for your own sake. Do you understand what I am trying to say to you?'

'Yes, yes Sholto I do.'

'Good man,' he said briskly. 'Now I must go and see your troop.'

☆ ☆ ☆

On the afternoon of 15 May, John had orders to go forward and recce a new gun position on the far side of the Rapido River. The Battery had been static for nearly a week. For the first two days the guns had been silent, and then from the evening of 11 May the whole front had erupted, firing thousands of shells on the enemy positions. News filtered through that the French Forces were advancing in the south and the Poles had launched an attack on the monastery itself. On 12 May a bridgehead was secured beyond the river.

John had settled down in this gun position. Unlike their

previous site under Monte Trocchio, they had not been harassed, only the occasional shell, and now inevitably they were moving forward into the unknown. His heart was thumping as he travelled in his half-track vehicle with Haddock driving and B.S.M. Cobber behind on his motor-bike.

They passed Monte Trocchio. The land the battery had occupied looked very different. The spring sunshine had dried the mud and all the shell holes had hardened into dark brown craters, like an artist's impression of a moonscape. There was not a sign of grass or vegetation. They crossed the river on a Bailey bridge and then skirted the edge of what remained of the town of Cassino.

Not a building was left standing, the rubble had by now mostly disintegrated, and the air was thick with swirling dust. Now and then, fingers of masonry stood up, a reminder that once this was part of somebody's home. The wind was from the East and the sweet sickly smell of rotting flesh filled their nostrils, it seemed incredible that the Germans had held out for so long.

Haddock seemed to sense what John was thinking.

'They must have been dug in deep, sir,' he said. 'Otherwise Jerry could never have survived that lot.'

'Many didn't,' John replied.

'No that's true. Bit of a pong, poor bastards. Still they are fucking good fighters, you have to give them that. They stuck it out for months, didn't they?'

'Yes.'

On the map, the Liri Valley looked flat, ideal it would seem for a quick advance by armoured forces. But in fact the ground was criss-crossed with irrigation ditches and rivers with steep banks. There was also virtually no cover, only thickets of oak too small to be of any use. There was only the one good road, the Via Casilina, otherwise only farm tracks, which often led off in the wrong direction or double-backed the way they had come.

John went down one of these hoping to find a farm house or some cover. They reached a collection of buildings which were flat and there wasn't a tree in sight.

'We shouldn't go any further, Mr Crabbe,' Cobber said. 'I reckon this is the most forward point on our map reference.'

'Yes it is, we must settle here, time is getting short.'

They looked at the field in front of them, once it had been full of maize, now it was burnt out stubble.

'No cover at all,' Cobber sighed. 'At least we had some trees on the Garigliano.'

'Is Jerry near?' Haddock asked.

'He is meant to be falling back to the Hitler line,' John said.

'Where is that?'

'Too bloody close for comfort.' Cobber mounted his bike. 'O.K. sir, the guns will be here before midnight.'

John found two walls standing at right angles, and parked his vehicle in the corner. The scene looke absurdly peaceful. A mist had hung over the Liri Valley for several days, fed by the exploding of thousands of shells. It had partially lifted and the sun was trying to break through, but visibility was only about half a mile. He could see the hedge at the far end of the maize field, but not the hills around. He could hear the battle raging on both sides, like distant thunder, but muffled by the fog, so it seemed far away. Likewise he could hear the groaning of tanks moving along the Via Casilina but they were out of sight. John knew that it was all too easy to be lulled into a false sense of security, all the same he had had an uneventful journey and the little ruined farm seemed almost a friendly oasis.

They had planted a regimental sign where the farm track met the main road, so there wasn't much to do except wait for Cobber to return with the troop of guns.

He made contact by radio with Pilling at his O.P. some way ahead, and then settled down with Haddock and his signaller Jenkins to have their evening meal.

Haddock produced a bottle of wine, from his seemingly inexhaustible supply, and the three of them drank and ate their cold bully-beef while darkness slowly descended.

'I wonder if the Poles have taken the monastery?' Haddock asked.

'I hope so,' John replied.

'It is a funny thing, isn't it sir? We are meant to be a British Army, yet there are Poles, French, Indians, Canadians, New Zealanders, and now even the Ities are meant to be on our side too, we are a rum lot, Fred Karno's army and no mistake.'

'Don't you know, Haddock,' Jenkins said quietly, 'that the British always fight to the last drop of someone else's blood?'

John had never been able to make much contact with Jenkins, he had been a school teacher in civilian life and, although always polite, had a chip on his shoulder. Normally he didn't say much but now the vino on an empty stomach had loosened his tongue.

'Oh come off it Jenky, there are lots of British too, what do you think we are?'

'Oh we are here all right,' Jenkins continued, 'and we run the show, when we are not giving way to the Yanks, and a right cock-up this whole campaign is.'

John felt he ought to say something but remained silent.

'But we have made it, better late than never!' Haddock said.

'Really! You are not as thick as that. Look at the facts. We have superiority in everything, particularly in the air, you never see a German plane. More guns, more tanks, more infantry, and what happens? We are nearly thrown back into the sea at Salerno, and remember those poor sods who landed north of the Garigliano, they bought it through sheer incompetence up top. And it's taken nearly four bloody months to break through here, and the Krauts are waiting for us on the next line, not far away. As for Anzio, the landing that was meant to spearhead the attack on Rome, they are still stuck on a tiny bridgehead having the shit knocked out of them. It is a farce!'

'But that was the Yanks' fault Jenky, they are in charge there.'

'Oh yes bloody Mark Clark, seeing himself as another Caesar entering Rome. But Alexander is in charge of the whole shooting match. He just sits in Caserta reading poetry.'

At last John felt he must interfere. 'Did you teach history in civilian life, Jenkins?' he asked.

'Yes, as a matter of fact I did.'

'Then you ought to know that a historian should keep a sense of perspective. What you have just been saying is a load of one-sided bollocks.'

'It is not, it is bloody not.' He paused and looked at John. 'Are you going to put me on a charge, sir, for insubordination?'

'Oh don't be such an idiot.' He took the bottle of vino and emptied it into their glasses. 'We are three men sitting in a ruined farm far from home, all in the same boat and needing each other, I am not going to be regimental, what would be the point?'

'Which means that we can let our hair down?'

'You seem to have been doing that quite successfully for the last few minutes.'

Jenkins managed a bleak smile. 'O.K. sir. Now be honest with us Mr Crabbe, I am right aren't I?'

'No not altogether. I don't know the secrets of the High Command, I am just a very junior Second-Lieutenant. But I have my view like you. It seems to me that we are only a side show, the main effort is being made on the second front across the Channel. But we have been able to tie down a large German army which can't be used against us in France.'

'But that wasn't what we were told by Monty when we landed in Sicily, we were to sweep up the country and on into Austria. As it is, over a year later we haven't even reached Rome.'

'Monty is no longer with us,' Haddock said.

'No. More's the pity. At least he knew what he was doing, and did not let the Yanks walk all over him.'

'There is another point Jenkins,' John continued. 'The Germans have had time to construct a series of well-fortified lines right up Italy. They had a head start.'

'Because we gave it to them, we have been too bloody slow the whole time. Look at Anzio, that was actually quite a good idea for a change, a landing near Rome. And what happened? We fart-arsed about on a small bridgehead and waited for the Krauts to come, who once again nearly pushed us back into the sea.'

John knew that there was a great deal of truth in Jenkins's account, and that his own defence had not been very convincing, but he was saved from further argument because the signaller had a routine check to make on the radio.

The guns arrived with Cobber shortly after eleven and they were all in position before midnight. As John prepared for bed there was the sound of aircraft above gradually getting closer. 'Good old RAF,' he thought, 'I hope they knock the hell out of them.' The screech of falling bombs shook him out of his complacency and he dived into the half-track vehicle just short of Jenkins, who fell on top of him. They lay flat, the comfort of the armour around them.

'You said that we never see a German plane,' John muttered.

'Well we haven't, sir, have we? Not for months, the bastards are getting cheeky.'

The raid was soon over, probably only about a half a dozen planes, but directed at their gun position.

The ground shook with the explosions for a few minutes, and then they could hear the aircraft moving away. John climbed up and began to clamber out of the truck to see if anyone had been hurt. As soon as his feet touched the ground he stopped. There were flashes of light all over the area, like fire-crackers.

'What the hell is happening?' he shouted at Jenkins.

'Get back, sir, get back into the truck.' He pushed John on to the floor. 'They are anti-personnel bombs, they bounce all over the bloody place and explode, full of nasty pieces of shrapnel. They are no use against armoured vehicles, they are designed to attack men out in the open, we'll be alright, just keep your head down until the fireworks stop. Silly sods, they must have mistaken us for the infantry.'

'Do they often use them?' John asked.

'Yes, on forward troops. They are nasty little things, they roll into slit trenches, there is no real defence against them if you haven't armour to protect you.'

John sat up suddenly. 'Jenkins, where's Haddock?'

'He went off to take some bottles of vino to the guns.'

'When?'

'About half an hour ago.'

'Oh God, I hope he is O.K.'

'Don't worry, sir. He is an old hand. He knows all about these anti-personnel bombs, he will be keeping his head down in one of the guns with all the others.'

'I hope to God you are right.'

'I am, sir, he knows the form. Look! Those bloody things don't bounce as high as the armour on the guns, they just career all over the ground like billiard balls.'

The sharp crackles died down suddenly, and then, like a motor bike engine, spluttered into silence.

'I am going to look for him,' John said.

'I would hang on a bit longer, sir,' Jenkins replied. 'They have a habit of starting up again when you least expect it.'

But John was already out of the truck. Jenkins followed him and they ran towards No. 1 gun. The smoke together with the evening mist had covered the area with thick fog. They stumbled as they made their way towards the maize field, John was running so fast that he came upon the first gun suddenly out of the mist and struck his head against the side of the armour. The gunners were beginning to scramble out of their refuge to inspect the damage. John felt dizzy from the blow on his head and gripped the side of the gun.

'Are you alright, sir?' He was conscious of the gun sergeant by his side.

'Yes,' he paused for a moment to catch his breath. 'Where is Haddock, have you seen him?'

'He was here, sir, before the bombing, delivering some vino. I expect he is with one of the other guns. Are you sure you are O.K.?'

John did not reply, Jenkins had caught up with him and instinctively he grabbed his arm and then ran off into the mist. They kept to the edge of the field along the side of the farm track, so as not to get lost. John thought that the last gun, No. 4 was the most likely place to find him. The fog was so thick that they had to slow down.

'Bugger!' Jenkins tripped and fell by the edge of the track.

John went to help his signaller to his feet, and then they saw him. Jenkins had fallen over two army boots. Haddock was lying across the path. His head had been almost severed by a piece of shrapnel. His chin had been pushed upwards by the force of the explosion, his face was untouched but there was an expression of slight surprise in his eyes. The blood, cold grey in the night, was still seeping from his throat.

☆ ☆ ☆

John was devastated by Haddock's death, he felt as though all the stuffing had been knocked out of him. Earlier, Captain Max Gregory had been killed and the signaller Mason. He had hardly known his troop Captain but Mason's death had upset him as they had got to know each other at Trimonsuoli. But Haddock was different. He was one of John's familiars, together with Sholto, Charles, Taffy and Cobber. In war personal relationships have an extra dimension, they provide an anchor and something to hang on to when life itself is so uncertain.

In John's case, being so unsuited to war, he had managed to take a grip on himself because those close to him were there at his side. Now one of his chief props was dead. Quite unreasonably he felt a growing resentment against Jenkins, with his superior attitude and cynical posturing. Haddock had not been like that, always cheerful, kind and uncomplicated. It had been his innate generosity, wanting to share his vino with the others, that had killed him.

In a different way John had lost Taffy too. The Command Post Officer at Battery H.Q. had been evacuated with jaundice and Taffy had been sent there to take his place. So he felt isolated and alone. Not entirely though, there was still Cobber.

The Sergeant-Major dropped all formality and spoke to John like a Dutch Uncle. 'We all miss Haddock,' he said. 'Especially Major Sholto, he has known him for years and brought him into the Regiment. You are not the only one. But you must harden your heart, Mr Crabbe, he won't be the last one to go. Remember it is much worse with the forward troops, like the infantry, their casualties are much heavier than ours. People die in battle, it is a fact of life. Oh and one other thing. Jenkins and Haddock joined up the same day, he will be missing him too, you know.'

But John could not bring himself to talk to his signaller about it, there remained a wide rift between them.

The next day was one of uneasy calm. There were plenty of enemy shells landing, and although none actually hit the troop position, there was always the feeling that they might at any moment. In the evening John was summoned to Battery H.Q.

Sholto seemed cheerful enough and he made no reference to Haddock.

'The Poles have taken the monastery,' he said, chewing on his cigar, 'which is good news. We can reasonably expect to breach the Hitler line soon, and then the enemy will pull back to another position just south of Rome. If the break-out of our forces from Anzio goes according to plan, that line should become untenable and we should then have the way open to Rome. The trouble is that up to now the enemy has been calling the tune, fighting copybook defensive operations, and then withdrawing in good order to the next line to fight again. They are being very clever, no doubt about that. This time we want to catch them up, engage, then destroy them, otherwise this campaign will go on for ever. Our casualties have been heavy because every twenty miles or so we get a bloody nose when we come up against Germans dug in and ready for us.'

'We are a good army trained in pursuit, so we have got to overtake them, it is as simple as that.' Sholto paused. 'That is the general situation. Now as regards the Battery. We must be ready to move forward fast, when the time comes, to give covering fire to the tanks and infantry as their advance gains momentum. These are the orders.'

He dealt with the other troop first and then turned to John. 'I want you to go at first light, Johnnie, in a Jeep and find a position on the edge of Aquino airfield. Don't go any further than the periphery because the town is still in enemy hands. Don't hang about, just plant the signs and markers and come back. Take Jenkins with you, he can drive, but not Cobber, he must stay with the guns. O.K.?'

'Yes Sholto,' John muttered.

'There will be a mist so you won't be visible to the enemy, but make the route for the troop absolutely clear, so the guns can occupy it without getting lost. Taffy will come up with a signaller from here to cover while you are away, but you shouldn't be long. Good luck.'

As soon as he returned John passed on the instructions to Cobber and Jenkins. He expected Jenkins to moan about leaving the radio, but he didn't say a word. Cobber was clearly not happy about the situation.

'I wish I was coming with you, sir,' he said.

'We will be O.K. Sergeant-Major.'

'Just be careful sir. If any unpleasantness starts, come back sharpish. We don't want bloody heroes, we just want you both back in one piece. I fancy that this idea comes from Colonel Alex.'

'In what way?'

'Well, Major Sholto doesn't like taking unnecessary risks with any of us, though he will always have a go himself, but the Colonel has been leaning on him and the battery commanders, that's for sure. I bet he told the Major to stay put and send the gun position officers on this recce!'

'Well, that's our job isn't it?' John tried to sound more confident than he felt.

'I only hope the mist doesn't lift.' He paused. 'Don't go after a bloody medal, Mr Crabbe, at the first sign of trouble, scarper, the Major will understand.'

Cobber had meant well, but his advice had done nothing to restore John's morale. He couldn't even talk to Charles Pilling on the radio because wireless silence had been imposed, unless the O.P. broke it in an emergency.

Jenkins spoke for the first time. 'When do we start?' he asked.

'I will collect the Jeep at 0400 hours.'

'In three hours' time.'

'Yes.'

'Well I am going to get some kip, goodnight sir.'

'Goodnight.'

John would have liked to talk about the morning. But there was a barrier between the two men, and both were conscious of it. John took out a torch and studied the map once again. He had marked it up before Sholto's briefing from the copy at Battery H.Q. showing the latest information. This indicated a track off the railway line, signposted to the airfield about a mile away. It was somewhere by the side of the track, directly behind the tank formations waiting to advance, that he had to find a gun position.

He rather wished that he had asked some questions at the

briefing. For instance, what other units, apart from the tanks forming up, might he find in this area? How could he guarantee that the piece of ground that he chose would be free by the time the guns arrived? On previous recces he had stayed there to stake a claim, but on this occasion he was to return to the Battery. He imagined that as the airfield was just short of the Hitler line, troops would be very thick on the ground.

He was tempted to go back and have a word with Sholto, but it seemed at the time a feeble thing to do. He decided to hope for the best, maybe when he arrived he would be able to work out something. The main thing was to find the track and plant the regimental sign showing the way off the railway line.

There was no question of sleep. Not wanting to be in the truck with Jenkins he curled up on what used to be the floor of the farmhouse between the vehicle and the wall. Nights are cold in Italy in May and the stone walls were moist, so he pulled the blanket around him, but he still shivered.

Taking Sholto's advice, he tried not to think of Lynne and Positano, but perversely he was able to conjure up her face in his mind for the first time since rejoining the Regiment. He saw her with great clarity on the night he brought her ashore from the sea, her hair wet and clinging to her cheeks, she had looked like a little girl, so young and vulnerable. He remembered her soft flesh as he hugged her trembling in his arms and her gentle laughter as she noticed his underpants wrapped around his knees.

Then he thought of Thomas and anger swelled up into his gullet. Thomas the school bully, now sleeping in a warm and comfortable bed at the Caserta H.Q. He had it made, walking about in his smart Staff Captain uniform miles from the shit and smell of death. 'An office boy from Caserta' Lynne had called him and she was right, poncing about with his boyfriends.

The anger did John good. He despised Thomas now and the spell had been broken, he would never be afraid of him again. The legacy from his schooldays had been finally put to rest. In a strange way this gave John a feeling of relief, in spite of everything he began to feel drowsy, and as he drifted into that twilight state between waking and sleeping, he thought of his friends in the Regiment. Although he missed Haddock, there were still the others, and the paramount thought in his mind as he started to get ready in the early hours, was that he must not let them down.

When they started off in the Jeep John decided to try and get through to Jenkins.

'Listen,' he said. 'We may well become separated up there. As I see it, the main object is to plant a number of signs in the quickest possible time, and the way to do that is to divide forces and arrange a place to meet later.'

'That makes sense.'

'So what I am trying to say is that if things get nasty, it should be every man for himself, don't try and look for me or anything like that.'

'Don't worry, sir, I won't.'

'At least,' John took a deep breath, 'let us drop this antagonism between us, we are both in the same boat.'

'That's all right by me, sir.' He paused. 'But be honest with me, this recce is a right proper bastard isn't it, Mr Crabbe? Dreamed up by our revered Colonel.'

'It will be tricky.'

'Too true. I am not being impertinent sir, but do we know what we are doing?'

'I hope so, yes.'

'So do I.' he leaned over and picked up his rifle from the back of the Jeep. 'Well good luck, sir, we are both going to need it.'

The railway had been used as a road by the Germans, in the same way as the Allies on their side of the Rapido River. It was a bumpy trip, but Jenkins drove well, weaving in and out of the mass of vehicles moving forward. Two of John's fears proved groundless.

They found the turning off to the airfield without difficulty, and the timing was perfect. They had planned to leave the railway at first light, and as they drove down the bank off the track, visibility began to improve slowly but surely. Also, the journey had been entirely peaceful, with no shelling or bombing. John planted the first regimental sign and climbed back into the Jeep.

'So far so good,' he said.

'Yes sir,' Jenkins replied. 'I only hope this bloody mist doesn't lift, we had better get a move on.'

'I agree.'

Then their difficulties began. The trouble was that there was no discernable route any more. Tanks had been swanning about the area and their tracks led off in all directions.

'What now, sir?' Jenkins asked.

'Stop for a moment.' John took out his map and with a protractor took a bearing from the railway to the nearest point of the airfield. The problem was that it was hard to find the exact point where they had left the railway. It was guesswork and John knew it. He then walked a few yards ahead and found the bearing on his compass.

'It must be to the right here,' John said. 'We will keep on this route until we get to the airfield.'

'That will take us right up to the enemy lines, won't it sir?'

'Yes, but we stop before the boundary.'

'If you say so, sir.'

They planted another sign at the edge of the route and drove on. Visibility was about 200 yards and John sat forward straining to see the airfield fence. After about ten minutes they stopped again. There was no sign of any other vehicles or tanks, they seemed to be completely out on a limb.

'We won't go any further,' John said. 'We can't be far away now. Stick in the markers and then we will go back fast on the reverse bearing and get the hell out of here.'

'That is good thinking, sir. Because I reckon we are in the middle of the airfield.'

'We can't be, we haven't passed the perimeter.'

'It could have disappeared sir, or the Krauts might have torn it down just to fool us.'

'No, I am sure we haven't reached it. Look! Turn round and be ready to leave. I will go forward on foot for a few hundred yards and see if I can find the edge.'

'But why sir, for God's sake?'

'Because my orders were to find a position close to the airfield and I want to see if that is where we are.'

'All right sir, but do hurry up, the mist is beginning to

lift.'

He was right. The sun was slowly starting to break through.

John stumbled forward. He knew that he was being an idiot.

The previous night he had been terrified of this recce, but now he felt a compulsion to ensure that they were in the right place. Jenkins's remark, 'do we know what we are doing, sir?' rankled, he just wanted to show the supercilious little sod that he was in control of the situation. And then there were the others. Pilling's remark that John was not cut out to be a soldier came back to him. He could hear him saying, 'My dear John, the position was miles from the airfield.'

This was the opportunity to prove himself, so he quickened his pace praying that he would find the elusive perimeter fence. A ditch appeared in front of him about three feet wide and full of water, it would be necessary to wade across it, so John decided reluctantly to turn back. The mist was dispersing fast so he broke into a run.

He tried to find his own footsteps for the way back, but there was no sign of them, he then realised that he may well be running in the wrong direction. He had only come a few hundred yards but that was enough, he was completely lost. He began to panic, cursing his stupidity, if he had not gone on this wild goose-chase, they would have been well on their way back by now.

Then suddenly he saw some figures coming towards him out of the mist, feeling a profound sense of relief that at last he had met someone to ask the way, he ran towards them. A cold sweat started in his legs and spread slowly upwards to the top of his head, as he raised his hands in surrender.

7

They made John run, prodding him with a rifle in his back, until he was close to collapse. Fortunately, they reached the town of Aquino before long and he was taken into the church with one soldier to guard him. He was numb with fear and shock. A tank battle was raging on the airfield and shells were exploding on the approaches to the town, but he was too exhausted to feel afraid.

As John slowly recovered he began to take in his surroundings. There was a hole in the roof of the church just above the altar. A large crucifix had been blown into the aisle and the head of Christ had become detached and rolled between the pews so that it lay a few yards from where he was sitting. Statues of saints were strewn in bits and pieces over a wide area, two legs clothed in armour were sticking out of one of the shattered windows, as though trying to escape from the carnage.

John turned to look at his companion. He was young, about his own age, and under the German helmet bright yellow hair protruded. He had his rifle at the ready and did not look at John, but just stared passively ahead. He did not appear particularly menacing, presumably guarding a prisoner of war was all part of a day's work.

Once the effect of the shock began to wear off, John began to realise how idiotic he had been. He must have strayed right into the middle of the airfield. The enemy patrol had been on the return journey when they captured him. They had not been all that far from Aquino which was behind the Hitler line. He wondered if Jenkins had escaped, he hoped so because he did not want him on his conscience.

Before long, John began to think about his present plight. He had been led to believe that if you were taken by the German army you could expect civilised treatment, but not in the case of the S.S. Were these S.S.? He had no means of knowing. Would they shoot him, or torture him? He felt again the cold sweat on his forehead as he had at the moment of his capture.

In his panic, he thought of Thomas safe at G.H.Q. and all those left behind in England complaining about food shortages and the rich living comfortably off black market goods. Then he remembered Cobber and Sholto, Taffy and Charles, they would despise him now for what he had done.

He started like a frightened rabbit as an officer came into the church. There was a brief conversation and then the soldier motioned John towards the door with his rifle.

It was bright sunlight as they emerged into the piazza outside, and John shielded his eyes against the glare. It was obvious that the Germans were withdrawing, but in good order. Staff cars and troop-carrying lorries were leaving the square at regular intervals down the narrow road leading to the north. John hoped the Allied guns, perhaps including his own, would not start shelling the town, it was certainly a tempting target. But the tank battle was still in progress on the airfield about a mile away. From the noise and black smoke billowing in the air, it was obvious that the artillery was fully engaged there.

A truck stopped in front of him. Troops were packed into the back and the sentry pushed John towards the front cab. He climbed in and found himself next to the officer he had seen in the church. There wasn't much room so the officer moved over so that John was able to perch uncomfortably on the edge of the seat.

'And why was an artillery officer behind enemy lines?'

John started, and looked at the other man in bewilderment.

'Oh yes, I speak English,' the officer said. 'It is not unknown in my country to speak a foreign language, unlike yours, the British are very insular.' He spoke with a strong German accent, but his command of English was excellent. 'Permit me to introduce myself, I am Hauptmann Kruger, in your army a captain. And you?'

'Second-Lieutenant John Crabbe,' John muttered.

'Thank you. Name rank and number is all your are required to give at this stage.'

'179870,' John replied.

'So. You are, I suspect, a very junior officer. Too young to be engaged in special operations behind our lines. Am I correct when I guess that you were on a reconnaissance for your battery guns and became completely lost?'

John did not reply.

The Captain had a pistol across his knees, he looked at John, and put it away in his holster. 'I do not think that you are going to play the hero, so let us both be comfortable. Cigarette?'

'I would like some water if possible.'

'Of course.' He handed John a water bottle. 'Finish it if you wish. There is more in the back.'

It was hot in the cab, and there was hardly a cloud in the sky. John gulped the water greedily.

'Thank you.'

'Thank you sir,' the Captain said sharply. 'I am your superior officer, am I not?'

'Thank you sir, very much,' John replied.

'That is better. Now I will give you advice. I am not your interrogator, you will meet him when I give you to the prisoner camp. It is by chance that you are with me and that I speak English. So. Listen. When you arrive at the camp, they will want to know why you were behind our lines, they do not like saboteurs, they might think that you were trying to contact the Italian brigands who are active in this area. You call them partisans, we call them scum!' He spat out the word. 'So tell them you were lost, which is the truth, isn't it?'

John hesitated.

'Isn't it?'

'Yes,' he mumbled.

'I hope they believe you, for your sake.' He paused. 'You were fortunate, Second-Lieutenant, that our patrol did not shoot you. Prisoners when we are retiring, are an —' he searched for the word, 'inconvenience. They must have thought that an officer might be worth the trouble. Yes, you were fortunate.' He lit a cigarette, and turned away.

John looked out of the window. The countryside was virtually devoid of troops. The bulk of the German army must have withdrawn much earlier, leaving behind a Panzer Division to fight a rearguard. The convoy was making good time, spaced at intervals of at least fifty yards. John tried to remember the map of the area in his mind. He calculated that at this rate they would arrive at the outskirts of Rome within a few hours. He was being taken further and further away from the Allied armies. But soon the situation changed, there were tanks and infantry all around them, and the convoy ground to a halt.

A dispatch rider came alongside and spoke to the Captain and it was then that the Spitfires struck, swooping low with machine guns chattering. There was a wood by the side of the road and they raced into it, soldiers tumbling out of the back of the truck. John threw himself on the ground, his cheek catching a sharp tree root, he could feel the blood trickling down his face. There were not many planes, but they made three runs, it seemed an eternity before they flew off. A soldier had landed on top of him. There was a fetid smell of stale sweat, the sweat of fear. When the German climbed to his feet, looking down at John he kicked him savagely on the arm. If the officer had not been there John had no doubt at all that the soldier would have shot him.

He sat up slowly and dabbed his cheek with his handkerchief. He moved his right arm and flexed his fingers. Nothing was broken, the boot had landed on the fleshy part above the elbow. He remained where he was, not wanting to appear conspicuous as the troops made their way towards the truck. He could see two fires, one in front and the other behind them, and there was a lot of shouting. The raid had certainly achieved a success.

The Captain was already on his feet. John was surprised to see him stop the soldiers mounting, and instead instruct the driver to take the vehicle off the road into the wood along a track just in front of them. John was seized with a sudden panic, perhaps they were going to lead him off into the wood and shoot him. He stayed quite still, his heart pounding. After a few minutes the Captain came over. In his hand were two tin mugs and a bottle. He handed John one of the mugs and poured a liberal shot of brown liquid into both of them. The label on the bottle was Vecchio Romagna. The last time John had drunk this brandy was in Positano.

'Cheers. That is what you say in England, isn't it?'

'Yes sir. Thank you.'

'Drink it. It is the last you will have for a long time. You see, even a Hun can be civilised with his prisoner.'

John felt embarrassed and said nothing. He took a good swig and immediately felt his panic subsiding.

'The road will be blocked ahead, so we stop here for some food. We still hold Aquino, your attack failed, so there is no hurry. Also your Air Force will be back, or should be if they know their job, and here we have cover.' He lit a cigarette and gave one to John. 'Players,' he said with a smile. 'You see we also have our booty in war.'

For the first time John was able to take a good look at the Captain. He was probably in his middle thirties, about the same age as Sholto. He had taken off his cap and his hair was sparse on the top of his head but bushy over his ears, he had an aquiline nose and a lean, intelligent face.

The brandy was beginning to restore John's morale. 'Where did you learn your English, sir?' he asked.

'Oxford. St John's College. I won a scholarship for foreigners. Then I taught English at Heidelberg until the war.' He paused. 'But I volunteered, I am not a conscript.'

A soldier came over with their food. He did not look at John but placed the German sausage, bread and cheese and apples in front of the Captain.

When they started eating the Captain said, 'Tell me about your life, before the war. I am not asking for military secrets.'

John warmed towards his captor. It did seem to him that he had been extraordinarily lucky to have found himself the prisoner of this cultured, intelligent man. He told him about his work in the theatre.

'Were you good as an actor?' the Captain asked.

Strange, Pilling had posed exactly the same question.

'I think so, sir, yes. Otherwise I would never have gone on the stage.'

'There is nothing either good or bad but thinking makes

it so.'

'To me it is a prison.'

'So, like me, you know your Shakespeare. I was going to ask you what you think of the war, but perhaps you have already answered me.'

'I didn't mean —'

'No, of course you were just completing Hamlet's sentence. But rather a suitable reply, is it not? Considering your present circumstances.'

'Yes.'

The Captain lit another cigarette. 'I will tell you what I think, Second-Lieutenant. It is absurd that England and Germany should be at war. We have a common heritage, our Führer agrees with that. But Churchill, in the pay of the Jews, has led you into disaster. You are allies of the Bolsheviks and the Jews. You are fighting the one man who could save Europe from both. It is a great catastrophe.'

John felt uneasy. This German Captain had treated him extremely well, and yet he was a fervent Nazi. Early in 1939 John remembered his headmaster at school praising Hitler and describing him as a bulwark against communism.

At the time, he knew in his heart that it was wrong to talk that way. He rejected it as he did so many of the values that were instilled into him at his public school. He assumed that all the upper class in England thought the same way, but he was wrong. Churchill did not.

'You do not reply to me?' the Captain asked.

'Sir, you have been very kind to me —'

'Kind! Do you think the German army are barbarians like your Russian friends? I treated you as a fellow officer from a civilised country like my own. What else did you expect?'

'I think sir,' John desperately searched for words, 'that you behaved towards me with extra consideration. I am grateful,' he paused, 'but I do not wish to discuss the war.' He stopped. There did not seem any more that he could say.

'So.' The Captain stood up and shouted orders to the soldiers who started packing up and climbing back into the truck. He turned to look a John. 'You are wounded in the face?'

'Oh no Sir. I just caught my cheek on a sharp root.'
'Have you a handkerchief?'
'Oh yes, I think so.'
'Give it to me.'
John handed him the rather grubby one. the Captain soaked it in brandy from the bottle and dabbed John's face.
'That should keep infection away.' He put on his cap. 'Come.'
The bombers came as they started to walk towards the truck. Bombs began falling over a wide area, it was clearly a major raid. Once again John hugged the earth. So much had happened to him during the last few hours that he was becoming fatalistic. Hamlet's words came to him. 'If it be now, 'tis not to come.' He covered his eyes with his hands, his private nightmare of being blinded was always with him. He was conscious of the Captain there by his side, a few moments ago they had been reciting *Hamlet* at each other. They might die together. 'The rest is silence.' Pity he was a Nazi, otherwise he could have made a friend of this kindly man. Thoughts raced through his brain as they both listened to the strident whistles of the falling bombs. He had heard that when one died, the whole vista of one's life telescoped in the mind in a few seconds, perhaps this was an omen, perhaps this was the end.
A bomb fell very close, John felt the blast above them like a hammer blow as it plucked branches off the trees and scattered them around. At the same time there was a flash of orange flame as the truck caught alight and a fireball came towards them, consuming the trees in its wake. They both jumped up and ran off into the wood. There was no air to breathe and as their lungs collapsed they staggered for a few yards and then fell together onto the ground. Slowly, very slowly, the air returned, then gasping and moaning, they gradually recovered.
The Captain was the first to rise and he helped John to his feet. They were three or four hundred yards now from the inferno that had engulfed the German truck. John had heard the pathetic cries of wounded men before, but this was almost worse. There was no sound at all save the crackling of the fire. All the men had been wiped out in a matter of seconds. Because he and the Captain had moved

away to eat on their own they were still alive.

The Captain looked up into the sky and shouted something in German. John could not understand the words but the rage and the frustration were clear enough. The revolver was still in the holster, but John felt with a sickening certainty that any moment he would be shot.

Then there was a shout in the woods behind them and they both spun round. About five men dressed in shabby peasant clothes came out of the shadows with an assortment of weapons pointing straight at them. The Captain made a movement towards his holster and then thought better of it and raised his hands above his head. One of the men in the centre of the group shouted to the others: 'Alt! Inglése!' and beckoned John to come forward. He then raised his pistol, pointing it at the Captain.

'No!' John cried. 'Don't, don't shoot him!'

One single shot rang out. What had been the Captain's left eye opened up into a neat black hole, there was hardly any blood. The figure remained standing for at least a couple of seconds, as though to attention, and then crumpled and fell.

'Tedésco finito,' the leader cried in triumph. 'Capitano morto!'

The men surrounded John, laughing and shouting. They shook his hand and the leader, a very tall man, slapped him on the back. 'Inglése Sottotenente. Bène!' He took John's cap off his head, ran a few yards and chucked it onto the fire. Then he took off his own coat and threw it to John, who put it on over his uniform. It was much too big, coming almost down to his ankles.

'Carlo! Carlo Chaplin!' one of the others yelled, amidst a howl of laughter.

'Taci!' the tall man snapped out suddenly. 'Vieni. Subito. Andiamo!'

Their mood changed completely and the six of them started climbing out of the wood. In about half an hour they reached a narrow road which snaked ahead between terraces of vineyards up into the foothills, the range of mountains in front of them seemed very close, etched against a bright blue sky. There was a muttered conversation between the group and two of them set off as scouts up and down the road, while the remainder stayed lying on their stomachs at the edge of the trees.

John began to feel a little more confidence in his new-found friends. After the party atmosphere when they rescued him, they now seemed to know what they were doing. He had yet to learn the Italian temperament, their ebullience appeared childlike, but under the cheerful enthusiasm there was a peasant cunning and ruthlessness. He wished they had not shot the German Captain out of hand, but he was glad they were on his side.

The road was quite empty and the silence was eerie. The scouts returned in a few minutes, and they set off all together up the hill. John felt self-conscious in his army boots and wrapped the coat around his neck to hide his uniform. The mountains ahead seemed to offer a haven and John willed them to hurry up, but they continued at a slow and steady pace. John realised, though, that if they were to be taken for a group of refugees on the trek away from the fighting they should not draw attention to themselves. He also decided that the foray had been well planned to take place during a bombing attack when any casualties would be assumed to be the result of Allied action. But all they had in fact achieved was the death of one German officer and the liberation of a very frightened English prisoner of war. They had managed to conceal their weapons up to a point, two of the band had machine guns pushed down their trousers and walked like wooden puppets, while the leader had a number of hand grenades stuffed down his shirt. From a distance they would pass muster, but if they came across any Germans on the road, John realised that they would not stand a chance.

Soon after a bend in the road a village appeared; as so often in Italy houses clung precariously to the flanks of a small hillock. They had been built higgledy-piggledy, facing in all directions, densely packed so it was not possible to see the narrow streets. The houses were all shapes and sizes and the only common factor was the reddish tiles on the roofs, in many cases gaping holes were apparent, the result John decided of neglect and not of shells or bombs. *Salitas* of steps zig-zagged down the hillside, reminiscent of Positano. He noticed on one roof the remains of some vines long since abandoned, and now dying in the warm spring sunshine. On the top of the village the tower of a church rose high, dominating the scene, and next to it a square structure like a small castle.

John was grateful when they came into the cover of the houses up the winding road. But they had not progressed far before the way ahead was jammed with people. There were carts drawn by emaciated horses, men and women on bicycles carrying children on the handlebars and an incredible amount of luggage strapped over the rear wheels. But most were on foot struggling with heavy suitcases, one woman had a pig in tow on a piece of rope. Caught in a no man's land between the two armies, virtually the whole village seemed to be trying to escape to the mountains. There was much shouting and gesticulating Italian style, but to little effect, the solid mass of humanity had ground to a halt.

The leader, who John had discovered was called Mario, cut a swathe through the throng by the simple method of using the butt of his pistol on the elbows of all and sundry. Soon they came to a *salita* and he led them up it at a brisk pace, using the same method to facilitate their progress. They traversed streets, crossed the back yards of houses, climbed fences and eventually arrived at the church. Mario clearly knew his way around. Once there he led them into the "castle". John decided that it had probably been a monastery at some time, but now it appeared to be a municipal building. He was surprised to see a lorry parked in the main hall, but without pausing the party went down some steps and arrived in a crypt underneath the church.

It was lit by candles and one paraffin lamp. John was immediately the centre of attention. Figures came out of the gloom, queueing up to embrace him, all asking questions in Italian of which he did not understand a word. Food appeared, bread and strong cheese and also some soup which tasted like grass and had lumps of meat floating about in it. John decided with disgust that it was probably dog or cat. But all his qualms were mollified by a bottle of red wine, uncorked, which was thrust into his hand. It was like vinegar but he drank it greedily, to him after all the adventures of this one day — twelve hours ago he had been with his battery — it was nectar.

Mario came over with a map and put his finger on the village. The light was so bad that John could hardly see but he did notice that the nearest town in bolder type was called Frosinone. The vino was beginning to take effect and when a large woman appeared with a bundle of clothes and started to pull off his uniform, he did not resist. He was unsteady on his feet as he clambered into a pair of corduroy trousers and a rough donkey-jacket. His head started to swim and he sat down with a bump, fatigue and the wine had rendered him legless.

'I have English, poco'.

John looked up and saw a priest standing above him. He tried to concentrate but the berrétta on the priest's head seemed to sway from side to side.

'Hullo,' he said carefully.

'You have due choices, amico.' He paused. 'Primo choice, you stay here aspettare le truppe Inglése, ma forse i Tedéschi come before. Avete capito?'

'Si.'

'Secondo, you come with Mario to montagna. Due choices.'

John looked round at all the friendly faces. The prospect of staying alone in this crypt in the hope that the Allies arrived before the Germans did not appeal to him at all.

'I will go with Mario,' he replied.

'Bene.'

'Molto bene.' Mario said.

☆ ☆ ☆

The next morning, John learned to his dismay that they were to stay in the crypt for at least another twenty-four hours. The road from Frosinone to Sora which crossed their path a few miles to the north was still being used by the Germans and was considered unsafe to traverse. Behind the road a series of mountain tracks led up into the Monte Ernici range and beyond through the Abruzzi to the Appenines, the lofty spine of Italy. The mountains ahead beckoned, and John knew they would provide a refuge. The German army, particularly in withdrawal, would never be able to cover the remote villages in the hills. But at this moment in time they were only a few miles away from the Via Casilina, Route Six as it was called, the main artery of their retreat, where the previous day he had been the unwilling guest of the German Captain who the partisans had killed in cold blood.

He shuddered. Not only was he sickened by the summary murder of the Captain, who had been kind and considerate to him, but he also realised his present desperate plight. He was no longer in uniform, he was an accessory to the killing of a German officer, and he was part of a guerrilla organisation who the Captain had described as brigands and scum. If captured, he knew that he could expect no mercy.

'Why?' John asked himself as he ate his breakfast of yet more bread and cheese washed down with ersatz coffee. 'Why me?' Like many conscripts in this war, he only wanted a quiet life, or as quiet as possible. He had done his best while with the Battery, in fact it had been an over-conscientious sense of duty that had led to his capture.

Ever since landing in Italy he had seemed destined to go out on a limb. First he had been persuaded to leave the transit camp near Naples and make his own way to the Regiment, this had resulted in his narrow escape in the bombing at Foggia airport. Now he was on his way to a prisoner of war camp which would almost certainly have guaranteed his survival until the end of the war, fate had landed him with a bunch of trigger-happy Italian peasants; God knows how it would all end.

He thought grimly that if this was a film, he would assume command of this band of partisans and lead them in daring raids on the Germans and be hailed as a hero. The British officer with a stiff upper lip altering the course of the entire Italian campaign. Gary Cooper perhaps, no of course, he was American. Errol Flynn. That's right, he would do. The Robin Hood of the Abruzzi. 'God,' John thought, 'I am so bloody feeble.'

With the priest acting as interpreter, Mario outlined the plan. He made it very clear from the outset that he was in command and that John was only a fairly useful passenger, as he gave the band the stamp of respectability. They were all local boys who had pinched some arms off German corpses and then melted back to their villages. They had already carried out three raids on the retreating enemy, always during the heat of battle, from the sidelines. They were proud of the fact that they had set an ambulance on fire. They were brave enough and quite ruthless. Mario's sister had been raped and murdered in Cassino before the Allied advance and he was out to kill any German he could find.

Word had come through that they were to join a concentration of partisans near Florence. Rome was expected to fall in the next few days, so the command, whoever that might be, had decided to group further north. John gathered that there was liaison with the British forces. All this would entail a long hard march through the mountains, a prospect John did not relish, but he decided it was better than staying in the village and waiting for the Allies or the Germans to arrive.

He was the centre of attention throughout the day. Women brought their children to look at him, as though he was a prime exhibit in a zoo. A fat girl tried to get amorous, and pestered him until Mario shouted at her, and pushed her out of the way.

Hunger, together with the boredom of waiting, accentuated his feeling of hopelessness. But at about four o'clock in the afternoon an enormous meal arrived. There was a vegetable soup, spaghetti with lumps of meat, grapes and the usual bread and cheese, washed down with a sharp red vino. The fat girl waited upon him shyly. John felt guilty and churlish. Food must have been scarce enough and yet somehow these Italian peasants had produced a feast. He smiled and muttered thanks, and wished fervently that he could speak the language to show his appreciation. The priest came and sat down beside him.

'Eat, eat good,' he said. 'Mario is *avanti* with you when no more day.'

It was a tremendous relief to John that they were going to move on.

'Catholic?' the priest asked.

'No, but Christian. I believe in God.'

'Bene.' He made the sign of the Cross, and touched John briefly on the head in blessing.

The lorry left the door of the church as soon as it was dark. John sat in front with Mario, the others packed into the rear of the truck, together with several more young men from the village. Fortunately there was a moon, all the same, travelling at some speed without lights was an unnerving experience. But there was so much to worry about that John, full of food and vino, relaxed a little. He had began to feel a degree of confidence in Mario, who managed the lorry with skill and verve.

They pulled up just before the main road. Mario switched off the engine and jumped out of the cab. A minute later he was back.

'No Tedéschi,' he muttered. Then, starting the truck, he turned to the left and at full throttle they careered down the road.

The noise was deafening, any Germans in the vicinity could not fail to hear them. Moonlight on the surface of the highway provided a certain amount of vision, but at this speed the lorry had to bend and twist to avoid the ditches on each side. It was probably only about half a mile, though it seemed much longer, before they pulled sharply to the right and began to climb a narrow mountain road. But Mario still drove fast. John hung grimly to the sides of his seat, it was a good half hour before they began to slow down.

They continued all through the night. John, conscious of the fact that every mile they were travelling further away from the German army in the Liri Valley, soon fell into a deep sleep. He woke with a start as the lorry came to a halt in the courtyard of a large house. Mario jumped out of the cab and stood with a machine-gun pointing at the front door. The men in the back tumbled out falling over each other and shouting. John, suddenly wide awake, pulled out his revolver and joined the others. It was becoming light now, although the sun had not yet risen above the mountains. The front door opened and a woman came out, There was an air of authority about her, and her housecoat was smart and expensive.

Mario shouted but she remained quite calm. When he stopped to draw breath, she gestured imperiously to him to drop his machine-gun. As he hesitated, she rounded on him and subjected him to a thorough dressing-down in rapid Italian. Very soon she was completely in charge of the situation. Eventually Mario lowered the weapon and the others, who were standing around wide-eyed at seeing their commander put in his place by a woman, did the same.

During the next few minutes the conversation became less heated and John recognised the word Inglése mentioned several times. Suddenly the woman turned to him.

'You are a British officer?' she asked in perfect English.

'Yes, yes I am.'

'I should have recognised you immediately by your boots. They are a dead give-away, no Italian peasant has boots like that.' John was so astonished by this turn of events that he did not know what to say.

She opened the front door. 'Go in there, my husband will be down in a moment, meanwhile I must get this rag-tail bob-tail crew under cover. There was a spotter plane over here yesterday.'

John found himself in a large sitting-room with dark pannelled walls. Stags' heads peered at him with sad eyes, and a huge hunting horn hung over the fireplace. There was a desk in the corner on which there were several family protraits, but in pride of place, a framed photograph of Mussolini.

John looked out of the window. The lady of the house was leading the band of partisans down a path towards the valley. The view was spectacular. The mountains, still pitch-black but crowned with white as the morning touched the peaks, towered above them. To the right a small river tumbled along a narrow gorge with the road cork-screwing just above it. The sun from the east had broken through, bringing the valley to life and producing little diamonds of light on the water.

'Buon Giorno.'

Startled, John turned round. An Italian officer was standing in the doorway. He was in uniform and had a feather in his cap. He was small and plump and seemed friendly.

'Good morning,' John replied.

'Ah! You are English?'

'Yes, I am a British officer. I don't suppose I look like

one,' he added.

'No, but perhaps that is just as well, if you are escaping from the Tedéschi. Don't worry, I have no reason to like our late allies. Are you the leader of this band of desperadoes?'

'Not really. They rescued me from the Germans, I had been captured.'

'I see. Let me explain. We heard your arrival and my wife went down to let you in. This was not cowardice on my part, Italian peasants are always much more frightened of a woman. Also, it gave me time to dress up, this impresses them you know, and we can claim that we are now your allies, or what is the curious English expression? Co-belligerents?'

'Yes, of course.'

'Where did they pick you up?'

John hesitated.

'Of course." The Italian smiled. 'You are right to be suspicious. I am so sorry.' He picked up the portrait of Mussolini and put it away in a drawer of the desk. 'We keep him there in case we have a visit from the Germans. Having an English wife and a son in London we have to be especially careful.'

'Where is your son now?'

'I don't know. We spent six years at our Embassy in London, our son Carlo went to Oxford and married an English girl. If the British are sensible they should send him back here in your Army to help with the reconstruction of our country. But who knows? Authority everywhere can be very stupid.'

John felt uneasy. The uniform, the photo of Mussolini, he had a horrible feeling that they might have blundered into a trap. The other man read his thoughts.

'Let me try and reassure you. My wife has been taking your friends to a hunting lodge a kilometre away. They will be fed and housed. We have had many nationalities here, British and American P.O.Ws who have escaped, aircrew who have been shot down, also an assortment of others, Poles, Yugoslavs, even Russians. We are one of the last staging posts. From here they walked across the mountains to Tivoli, their final stop before making their way to Rome.

Once there I understand that an Irish priest in the Vatican has been very helpful. The City has many hundreds of Allied fugitives. I do not think they will have long to wait. Rome should be liberated soon now, should it not?'

'I hope so, yes.'

'So do I. Have you heard of N. Section?'

'No.'

'It is an intelligence service run by the British with Italian co-operation. The job is to help Allied escapers. The organisation has been built up over the last few months and now works quite well. We get information and assistance from the Italian Committee for National Liberation, C.N.L., in Milano.'

'Good Lord, I didn't realise all that was going on.'

'Yes. Lucky for you, my friend.'

'How did you become involved? I mean, you were fighting us.'

'Not at all. When Italy came into the war I returned home from London and they did not know what to do with me. Being bilingual with an English wife and a son in England they were suspicious. But I had performed my duties correctly at our Embassy, so they could hardly arrest me. So I was posted to an Alpine unit in the Appenines. I was, so to speak, pushed out of the way. Therefore it was not difficult to disappear, once peace had been made with the Allies, and there was confusion everywhere and divided loyalties. Many of all ranks did the same. The Germans were too busy to care very much, they never had a very high opinion of their allies, so I retired to our mountain retreat and no one seemed to bother. My wife had a number of contacts with anti-fascist elements and so we became part of the human parcel service. Oh, we must introduce ourselves. I am Capitano Giovanni Bartolini. And you?'

'Lieutenant John Crabbe.'

He bowed. 'Lieutenant, I have not betrayed my country. Mussolini did that. In fact,' he spread out his hands in a gesture of resignation, 'I am being useful for the first time in this war.'

John smiled. 'I think you are both very brave.'

'Oh no, I am not brave. Eleanor is the courageous one,

she organises everything, I am just a dogsbody, is that not the English phrase?'

John laughed. 'I don't think you are a dogsbody, Captain, and I am very pleased to meet you.' He extended his hand.

'Bène.' Giovanni cried. 'So now you trust me. Eccellènte! Perhaps I should give you a token of good faith. I have a sword upstairs, molto elegànte, shall I surrender it to you like a character in an Ivor Novello musical, would you like that? It would impress your new friends.'

'What nonsense you are talking.' Eleanor had come in by the front door. 'You are very lucky, young man.' She turned to John. 'Your friend Mario knew nothing about us. You all stumbled on this house by accident, God knows where he might have led you. I will go and organise some breakfast.'

After she had gone John asked, 'Where are we?'

'Subiaco.' Giovanni took out a map from the desk, and John studied it by the window. 'We face north, there are three peaks, Monte Livata, Calvo and Autore, that is the highest and about 1800 metres.'

'Over 5000 feet. That is higher than anything at home.'

'They are beautiful, are they not? But it makes it difficult to use our wireless, we can get a signal north-west to Terni where we have a section, and sometimes even to Perugia, but the wireless is dangerous, we only use it in an emergency, the telephone is safer.'

'Really? The telephone?'

'Oh yes, it works, so far. Our codes are good, you know. Just trivial family chatter hiding our message. The Tedéschi look for wireless messages, they do not think we would be so stupid as to use the public telephone system, so it is far safer.'

Mario joined them for breakfast. As they spoke in English most of the time, he sulked and hardly said a word. John also thought that his nose had been put out of joint because he liked to be the leader, and now was relegated to playing second fiddle.

'Your troubles are over, Mr Crabbe,' Eleanor said. 'You can just wait here until Rome is free and then potter down the road. If the Teds should pay us a visit, which is highly unlikely, they have other things on their mind, there are plenty of places to hide you.'

John felt a profound sense of relief. It was extraordinary how things had worked out. Only two days ago he had been a prisoner, and now the future seemed incredibly rosy. He fell into a daydream. He saw himself entering Rome like Caesar, spending a few days leave visiting the sights and eating out at expensive restaurants, before being reunited with his regiment. And then he would have a tale to tell all his friends, escaping over the mountains with the partisans, he mustn't overdo it, of course, but he was beginning to feel more like Errol Flynn every moment. Even Charles would be impressed, and Sholto, and dear old Taffy would say, 'Good for you, boyo; good for you.'

His happiness was overflowing and he stuttered out his thanks, words tumbling over each other.

'Steady the horses,' Eleanor interrupted him. 'Many a slip between cup and lip. Don't count your chickens before they are hatched.'

Her mixed metaphors were too much for him and he started to giggle. Soon the tears were pouring down his cheeks.

'Forgive me,' he said. 'I can't help it, I am just so happy.'

Mario suddenly growled in Italian, and John looked at him guiltily, he had forgotten that he owed him his freedom. He started to say something, but Mario cut him short.

The conversation continued in Italian. John could not understand of course, but it was obvious that Mario was determined to have his say. After a time Giovanni held up his hand.

'I will interpret, if Mario will allow me.' He paused and looked at John. 'Mario wants you to go with him to the north. He said he rescued you and killed a German officer because he was about to shoot you. He says you owe him your life. He makes the point that there are British officers attached to the partisans, and why should you not be one of them?'

Mario spoke again briefly, looking straight at John.

'What was that?' John asked.

Giovanni was silent for a moment, and then replied, 'He asks if you are afraid?'

'Oh, it is too bloody stupid,' Eleanor interposed. 'He just regards you as a trophy to show off to his friends. It would be much more dangerous anyway, with you in tow, you don't speak a word of Italian'.

'That's true,' Giovanni said. 'I think you would be much wiser to stay with us. But then the decision must be yours.'

John avoided Mario's gaze. 'Where does he want to get to?' he asked.

'Perugia. The partisans are fairly well-organised in the Umbrian countryside and it is an important centre of the escape route. Let me make a suggestion. No one can leave here for a day or two, papers must be arranged and we will do our best. So let me tell Mario that you are considering his proposal.'

John nodded, but during the further exchange in heated Italian, he knew that there was no decision for him to make, it was quite crazy for him not to wait and go to Rome.

Mario left after breakfast to join his men, while the three of them drank their coffee as the sun began to stream in from the side window.

'Are there any British in Perugia?' John asked.

'Not until a few days ago.' Giovanni replied. 'But they have one now, an officer from Bari. Apparently she is a woman, quite young and half Italian. I spoke to her on the phone, you would never know that she was English, her accent is perfect.'

☆ ☆ ☆

It was after breakfast two days later on 21 May that they learned the Germans were coming. Since their arrival John had lived like a lord. On the first day after a bath and a change of clothes, Giovanni had started right away to try and teach him a smattering of Italian. 'You will never be able to fool the Italian police,' Eleanor had said. 'But with any luck the Teds won't rumble you, they are a pretty stupid lot.'

They ate well. Vegetables were in short supply but there

was plenty of venison, poultry and eggs, and a good supply of grapes. Vino and brandy were produced for the evening meal. The Bartolinis had clearly looked after themselves. It was like the sort of holiday in the mountains that John had always dreamed about. They all awaited anxiously the fall of Rome, when it would be safe for John to, in Eleanor's words, 'potter down the road' and find a British unit. Communications were kept open, including the wireless at regular intervals. Giovanni thought this was a legitimate risk because information was the absolute priority. Mario, who was no fool, co-operated to the full. He kept his gang in the hunting lodge under a strict discipline, and posted scouts at strategic points to keep an eye on the road up to Subiaco.

It was a wireless message from Terni relayed from Milan that first alerted them to the danger at nine in the morning 21 May. The coded order was brief. 'At first light patrols entered Fiuggi, units in the area disperse.'

Eleanor was the first to react.

'Our network is working bloody well, good stuff,' she said. 'We have time to take emergency action. John, go and fetch Mario, but for God's sake keep your head down if you see a spotter plane.'

By the time John and Mario returned, the breakfast had been cleared and Giovanni and Eleanor had a map spread on the table. The ensuing conference was carried out in animated and at times explosive Italian. Eleanor and Mario had a set-to, both trying to shout down the other. John felt frozen in panic, he was more frightened now than he had ever been since landing in Italy, particularly as he did not understand what on earth was going on.

'Where are they?' He appealed to Eleanor. 'Where are the Germans?'

'Hold your horses,' she replied, and gestured to Giovanni to take over the conversation with Mario. 'Several hours away, if they come at all. It took you twelve hours to get here. Fiuggi is about half way. Didn't you understand a word?'

'No, you were talking too quickly.'

'Italians do talk quickly. So much for all your language lessons.'

'Tell me what is happening, please,' John cried.

'All right, keep your hair on. The Teds are obviously doing a trawl. It is a habit of theirs once they begin a general withdrawal. They go to out-of-the-way places and try and pick up anything they can find. They know about N. Section, of course, but it is all guesswork. They won't find anything here, we will make sure of that. But that silly fool,' she pointed at Mario, 'wants to stay and fight and so blow the whole bloody operation. Oh God, give me patience!'

'How about me?'

'Oh we will hide you, don't fuss yourself. It is this mob I am worried about.'

But Giovanni had calmed Mario down. They talked over the map for several minutes and then the two men left the room. Eleanor took John over to the map.

'Gio is very good. He can keep cool while I lose my rag. I leave the strategy to him, he is the soldier. This is the general picture. The road from Rome to the east coast at Pescara lies to the north. We thought the Teds were going to sit on that as a last defence of Rome, but the grapevine tells us that they are beginning to pull back. Mario and his merry men can either make for Arsoli, twenty kilometres and a road all the way, or take a forty kilometre trek across the mountains to Avezzano, a bloody hard slog. They are both on a railway line which we think is still working, but Avezzano is a junction. The main thing is that they have got to get out of here sharpish. The order said "disperse" and it means just that. Pity that their new papers haven't come through, but that's life. They will just have to manage.'

'Wouldn't it be dangerous, travelling by train?'

'Dodgy, very dodgy, but how else do you think they are going to reach Umbria; walk? It is nearly 300 kilometres.'

She left him abruptly and went into the kitchen. John climbed the stairs to his bedroom and looked out of the window. Mario was herding his troop along the track from the hunting lodge, and soon they disappeared from view into the back of the house. Giovanni followed. He had discarded his uniform on the first day, and wore breeches, riding boots and a hacking jacket. He looked rather endearing, an Italian dressed like an English squire.

John looked down the valley, his heart thumping, and his eyes skinned for the sight of little grey men advancing. Eleanor had reassured him to a certain extent but he was still really frightened. He had seen many films of fugitives hiding from the Nazis, but this was real life. He wondered where they would hide him and for how long.

Ever since he had heard that there was an English girl in Perugia he had thought about Lynne. It must be her, coming from Bari and speaking perfect Italian. He had day-dreamed about entering the town with his regiment and running into her arms. He could talk to her about N. Section and about all his adventures, and they would re-live Positano all over again.

Now stark reality blotted out any cosy thinking. He was a long way from his regiment and from Lynne, and the Germans were in Fiuggi. He froze by the window unable to take his eyes off the road. He tried to pray, but as always on these occasions the words would not come. The door opened suddenly and he leapt to his feet. Giovanni was standing there, and there was a look of fear in his eyes.

'We have had word from Fiuggi,' he said. 'They are looking for a British officer. You must leave at once.'

☆ ☆ ☆

John and Mario left within the hour to cross the mountains to Avezzano. The plan was that half the troop would go to Arsoli, which was situated on the main highway from Rome to the east coast about forty kilometres from the capital. There they would join up with partisans known to be operating in the area. But this route was considered too dangerous for John. Not only was Avezzano further away but it was a larger town with a number of safe houses and a good centre for travel. So it was decided that Mario, John, and two others would take the lorry until it ran out of petrol and then go off on foot.

'Keep your pecker up, old boy,' Eleanor had said, 'Sorry it had to come to this. There must have been a survivor at your little party with the Teds who spilled the beans. Never mind! We have filled your haversack with food, I have told

Mario to look after you, I am sure he will, not such a bad bloke on the whole.'

John had thrown his arms around her and hugged her hard.

'Oh my goodness! You will have me blubbing in a minute.' She kissed him on the cheek.

Giovanni took his hand.

'We will meet again in London, of that I am sure. Perhaps I will see you on the stage of one of the theatres. Not with Ivor Novello, though, that is not your style, is it?'

'No, not really.'

There were two main peaks to cross to reach the road and railway from the South to Avezzano, M. Autore and M. Tarino, the latter was about 6000 feet. The simplest way would have been to go back down the road almost to Fiuggi and then take the track round Tarino along the river Aniene. This was clearly not an option with John in tow, so they made for the route east from Subiaco where the road petered out just before the summit of M. Autore.

They took the lorry and began to climb almost at once. M. Calvo, which Giovanni had pointed out from the house, stood about a mile in front of them, a huge obstacle of rock barring their way. Then the road turned suddenly to the left, and soon they were negotiating the first hairpin bend. There were nine in all and they came thick and fast, with only a short distance between them. The route was narrow and as the lorry twisted and turned, the rear wheels only skirted the edge of the track.

John, not very keen on heights, looked straight ahead and wondered how their two companions in the back were faring, it must have been like a roller-coaster. He looked at Mario who seemed quite unconcerned, he did wonder though what would happen if they met something coming the other way, or if the brakes failed, or finally if they ran out of petrol while on this incredible zig-zag course. He tried shutting his eyes, this made him feel sick, so he just held his breath and willed the crazy spiral to end.

It did eventually and the road straightened. Then a strange thing happened. Mario started to sing. He had obviously been worried as well and showed his relief in a burst of song. *Rigoletto*, John thought, but he wasn't sure, blossomed forth in a rich baritone with all the frilly bits.

'Bène, bène!' John cried, his spirits soaring as he slapped Mario on the back.

The Italian stopped for a moment, grinned, and then started off again. In spite of all his fears John could not help smiling. It was an extraordinary situation in which he found himself. He had joined the Army as an unwilling conscript, then after a series of adventures over which he had no control, landed up in a clapped-out lorry, climbing up a mountainside to escape from the Germans and listening to a recital of grand opera.

Before long they arrived at a small plateau. They passed some cattle grazing and came to a hill farm with a number of out-buildings. Mario pushed the map over to John and pointed to the name, Campo dell' Osso. From his knowledge of Latin, John had no difficulty in translating "Field of Bones." He hoped it was not an ill omen.

The farmer was wary at first, but after Mario had given him the lorry as a present, they all relaxed and a meal was laid on. The family was kind and hospitable, and John was to find the same thing throughout his travels. The *Contadini*, country people, were always ready to help, although they knew the risks that they were taking. He shared the common prejudice of the British Army against the "Ities", running away in battle and then oiling up to the conquerors; but already he had begun to change his views. Mario, in particular, had started this process.

They decided to spend the night at the farm. The other two partisans were posted to watch the approach and they had an excellent field of vision, and it was thought that no one would be able to negotiate the road in darkness. It had been difficult enough in broad daylight.

For the rest of that day Mario worked on John's Italian, as Giovanni had done, but he was a harder taskmaster. John's head was reeling by the time they went to bed, nevertheless his understanding of the language was improving.

The plan was for John and Mario to leave on foot at first light, and the other two to follow during the afternoon, they could always pass as farm workers if the Germans should arrive. The important thing was to get John on his way, and dividing forces made them less conspicuous.

The going was easy to start with, as the road continued for a mile or so, climbing sharply towards the summit of M. Autore over a thousand feet above them. The mountain acted as a shield from the winds off the Adriatic, which accounted for the reasonable pasture at the farm. But as they climbed the gusts became stronger, and when the road had petered out the rocky terrain was tough.

They reached the summit at about midday. The wind was now gale force and the sun was surprisingly hot. John willed himself to look at the view, his head swimming as he clutched onto his cloth cap.

'Avezzano.' Mario pointed to a town covered with heat haze. It looked fairly large. 'Capistrello.' He indicated a village on the edge of the plain, about ten kilometres south of the town. That was to be their first objective.

They found a hollow behind some rocks, sheltered from the wind, and rested. They had a drink of water and some cheese. In an instinctive gesture Mario put his arm round John and smiled at him. He was happy now, on the way north with his prize possession, a British officer. He had wanted this all along and so all the antagonism had vanished. They studied the map together, and Mario talked slowly about their route. John was delighted to find that he could understand the drift.

Beyond the summit of M.Autore there was an escarpment of sheer rock, running for several miles, denying them access to the plain. There was a track just above it winding south to M. Tarino and a tiny hamlet on the end of a road, Campo Staffi. Near here as the road twisted back towards Fiuggi and danger, there appeared to be a gap in the rockface where they could make the descent to Capistrello.

It did not look all that far on the map, but when they found the path and started their trek the wind tore at them relentlessly. Luckily it was all off the plain, otherwise it could have blown them over the side. All the same, their eyes were streaming, and the sun beating down caused sweat to trickle down their faces. Progress was slow. They both knew that if they did not make the village by nightfall they would have to spend the night on the mountains when the temperature would plummet.

John was surprised with himself. Not only was he able to keep up with Mario, but often he was in the lead. He did not know what to expect from the next village, but the thought of a bed under cover spurred him on.

They did reach the village while it was still light. Mario knocked on the door of the first house. A woman appeared almost at once and peered at them suspiciously, Mario started to talk to her but she shook her head vigorously and put a finger to her lips.

'Polizia,' she whispered, and gestured to them to go away. She tried to shut the door, but a man came up behind her and flung it open. He was in uniform and held a revolver in his hand.

'Carabinièri. Documenti, carta d'identitá', he said and motioned them to come inside.

☆ ☆ ☆

The policeman sat twitching on the far side of the kitchen table. In front of him were three pistols, his own and the two surrendered from John and Mario. The family of the house, father, mother and a little girl, stood behind them, silhouetted against the window, motionless like cardboard cut-outs. John and Mario were seated facing the officer, who looked unhappy and was clearly uncertain of what to do next. His driver had gone off somewhere in the village and he was obviously aware of the fact that being alone the two men might try to overpower him. He was vulnerable and nervous.

Mario spoke to the policeman quietly. He said that they had no desire to fight an Italian, which was why they had handed over their weapons. He pointed out that the Allies would soon be taking over the areà, and if he wanted to keep his job, John, a British officer, was in a position to help him.

A signed document by the Lieutenant saying that he had been of assistance would ensure that he would be recognised as a friend by the Allied authorities. In fact he would probably be promoted. All he had to do was go back to Fiuggi and tell his German friends that he had found nothing. Furthermore, Mario added, the document would be even more complimentary if the officer could give them some information as to the safest way to Avezzano.

John did not understand everything, but enough to be aware of what was happening. He thought he might make his own modest contribution to the dialogue, so he stood up, saluted and held out his hand. This was a mistake because the policeman, startled by the sudden movement, siezed his pistol and pointed it at them. John's hand closed over the officer's and as he began to shake the pistol went off, shattering the window behind them. It all occured so quickly that no one knew what was going on. The farmer and his family ducked under the table, and the door burst open and the police driver came running into the room.

Mario began to laugh, pointing to John's hand still outstretched in welcome. The policeman, realising that all John had intended to do was to shake his hand, looked nonplussed for a moment, and then began to laugh as well. The family stood up slowly and the driver, framed in the doorway, must have wondered if his officer had gone stark raving mad.

John's action had certainly broken the tension if nothing else. Mario and the policeman continued to find the whole episode hilariously funny and the farmer, sensing the remarkable change in the general atmosphere found a bottle of vino and some glasses.

Pen and paper were produced, and Mario wrote a long screed in Italian, while John also wrote a message in English which read:

'To whom it may concern. The police officer has been of great help to me and the partisans in enabling us to escape from the Germans.' He stopped for a moment and then decided that his testimonial was much shorter than Mario's, so he added, 'At considerable risk to himself. He deserves the highest commendation.' Signed: J. Crabbe Lieutenant R.A. Home Counties Yeomanry.'

In his very limited Italian accompanied by various gestures, he endeavoured to explain the meaning to the police officer, who seemed pleased. John then signed both documents.

They spent the night at the farm. The two pieces of

paper worked wonders, and the two Carabinieri were most co-operative. The driver, who was a local boy, came with Mario and John the next morning to show them the way down through the rock face, and the officer had told them to avoid the main road altogether until they reached Avezzano, as the route and the railway were full of Germans.

There was a road from Campo Staffi which ran along the top of the escarpment for about two kilometres, and then changed course back away behind them. It was on the sharp bend that the police officer showed Mario and John the descent, and then after exchanging friendly greetings, left them to return to the village.

There was no path at all, only a narrow gully between the rocks, and at the far end of it the valley stretched out in front of them. They could not see a way down from where they stood, the funnel could well have ended in a precipice.

'Coraggio!' Mario had said, and gripped John's arm. They proceeded slowly down the shaft which ended on a ledge. About twenty feet below the mountainside sloped away more gently but the drop in front of them was sheer, and once out of the gully the wind struck them with full force. John, his eyes streaming, clutched on to a piece of rock as he felt his head swimming.

'No, no, I can't,' he said, shaking his head violently.

Mario acted immediately. He turned and slipped over the side grasping the edge of the narrow platform with both hands. He hung there for a moment, and then let go. He landed and flattened himself against a piece of rock for support, and then shouted against the wind.

John shut his eyes and jumped. He ended up in Mario's arms squashing him against the rock.

'Bène.' Mario smiled at him. 'Bène. Mio portafortuna!'

The going was rough now underfoot, but not too steep. They felt rather vulnerable out in the open but there were woods to the north, about 3000 feet below. They did not stop until they reached them, and looking on the map Avezzano was only about ten kilometres away.

The sun was beginning to set by the time they reached the cover of the trees. They were both exhausted and lay on their backs for a while without speaking. Then as they finished their food and water, Mario spoke slowly and deliberately.

'Non fa niente, stà zitta. Al Campo Staffi, a mancato poco de morire per colpa tua, lasciami fare. Andiamo a dormire qui questa nòtte e partiamo domani mattina a l'aurora. Capistrello è a basso della montagna e da là, ce tante strade piane che va a Avezzano.

Siamo fortunati che non abbiamo incontrato i Tedéschi — vanno nelle stràde majore. La Trattoria Firenze e vicina a la staziόne e il padrone va a dire còsa fanno. Capischi?'*

John nodded. Although he had made little progress in speaking Italian he could now understand Mario quite well.

Darkness fell quickly in the forest, and with it the temperature dropped sharply. It had been hot on the lower slopes and John's clothes were dank with sweat, now the moisture began to dry out in the cool air and he began to shiver violently. It was pitch-black, he could not even see Mario at his side, and then suddenly he felt the arms of the other man around him. They hugged each other from shoulder to toes, and the warmth of the two bodies embraced them both.

Mario started to snore softly, but sleep evaded John for a while. As he felt the stubble of the other man's chin against his cheek he thought about how the relationship between the two of them had changed. Now Mario regarded him as his "portafortuna", his mascot. He must have realised that John was no hero, but that did not matter. He was determined to bring him safely to their destination.

John for his part had begun to trust Mario completely. He was absolutely dependent on him in the crazy situation in which he found himself. He no longer bothered that he was not behaving like a war hero in a film, he only felt a growing affection for his protector and his friend. His love for Lynne was quite different, there was of course the romantic yearning to find her somewhere along the line. But he was too cold, tired and frightened to indulge in fantasies, daydreams were a luxury he could not afford at that moment. The reality was the firm grip of Mario's arms around him.

---

* See Appendix on page 250 for translation.

As soon as it was light enough to move they set off together, cold and very hungry. With an instinctive gesture Mario took John's hand. They found a track which dipped sharply down onto the plain. They were out of the wood before the sun had risen above the foothills. The air smelt sweet and the dew sparkled on the edge of the path. John was acutely aware that this was the most dangerous part of the journey, God only knew how many hazards lay ahead before they reached the Trattoria Firenze.

They had a vague plan that if they were stopped Mario would say that John was a deaf mute brother, but neither of them really thought this would fool anyone.

They did not see the road at first because it was in a hollow, but as they climbed a gate it lay a few feet below them. A farm lorry rumbled past full of chickens. Mario cursed in choice Italian and John realised that if they had been a minute earlier they might have been able to get a lift. Then the RAF came to their rescue once again. Two Spitfires flew low above their heads and began to strafe the main road a few miles to the east. The sudden noise caused the lorry to swerve violently and end up with its nearside wheels in a ditch just ahead of them. The tailgate flew open and the chickens tumbled out on to the road, squawking and falling over each other to escape. Then there followed a typical Italian scene. The driver and his mate cursing and swearing at the top of their voices and waving their arms in the air, starting to try and round up the birds. The trouble was that a number of them were off down the road at the rate of knots. John was surprised at how fast they could travel. He and Mario joined in the fray, but John had never picked up a chicken before, and after he had been pecked several times on his hands, he decided to adopt a more passive role and ran back up the road to try and recapture the ones that had got away. This was easier said than done. He waved his cap at them and kicked out in all directions, but the chickens had tasted freedom and were not going to give in without a fight. They flapped their wings at him and stood their ground with their beaks snapping. John decided that Italian hens were very aggressive.

It took half an hour to recapture most of the birds, and it was another half hour at least before they managed to get the lorry back on the road. The driver and his companion were very friendly. There was shaking of hands all round and several 'molto grazies'. Then Mario, after talking to the driver, pointed to the back of the lorry.

'Giovanni, mio amico, 'ide, ide, con le pollastri, Si, me speak Inglése. Bène?' With that he jumped into the front seat.

John climbed over the tailgate into the fifty hysterical chickens. He fought his way to the front, being careful to protect his hands, already bleeding from his previous encounter. He kicked and pushed the birds with his knees until he had enough space and then lay down, rolling himself into a ball like a hedgehog for protection.

It was not a comfortable journey. The noise was deafening. The chickens crawled all over him, shat on him, and from time to time gave his bottom the odd peck. The lorry pitched up and down on the bumpy road so his left knee thumped against the floor boards and his head against the partition behind the front seats. But he accepted all this with a good grace because he knew that the squawking birds were good cover if they should be stopped.

And this proved to be the case. The truck halted at a road block just outside the town. John heard German voices, so he flattened himself hugging the floor. Here the chickens proved to be his friends. They swooped en masse towards the tailboard screeching and flapping their wings, prepared to repel any invader. There was the sound of laughter at the back of the vehicle and after a moment or two the lorry was on its way again.

At last they stopped. There was a sound of Italian voices and John sat up. They were in some sort of warehouse and men began to unload the birds. He waited until the back was empty and then clambered out. A gale of laughter greeted him from the assembled men, and 'Ecco' punctuated the mirth. This is a very expressive Italian word which can mean a number of things, but here it meant 'look at the poor bugger'. John was aware that he was a sight. His hair was covered with bird shit and so were his clothes, while his hands were bleeding.

Mario joined in the fun for a few moments and then with a cheerful 'arrivederci' he led John out into the street.

'Va piano. Fa il pòvero ingènuo' he spoke slowly. 'Ma è un pòvero ingènuo, non ce problemi.'

The chicken farmer had given Mario directions on how to find the railway station, and as they walked through the streets no one paid them much attention, presumably they were used to seeing one of the *Contadini* who obviously lived in a chicken coop. The square in front of the station was full of Germans, debussing from lorries, and Mario gripped John's arm.

'Coraggio' he said softly.

John comforted himself with the thought that he did not look the least like a British officer.

They found the trattoria and made their way to the back of the inn. A young woman let them in, she was clearly expecting them and didn't turn a hair. They descended some steps through a cellar full of wine bottles and then through a door into a large laundry room. A camp-bed was situated in the corner. A man sat up and peered at them.

'Hullo,' he said. 'I'm Roger. Come and join the club.'

☆ ☆ ☆

The Trattoria Firenze looked after them with great efficiency and they were provided with papers. John and the other British officer, Flight-Lieutenant Roger Cowan, were Yugoslav academics from Belgrade on their way to take part in secret work for the Germans at Perugia University, while Mario was a police official of the puppet Mussolini Government set up in the north acting as escort, his identity card was particularly impressive, the *Fascio* embossed in gold. It was a good cover because they would be unlucky if they met either Germans or Italians who spoke Yugoslav.

It was an extraordinary experience staying in the basement of the Trattoria. While German officers wined and dined above in the restaurant, the atmosphere below was quite relaxed. The Padrone provided excellent fare for the Germans, his cafe was virtually the local officers' mess. But shrewedly he knew that the Allies were only about twenty miles away, so he was in the process of changing sides, aided by his daughter who was sleeping with the local partisan leader, the bearded Giuseppe; together they ran the "Parcel Post" service.

'Brown Job, are you?' Roger Cowan asked John as they all settled down to a meal.

'Yes, a Gunner officer.'

'Which regiment?'

Here Giuseppe intervened. 'Scusi! No! It is a rule in N. Section that there is no talk about the past, in case of capture it is better that you know nothing. Capischi?'

'O.K.' Roger replied. 'Sorry and all that. By the way Crabbe, Giuseppe here is an honorary British officer with the rank of Major. Isn't that so, Gussy?'

'Yes, that is so.'

'And he speaks excellent English, has ears in the back of his head, and is the boss, so we do what we are told!'

'The reason is that we know the local situation. It is still possible that the Tedéschi will defend this town, we do not know. But if they do we will be in the front line, so I am afraid you cannot stay here. Tomorrow you will travel north.'

'How?' John asked.

'By train from Avezzano station. It is all arranged. It is possible to reach Perugia after three changes, but of course these are not normal times. But your papers are good and you should be O.K.'

John had been overjoyed to meet another British officer, but unfortunately he disliked Cowan on sight. He hated being called by his surname for one thing, it reminded him of school, and there was a casual arrogance about Roger which got his back up. Mario obviously felt the same, so after the meal he went off into the adjoining room and lay on his bed.

'Good riddance,' Cowan said when they were on their own. 'Your pal Valentino gets on my tits. Bloody Wops, turncoats, all of them. Mind you, Gussy is better than most, he did pick me up after I pranged my Spit, just outside the town.'

John was further irritated by the fact that Roger was talking about the immediate past, though Giuseppe had asked them not to. But he did not want a row at this point, so he merely asked, 'Were you hurt?'

'Twisted my neck. Vertebral column caught it, but spinal cord is O.K., so no serious damage.'

'You seem to know a lot about it, to me it would just be a neck ache.'

'Started as a medical student at Saint Bartholomew's, but gave up to join the RAF. I wanted to fly when war came.'

'I see.'

They talked for a while, but John was reticent about himself. He did not mention that he had been an actor, anticipating a snub from the other man.

'Cagey bastard, aren't you?' Cowan said at last. 'Do you think I am a German spy, or something?'

'I am just tired,' John replied. 'I think I will go and lie down.' He went into the other room and gave Mario's hand a squeeze as he passed his bed, unaware of the fact that Roger had followed him in.

'Crabbe,' he said, standing in the doorway, 'we had better get one thing straight, I outrank you and so I am in charge from now on. Also, I speak a bit of German so I will talk to the Huns, and your friend,' he underlined the word unpleasantly, 'can talk to the Wops. All you have to do is keep your trap shut, savvy?'

John blushed furiously. What was it about him that invited ridicule from a certain type of man? He lay on his back looking at the ceiling, shaking with anger.

'Coràggio, mio amico,' Mario called out softly. 'Cowan bruto vigliácco.'

'In English, a right proper bastard,' John replied.

The Italian chuckled. 'Si, si, Bastardo. Non fa niente, Giovanni, non fa niente!'

The next morning the three of them managed to push their way on to the train, which was packed solid with Germans. They were virtually the only civilians, their papers had got them past the barrier without difficulty. It was a strange sensation standing in the corridor surrounded by soldiers in their field grey. The paradox was that they were far safer here squeezed in amongst the troops than they would have been as two lonesome figures on a mountainside.

The stench of bodies in the stuffy carriage was overwhelming. John had taken a bath before they left and had sprinkled some purple crystals into the water and then enjoyed the warm luxury. Roger had remarked at breakfast that he smelled like a French tart. As the train started with a jerk, a fat soldier was thrown against John, squashing him against the window. It was beginning to get hot, the sun was already streaming through the glass. Sweat was dripping down the man's face in three distinct rivulets, which met together on his chin and then splashed on to his collar, edging it with black. His nostrils twitched only a few inches from John's face and it was apparent that he was sniffing the bath salts. He said nothing, but soon it was obvious that the fat lout was becoming sexually aroused.

There was no finesse as he began to undo John's fly buttons, he pulled two of them off, and spread-eagled against the side of the carriage and unable to move an inch, there was nothing John could do about the violation.

'Nicht Jude.' the man began to snigger. 'Nicht Jude.' He made the sign of cutting his throat. 'Fur alles Juden.' His lips parted in a a grimace, and the blast of halitosis through his discoloured teeth made John retch.

It was only the arrival at Sulmona, their first change, which saved John from the appalling prospect of a return match, which the fat man was clearly expecting.

Once on the platform he felt dizzy, and would have fallen if Mario had not supported him. He was trembling all over, including his lower lip which he could not control. The troops stayed on the train which was bound for Pescara on the east coast, so the small waiting room was empty and they were able to talk.

'What on earth is up with you, Crabbe?' Cowan said sharply. 'You look as though you have seen a ghost. For Christ's sake pull yourself together, man. Remember you are a British officer. Now,' he paused, 'there is a military police post on the other platform, I'll go and talk to them and find out about the train. We are supposed to be important people, we should behave as such. Wait here.'

'Bastardo.' Mario repeated. 'In l'Inglése, piú forte?'

'A first class shit,' John muttered.

He went out onto the platform to find some air. A breeze had sprung up, and he began to feel a little better, but still his damned lip would not stop shaking. There were a few people waiting, but no troops. His eye was caught by a truck on a siding from which soldiers were unloading huge shells, and then he saw the barrels, two of them pointing up beyond a low stone wall. Sulmona station was in the middle of a heavy artillery position. Their guns would have a range of nearly twenty miles, all the same it brought home to him the fact that the front line was not all that far away, and the sooner they were on their way north the better.

When Mario came up John took his arm and pointed. The Italian whistled softly. The same thought struck both of them. If Cowan was rumbled there would be no escape, they were slap in the middle of a German regiment. So their relief was very real when they saw him coming. Reluctantly, they had to admire his air of insouciance as he strolled across the railway lines.

'They want to see your papers. It is O.K. Don't look so scared, I have softened them up. The Sergeant was most impressed with my credentials and said he realised the importance of our journey. These tickets will entitle us to seats.'

At this moment, out of the corner of his eye John saw one of the long barrels elevate to a higher trajectory, and then the other followed suit. Mario noticed the same thing and as often in their relationship thoughts occurred to them both at the same time. They hoped fervently that Cowan had not noticed the guns.

He hadn't. The report from a field piece of that calibre is quite spectacular, particularly as in this case two went off together, followed by further bangs all around the station. Roger flung himself onto the hard concrete face downwards, cradling his head with his hands. When the firing stopped he looked up to see John and Mario looking down at him. Mario could not keep a straight face.

'Can I help you up Cowan?' John asked innocently, and as he walked over to the Police office he was aware that his lip had stopped trembling.

The franking of their documents was only a formality. Roger had clearly made an impression on the German Sergeant, who wished them a good journey, and the tickets did indeed secure them seats when the train came in about two hours later.

John had always loved railways since he was a small boy. Whilst living in Bayswater in London, he had often played his special train game. His home was about ten minutes' walk from Kensington Gardens, so he used to set off at a brisk pace. The built up area, through which he went, was the suburbs of London and the Park was the open county beyond. Each street intersection was a station, and if he had to stop, that was at a signal. He had discovered that by walking fast close to the wall or railings the doorways seemed to fly past at great speed. He clicked his teeth together and swayed gently as his train rocked over the points. Once he reached the Serpentine he let his imagination run riot, he was the Riviera Express thundering towards the West Country, he used to become totally absorbed in his game. He played it while he was at his public school, far too old for such childish fancies, Thomas would have despised him for it, and Cowan too, the grown-up equivalent of his school bully. Now his fantasy had become reality, but never in his childhood dreams had he ever envisaged a situation like the one he was experiencing at that moment.

Mario was by his side and the proximity of his body brought comfort and a feeling of security. Cowan opposite was pretending to be asleep. They had not spoken since Sulmona and it was easier to mask a strong fit of the sulks by giving the impression that he was so relaxed that he could doze off.

'It is a pity he is such a shit,' John thought, and then began to indulge in a little self-examination. 'I am jealous,' the realisation came as quite a shock, 'jealous because this RAF officer is doing very well, he had taken charge, he has already persuaded the Germans to get us seats on this train, he could be cast in the role of a British officer leading the partisans to victory. He is a very useful chap to have around, Mario detests him but respects him all the same and would do what he was told, and so would I.' This was a sobering thought, but it still was a pity that he was such a shit.

John looked out of the window. A farm slid past, the red roofs, shutters and Cypress trees had become so familiar, and the blue mountains to the east shimmered in the hot sun.

'Colazióne?' Mario opened his bag and produced food and vino that the Padrone of the Trattoria Firenze had provided. He had been generous, there was bread, ham, cheese, grapes and chocolate. At the end of the meal, Cowan produced a packet of cigarettes and handed them round without comment. Mario and John had not had a smoke for days and had no idea that Roger had some up his sleeve.

'Molto grazie,' John said, trying to be friendly.

Cowan ignored him and looked out of the window.

At L'Aquila the train filled up with crowds of excited Italians who had obviously been waiting for a long time for the train, and at Rieti still more. Fortunately no one had tried to engage them in conversation, possibly because they took John and Roger for Germans in civilian clothes and avoided them. Mario cut short any approach with a suitable display of bad temper.

They reached Sellecchia, a village about ten miles short of Terni, just as the sun was beginning to set. It was a pretty little place with a brook running alongside the track, the inevitable church perched on the top of a hill and over to the east a small lake, di Ripa Sottile, its bright blue water shining like glass in the still air.

The first sign that all was not well was when the engine was uncoupled. This time it was Mario who acted. He left the train suddenly, ahead of the general movement onto the platform. A quarter of an hour later he beckoned to them to get off the train, and a taxi was waiting for them outside the station.

The line had been cut by an air raid earlier in the day between Sellecchia and Terni. Mario had seen the station master and shown him his gold-embossed passport. This official, standing in front of a portrait of Mussolini, had telephoned his brother-in-law, the local taxi driver and youth leader of the boy Fascisti, who had undertaken to drive them to Terni station.

Mario and the driver Anillo chatted together during the journey. Anillo was eager to praise Il Duce and tell Mario all about his activities with the young Fascisti. Just short of the town Mario suggested that they stopped and the driver pulled the taxi off the road. They walked back to an *albergo* which they had just passed, and had a three-course dinner.

Afterwards John and Roger went on ahead to the car, while the two Italians settled the bill; it was pitch-dark now and there was no moon. Mario joined them about five minutes later alone. Anillo was meanwhile sitting on a lavatory seat with his neck broken, where it was unlikely that anyone would find him until morning.

'Bruto Fascista,' Mario said briefly. 'Avanti, Perugia.'

8

The American Military Police were courteous but firm when they threw them out of the Grand Hotel in Rome. Sholto, Pilling and Taffy had been drinking in the bar, then set off in search of food. They walked into the dining-room where all the tables had been put together to accommodate a party of about sixty senior U.S. officers presided over at the far end by a three-star General. All would have been well if Taffy had not felt friendly. Sholto and Pilling realised that they were gate-crashing a private dinner party and started to withdraw; not so Taffy. He wanted to cement an entente cordiale with his American buddies. Before the two police on the door could stop him he made straight for the General.

'I must shake your hand, General,' he said, noticing the stars just in time. 'I wish to give you the best wishes of my country which is Wales, and my regiment which is English, but none the worse for that.'

'Thank you, Lieutenant.' The General stood up and extended his hand, dismissing with a look the M.P. who was hovering in the background.

'Where are you from, sir?' Taffy asked.

'Texas, Lieutenant.'

'Oh, I am from Cardiff. From Cardiff to Texas, hands across the sea, sir.'

At this point Sholto intervened. 'I am sorry we have interrupted your dinner party, General, but we were looking for somewhere to eat.'

'There are plenty of diners open in the Via del Corso, Major,' he replied. 'There is certainly no shortage of food in the Eternal City.'

'Thank you, sir.'

'You're welcome.'

But Taffy still wanted to stay and chat, which is why discreetly the Military Police led the trio to the front door.

They took a taxi up the Via del Corso, and the driver put them down at a ristorante near the Villa Borghese. The whole street was alive with Rome's cafe society and American soldiers eating out. Waiters plied their trade between tables on the pavement and the noisy trattoria within. Lights blazed and the sound of popular music issued from both sides of the street at the same time, providing a strident cacophony of sound. Rome had been declared an open city, all the same a couple of German fighter-bombers could have flown down the lights of Via del Corso and made a very large killing indeed.

They entered the restaurant and the Padrone led them to a table in the window. The establishment was nothing like as grand as those further back towards the city centre. There were no Americans, only a few Italians, who unlike the arrogant types in the bar of the Grand Hotel were rather subdued.

Charles Pilling looked around with a snort of disgust.

'This is typical, isn't it?' he said. 'Just because we are bloody British, even the taxi driver knows where to take us. Not to any of the dozens of proper restaurants that we passed, only the smart Romans and Yanks go there, but to an obscure cafe right at the far end. Fuck it. Just because Lt-General Mark Clark entered Rome first we British are treated like shit. I am going to eat in the smartest, ritziest restaurant in Rome. Bugger the bloody Yanks.'

'May I remind you, Charles,' Sholto said, 'that officially Rome is out of bounds to us?'

'That is my whole point, Sholto! How dare they? Who started fighting the Krauts in the first place, anyway?'

It was true. Rome had been declared out of bounds to most of the British units, many of whom had fought continuously from El Alamein, across North Africa, invading first Sicily and then Italy and, once they had reached Rome, found that they were not allowed to share in the liberation. The Home Counties Yeomanry were stationed in a rest area about ten miles north of the city. On reading the restriction order Lt-Colonel Alex had said:

'I myself am going to pay a visit to Rome, and I suggest every member of the Regiment does the same.'

As far as the Battery was concerned, Sholto worked out a roster to enable as many men as possible to go. He, Charles and Taffy arrived exactly a week after the capital fell to the Allies.

'Per favore,' the padrone interupted them discreetly. 'I speak English, so I understand. It is difficult for you to find room on the Via del Corso, the restaurants will be full of drunk Americans anyway, and they will charge you too much money, parimente the food will not always be good. Here it is *tranquillo*, there is room and I promise you good food, that is why the taxi come here, he tries to help you.'

'Well you can't say fairer than that,' Sholto remarked. 'We eat here, yes?'

The other two agreed, Charles reluctantly. Taffy became friendly again.

'Shake hands, boy,' he said, grasping the padrone's in a vice-like grip. 'How do you do. What is that in Italian?'

'Come stati.'

'Come stati, buono. I come from Wales you know. What is Wales?'

'Il paese di Galles.'

'Bène. I live in Cardiff —'

'Presumably Cardiffo, for God's sake leave off Taffy, I am starving.'

But Taffy was in full spate. 'He is a nice little chap, though, isn't he?' he continued after the Padrone had withdrawn. 'There was a man who sold ice cream on Barry Island just like him, come to think of it, he was Italian too.'

'I only hope he is right about the food,' Charles said, 'otherwise I am off to sup with Rome society down the road.'

'Oh we saw enough of them in the bar at the Grand, didn't we? A nasty, supercilious lot, lounge-lizards, I call them. They looked at us as though we were something the cat brought in. Who is winning this bloody war, anyway?'

'They were frightened,' Sholto said.

'Oh no they weren't,' Charles disagreed. 'Did you see

that bloke by the bar with the long cigarette holder, bloody ponce looked down his nose at us.'

'They were scared stiff,' Sholto persisted. 'They don't know what to expect. They are rich and pampered and many were probably ardent fascists. The new administration hasn't made much impact as yet, but they know it is only a question of time before their little world collapses about their ears. So what do they do? As an act of bravado they continue to haunt the same bars, appearing casual and relaxed, hoping their fears will go away.'

'How do you know all this, Sholto?' Taffy asked.

'I was watching the man you mentioned, Charles. When I went to the bar to order some drinks there was a space beside him. It must have appeared that I was making straight for him, there was a look of panic in his eyes and he dropped his glass of brandy on the floor.'

The meal was excellent, even Charles agreed. It was not until the coffee and cigars that Sholto said suddenly:

'I waited because I did not want to spoil your evening, but you have to know sooner or later. I am afraid John Crabbe is dead.'

When Jenkins the driver had returned alone from the recce for a gun position by Aquino airfield, they had no idea what had happened to John. But when the Battery moved forward the next day and the airfield fell to the Allies, there was no sign of him, so it was a fairly safe assumption that he had been taken prisoner. Before they could reply Sholto went on:

'There was a bombing raid on Route Six near Frosinone on the day John disappeared. A direct hit was made on a truck full of troops, our M.Ps. found one hell of a mess, bits of charred corpses all over the place. They also found,' he paused, 'a British officer's Artillery cap, badly burned.'

Still the other two remained silent.

'If he was taken prisoner while wandering around Aquino airfield, he would probably have been travelling back up Route Six at just about that time, and there were no other prisoners taken that morning as far as we know. At any rate, he has been posted "Missing believed killed".'

Taffy was the first to speak. 'It cannot be certain, though, can it Sholto? I mean they did not actually find Johnnie did they, only the hat. There must be some hope mustn't there?'

'Of course, but we must face the facts, things don't look too good.'

'I'll say they don't,' Pilling said savagely. 'And it is all due to our bloody Colonel playing silly buggers. All right, we are fighting a war and people do get killed, a lot of our chaps have died before Johnnie, but what makes me so fucking mad is that his death was absolutely unnecessary.'

'Steady, Charles boy,' Taffy said.

Pilling ignored him. 'The Colonel likes to be thought of as a martinet, he cracks the whip to keep us on our toes, so he picks on Johnnie, nice gentle Johnnie who doesn't know his arse from his elbow, to go right up to the enemy lines to find a gun position. It is a bloody scandal.'

'Balls,' Sholto came in sharply. 'The Colonel didn't send John, I did. The C.O.'s order was to send gun position officers to reconnoitre ahead so as to ensure a quick advance when the time came. It was a good order and as it was it paid off. We used John's markers, he did the job.'

'And died for it.'

'As you said yourself, it does happen in war.'

Taffy broke the ensuing silence. 'He was conscientious, you see, Johnnie, very conscientious. You once told him, Charles, that he would never make a soldier and he wanted to prove you wrong. Just think about that before you blame the Colonel.'

Charles opened his mouth to speak, but bit his lip instead.

'When Jenkins the driver came back, he said that John was determined to find the perimeter fence, so that the guns could be brought right forward to the proper place. He was afraid of ridicule, you see, I think he had a lot of it in his life. And when the guns did get up there, we found that there wasn't a fence at all, just a little narrow ditch. Ironical, isn't it, really?'

Sholto said: 'I will write to his mother. But you two met this girl of his in Positano, tell me more about her.'

'Oh, she was a real smasher,' Taffy said. 'Very cool and intelligent and bloody marvellous to look at. I would never have tried my luck there, I am not in her class, if you see what I mean.'

'We do,' said Pilling.

'You tried though, didn't you Charles? But you had no luck at all. She only had eyes for Johnnie. She said she was an interpreter at G.H.Q., but we thought she was probably in Intelligence.'

'She was recalled early off leave,' Charles added. 'And they sent a special car for her, you don't do that for just an interpreter.'

'Do you think it was merely a holiday romance, or did it go deeper than that?' Sholto asked.

'Oh Johnnie adored her,' Taffy replied. 'He was inconsolable after she left. We tried to cheer him up but he wouldn't even get drunk.'

'He must have been in a bad way then,' Sholto said smiling.

'But you see what I mean — we could not find any way to comfort him, so to speak.'

'How about her?'

'That was the surprising thing,' Charles said. 'I think she genuinely fell for him. We both thought it odd, after all, Johnnie was hardly the glamorous type, was he? She was all motherly and protective with John and,' he paused, 'she took him to bed.'

'O.K. I will try and contact her, there is a Spook H.Q. at Bari I understand, they would probably know where she is.' Sholto stood up and looked at his watch. 'Half an hour before our transport arrives at the Grand,' he said. 'Let's take a taxi and go on a Grand Tour.'

The driver took them across the Tiber at the Ponte Ulberto to St Peter's and the Vatican. Here they strolled for a time around the empty piazza. The peace was shattered by the arrival of American M.P.s in a Jeep. Pilling took a deep breath, prepared to do battle, but the police were polite enough, while pointing out that there was a curfew in force and they should stay in their taxi.

They recrossed the river over the Victor Emanuele bridge and on to the Piazza Venezia, where the grandiose monument to the said King came as quite a shock as they rounded the corner of the square. A grotesque wedding cake in white marble. The driver took them slowly alongside the old Roman Forum pointing out the sights in fractured

English, and then stopped by the Colosseum. It looked jet black and sinister, etched against a light moonlit sky. A grisly relic of Rome's history. It matched their mood. There was no pleasure any more in their night out, for there was an empty seat in the cab.

☆ ☆ ☆

When John and Lynne finally met it was an anticlimax. He had dreamed of the scene, beloved of Hollywood films, when the two lovers, positioned conveniently just within a wide angle shot, ran from opposite sides to meet centre screen and in the ensuing embrace he lifted her off her feet and she kicked off her shoes; slow fade. It wasn't like that at all.

Mario drove the car into the safe house, a farm between Bastia and Perugia as the dawn was breaking. A big man with a black beard greeted them unenthusiastically.

'Come in, come in.' He turned to Mario. 'Hide the car at the back of the barn, we will be in the house. Oh, you are the partisan are you?' He repeated the instructions in Italian.

Once in the kitchen he poured some coffee.

'My name is Captain Gonshaw-Bliss. Yes all right, I was known as "Gone for a piss", but my patience threshold has worn pretty thin of late.' He looked at them both with eyes red through lack of sleep. 'Are you both RAF?'

'I am,' Cowan replied. 'He is a Brown Job.'

'Ranks? I don't want names.'

'Flight-Lieutenant.'

'Second-Lieutenant, R.A.' John added.

'Well you are not staying here. The line to the south has been broken, some fifth columnists, must be. The Teds are all over the place at Terni, how did you get through?'

'The train stopped before we reached there and Mario got hold of a taxi.'

'And murdered the driver in cold blood,' Cowan added.

'E was Fascista'. Mario came into the room and poured himself a cup of coffee. The Captain looked at him with interest.

'You speak English?'

'Poco, from Giovanni here. Mio amico. Lúi' He glowered at Cowan. 'Porco.'

The Captain addressed him in Italian. Mario, delighted to find a British officer who spoke his own language, at once launched into the story of their adventures. The Captain could not get a word in edgeways, but it did not matter because Mario gave him a detailed description of everything that had happened since he rescued John near Frosinone. He stood centre-stage, and declaimed with a series of sweeping gestures. John half expected him to burst into grand opera, as he had on the mountains above Subiaco. When he looked at John, the dark eyes softened, and when at Cowan, they flashed. My God, what a wonderful actor he would have made, John thought. A stunning Mercutio in Romeo and Juliet, full of Italian fire.

The Captain was clearly impressed, but Cowan, with his nose severely put out of joint, decided to be bloody-minded.

'Where do you propose we go, then?' he asked sulkily.

'Up to the Pratomagno hills between Arezzo and Florence, you will leave as soon as we can lay on suitable transport. As I said, the line south is broken, it is not safe any longer to move our traffic that way. The partisans virtually control the Pratomagno, the Teds simply do not have the resources to police that area, and there is a log jam of liquorice-all-sorts building up in Tuscany. Yugoslavs, Greeks, Poles, even some Russians, though God knows where they came from, quite apart from British and Americans. The floodgates have opened from the north, and they all have to be contained there until our armies reach them, and God knows when that will be. Two more British officers up there will be a help sorting out the mess.'

'I am staying here,' Cowan said shortly. 'I joined the RAF to fly, not to skulk about in the mountains. I will make my own way south. Savvy?'

Captain Gonshaw-Bliss fixed a bleary eye on Flight-Lieutenant Cowan. 'You will do as I fucking say, mate. It would make no difference if you were a Group Captain. You obey orders, understand?'

Cowan glared at him and did not reply.

'Otherwise,' the Captain leaned forward, 'I shall put you under arrest for endangering the operation. Savvy?' He underlined the last word.

'Splendido.' Mario said, with a broad grin on his face.

'Now, all arms on the table,' the Captain continued.

Mario placed two hand grenades and a Luger pistol, John the Service revolver he had taken from the German Captain, and Cowan shook his head.

'I shall have to search you, stand up please.'

He frisked them quickly and efficiently, Cowan opend his mouth to protest, but decided against it and said nothing.

'O.K. Now all go and get some kip. There are some beds in the room at the back. Breakfast at ten, Carla should have returned by then, she is off trying to find some transport for you all.'

'Carla?' John asked.

'My second-in-command. She will go with you to Arezzo. Petrarch's birthplace, Mario.'

'Scusi?'

'One of your poets. Never mind.'

John was too nervous to sleep. The idea of escaping into the Pratomagno where the partisans were in control was a comforting one, a refuge at last, after being on the move for so long, but they were not there yet, and all the Captain's talk about fifth columnists and the Germans apparently expecting them in Terni had unnerved him. He wondered who this Carla was, presumably the local Italian agent like Giuseppe and Captain Bartolini. The other two were snoring loudly, Mario in long regular notes rising from baritone to tenor and then sinking down to baritone again like the ebb and flow of the waves on a beach. Cowan just emitted a series of piggy snorts punctuated by whistles. Their breathing habits seemed to encapsulate their different personalities. John could not sleep anyway, the cacophony was getting on his nerves, so he dressed and went back to the kitchen were he found Captain Gonshaw-Bliss tucking into eggs and bacon.

'Hullo,' he said. 'Meet Giuliana and Luigi, I have taught them to cook a *prima colazione inglese*.'

John tried a few words of Italian in greeting to the middle-aged couple cooking at the stove and was rewarded by a kiss from Giuliana.

'They are a lovely pair,' the Captain continued, 'can't

bear the Tedéschi, their son was taken away for slave labour just before Christmas, they joined our organisation soon after. But —' he added flatly, 'I am going to close down this outpost as soon as I get rid of you lot, go to ground somewhere and take them with me. Things are getting too hot.'

'Is there really a traitor among us?' John asked.

'Must be. They were waiting for you at Terni station, we know that. The fact of the air raid and the train stopping was just bloody good luck. Also we haven't heard from Giuseppe in Avezzano since he told us of your departure; it may not mean anything, but it is worrying.'

Giuliana put a plate of eggs, bacon and fried bread in front of John.

'Incidentally,' the Captain continued, 'that Flight-Lieutenant of yours is a right proper shit, isn't he?'

'Yes,' John replied with feeling.

'Unusual, actually. We have had lots of pilots. Yanks, British, even the odd Czech or Pole, some of them are a bit prima donnish, but you expect that really, after all it is often a short life, a fighter pilot's, but they are usually grateful for what we do for them. Not so your friend, he must have been an absolute pain in the arse for his squadron, and Mario would cut his throat given half a chance.' He turned and looked at John. 'You couldn't sleep?'

'No.'

'Nervous?'

'Yes.'

'I know the feeling. At first it is a bit of a game, all this cloak and dagger stuff, but then after a time it begins to pall. One yearns for regimental life again with friends all round, getting drunk in the mess, going on leave, and when you do go into battle being part of the team. Here you are on your own, and it wears you down after a time.'

Captain Gonshaw-Bliss's revelations were interrupted by the arrival of the others. Over breakfast Cowan was ignored, Mario and the Captain made John speak Italian and he was surprised and gratified to find that he was beginning to speak and understand the language in a limited way. Mario found his efforts funny and roared with laughter when John made some howler.

'*Grossa* means pregnant,' the Captain said, 'not full of breakfast.'

It was then that John looked up and saw that Lynne had come in unnoticed, and was at the far end of the table. She was wearing a cheap black cotton dress, no make-up, and her straggly hair fell in loose strands around her neck. There was a hollowness in the cheeks now and her eyes seemed even more deep set, high-lighted by the shadows under them, but it was Lynne all right.

With his heart pounding John tried to catch her eye. But she was eating her breakfast, she did not seem to be deliberately avoiding his look, just hungry and enjoying her meal.

'Well,' the Captain said, 'I had better start the briefing. Carla will give a simultaneous translation in Italian.'

Lynne did look up then, but there was no recognition in her eyes as the Captain spread out the map on the table.

'A truck carrying one tractor and two crates full of spares will come into here in about one hour's time. There will be a tarpaulin in the back under which the three of you can hide. Carla will be in front with the driver, who is working for us. She will conceal a pistol under the seat, no one else will be armed. The Krauts are used to lorries carrying farm machinery travelling from the Perugia area to Arezzo and Florence, so there should not be any trouble. This area is not much occupied anyway.'

'So the only one of us armed is this Italian girl?' Cowan asked angrily.

'That is so.'

'Why, may I ask?'

'Because she is in charge of the operation. If the Teds do search the back, which is unlikely, you could be three peasants cadging a lift, but not if your are bristling with arms. O.K.?'

Cowan did not reply.

'The main hazard is getting across the Arno and up into the hills. The Ponte Buriano, seven hundred years old, if you are interested, crosses the river a few miles north-west of Arezzo. The enemy are always there in force, to prevent access to the Pratomagno. The lorry will stop and put you down at a house in the village about a mile from the bridge, and you will stay there until nightfall. At twenty-two hours start making your way to the marshy land just west of the bridge; at the same time the partisans are going to stage a mock attack on the other side of the Ponte Buriano to draw German patrols away from your area. They promised to make a lot of noise. Then you swim across, it is fairly shallow around there. Oh by the way, can you all swim?'

Mario shook his head.

'John will help you over, at your height you could probably wade. On the far side make for some trees in front of a group of houses. Partisans will be all over the area and look after you. Any questions?'

'Mines?' Cowan asked.

'Our local information, which is pretty good as a rule, says that the Krauts have not bothered. They man the bridge, and mines would be a hazard for their own patrols.'

'How do we see the houses once we are over?' John asked, wondering if his voice would cause any reaction from Lynne. It didn't.

'God willing, there will be a full moon.'

'One last question.' Cowan spoke with heavy irony. 'I take it our lady C.O. can speak English?'

'Oh yes,' Lynne replied brightly. 'I can, actually. And I know a hawk from a handsaw.'

☆ ☆ ☆

There was a tractor in the back of the lorry, forward of this were two crates of spares, which left a space of about six feet before the rear of the cab. The tarpaulin was on the floor there for a hiding place should it become necessary. As the tractor could not be unloaded without a ramp, they were well protected against any casual search.

Cowan lay on the floor ignoring John and Mario who were sitting on the packing cases. Lynne was in the front with the driver as arranged.

It was possible to forget the war for a moment. There was not a great deal of traffic and it was good to be on the move again towards, hopefully, their last refuge in the Pratomagno. The road skirted the northern edge of Lake

Trasimeno, miles of blue water with bossy little waves, and even producing sea horses out from the shore in the quickening wind.

'*La Donna è Mobile*,' Mario began, and John was able to join in by humming and whistling because he knew the tune. *Toreador* followed. John thought this a little odd as Bizet was Spanish, or was he French? Anyway they drummed their feet against the cases to act as castanets. Then surprisingly Mario switched suddenly to *John Brown's Body* which he sang in very fractured American. Not to be outdone, John gave his rendering of a couple of Fred Astaire songs, *No Strings and No Connections* and *Dancing Cheek To Cheek*, and finally *The Isle Of Capri*. The trouble was, though, he only knew half the words.

'Capri, molto bella,' Mario said with feeling.

'Si, si,' John replied, remembering standing with Lynne where Tiberius had stood. He had a great urge to tell Mario all about it. He might some day, but not with Cowan within earshot to spoil it all.

'Núvole,' Mario said, pointing south. They had left the lake now and were passing vineyards terraced on hillocks. The anvil was clear enough, black in the centre with curling whiskers of white on the crown. 'Arriva il temporale.'

He was right. By the time they dismounted at the group of houses near the Arno, huge drops of rain began to patter onto the dusty road.

Lynne led them into a room where a cold meal was laid out for four, and she went off to the kitchen to prepare soup. It was all ridiculously unreal. The last time John had been with her was in the little room in Positano eating supper together against the background of the lights of Praiano twinkling from the far side of the bay, and that was about six weeks ago. Now they were at a meal together again, but as strangers. John realised that there must be good reasons for Lynne not to acknowledge him, but all the same he longed for some action from her, some sign. When it came he was quite unprepared for it.

'Will one of you give me a hand?' she asked in English, putting her head round the door.

'Of course.' Cowan was there before John could open his

mouth to answer.

'Bella, bella ragazza,' Mario said appreciatively. 'Molto intelligente.'

John felt a sharp jab of jealousy. Mario had chatted with her as they entered the house, and now Cowan was alone with her in the kitchen, just because he had been half asleep. Though it was only four o'clock in the afternoon it was almost dark outside and this served to deepen his depression. The carafe of wine on the table was nearly empty, so he filled it up from a large carboy in the corner of the room and recharged his glass and Mario's. A flash and crack of thunder made him jump so that he dropped his and it shattered on the floor. Mario fetched another from the sideboard.

'Coraggio,' he said, putting his hand over John's and squeezing it gently. 'Coraggio, mio amico.'

It was stifling in the room but John started to shiver. Then, as Lynne and Cowan came in from the kitchen, hailstones the size of golf balls began to crash against the windows. Conversation was impossible while the racket lasted but the hail stopped as suddenly as it had started, leaving only the noise of the rain splashing down the panes.

Lynne and Mario chatted together, he was obviously fascinated by her, Cowan tried to interrupt at times without success. John was silent for he was almost going round the bend with frustration having to watch Mario whom he loved, play the big seduction scene with Lynne, employing all his Latin charm like Rudolf Valentino, peering at her through hooded lids, white teeth flashing, lips parted in anticipation. The only recourse John had was to hit the bottle, which he did with enthusiasm.

'Second-Lieutenant,' Lynne said sharply, 'We have a long night ahead. I suggest you make that your last glass.'

Cowan sniggered, Mario chuckled affectionately, while John felt his cheeks redden as if she had physically slapped him with her own hand.

The rest of the meal was sheer misery but when they had finished and Lynne began to pile the plates she turned to John.

'I think it's your turn to lend a hand, there is washing-up and we must remove all trace of our occupation.'

Mario looked disappointed but this time John did not need a second bidding. Lynne closed the door, caught him by the shoulders and shook him.

'Johnnie you are dozy, I gave you a chance earlier.'

'I know. I'm sorry.'

'That doesn't matter now.' Without letting go she kissed him fiercely on the lips, then smoothing the hair back off his face she took his head in her hands.

'What have you been up to? Johnnie darling, you do get into scrapes. Less than two months ago you were on leave with your friends from the regiment and now you turn up with the partisans, or one partisan anyway, Casanova outside champing at the bit.'

'It's a long story.'

'There is plenty of time.'

John picked up a drying-up cloth and stood by her side as she washed the dishes. He told her the whole story, and as he did so a great flood of happiness swept through him. He closed his mind completely to the immediate hazards that lay ahead and was able to live for the moment only in what was after all such an ordinary domestic situation.

'Things just happen to you, don't they, Johnnie?' she said after he had finished. 'Most people can organise their own lives up to a point even in the middle of war, but with you the unexpected always pops up and alters everything. But you seem to take it all in your stride.'

'I don't. All I want is a quiet life. But it never turns out that way.'

'No darling, it doesn't'.

As they began to stack everything away John asked:

'What will it be like tonight?'

'I don't know. Up to now they have smuggled people over the bridges, but the Germans have become much more thorough in their searches, so this little swim has been planned for us. This is a long way behind the lines, the Germans here are not crack troops, it really depends on the partisans across the river, if they create a big enough diversion we should be O.K.'

John wanted to ask more to seek reassurance but then he realised that Lynne had enough on her plate without his whingeing. Instead he said:

'You were rather savage with me over supper.'

'Yes, very schoolmarmish. Thank God you cottoned on to the fact that you should not recognise me.'

'Why?'

'The first thing I learned was to avoid complications. What would have been Cowan's reaction if he knew you and I had slept together under a full moon in Positano? Or Mario for that matter.'

'Mario would have burst into song.'

'You like him, don't you?'

'Yes, I love him.'

'And Cowan?'

'I hate him.'

'You must forget all that tonight, and about me too, until we are safely over the river. Understand?'

'Yes.' John shivered again but tried to disguise the tremor in his voice. 'Yes, I understand.'

☆ ☆ ☆

Nothing went according to plan. The trouble was that the Germans had chosen that particular evening to send out a patrol in some force over the Ponte Buriano. They had not mounted an operation like this before, because this was not considered to be a war zone. The enemy strategy was to fight a rearguard action around Lake Trasimeno to enable the bulk of the German army to withdraw to the Appenine hills, called the Gothic Line, which lay north of Florence, and hold the Allies there until winter set in. To facilitate this the retreating Germans blew all the bridges in Florence except the Ponte Vecchio.

But that was in the future. The local German commander, though, was not happy. First he was in a backwater and could do little to increase his chances of promotion; second, he hated Italians, erstwhile allies who had changed sides and betrayed the German army, but the third reason was the one that exercised him most. The Pratomagno was full of bandits, so called partisans, he knew this and could do little about it. He tried to get the Luftwaffe to attack them but German planes had almost disappeared from the skies by this time, and were not inclined to carry out raids on a few

Italian peasants, they had more important tasks to perform. He himself had not the resources to mount any attack into the hills where the irregulars held sway. So he was angry and frustrated. Hence this raid.

Front line soldiers of the Wehrmacht behaved no better and no worse than their counterparts amongst the Allies, the S.S. being the odious exception; John had been treated well enough during his brief period of captivity. Troops behind the lines though, were often of low calibre, the piggy man who had tried to ravish John on the train was a good example, and the units stationed around Arezzo were bored. Normally a raid would be carried out at dawn, when the potential victims were asleep, but in this case the Commander judged correctly that after a meal and a few drinks, his men could be relied upon to behave brutishly. They were entitled to a bit of fun to break the monotony. The patrols were ordered, therefore, to visit the few villages on the plain, just across the Arno, soft targets who would offer no resistance, as the partisans with guns were all up in the hills.

The order from H.Q. was quite specific.

"To carry out at 22.00 hours punishment raids on the villages mentioned, where shelter has been given to bandits, communists, and enemies of the Reich. Heil Hitler!"

This gave blanket approval to the burning of houses, raping of a few local girls, and hanging of anyone who resisted. Throughout World War Two the German army had a penchant for hanging people in all the occupied territories, which now included Italy.

But the German patrol had not reckoned on finding a well-armed force of partisans deployed just over the bridge to create a diversion for Lynne and her party. The two sides met head-on just in front of the group of houses only a few yards from the river. It was difficult to say who was the most surprised, but the Italians, who knew a German helmet when they saw one, reacted first, and the hapless patrol was met with a hail of fire, which was the last thing they had expected. They started to beat it back over the river but the officer in charge, a young lieutenant, was made of sterner stuff and standing in their path threatened to shoot any soldier who tried to pass him. So a small battle started for the possession of the Ponte Buriano.

All this should have provided an ideal opportunity for Lynne and her party to ford the Arno downstream of the bridge, but the fireworks had started too early when they had not the least idea what was happening. They wrongly assumed that the partisans had misjudged their timing and begun too soon. Also the diversion that had only been planned to last ten minutes or so to draw the enemy patrols away from the marshy land west of the bridge, was developing into a nasty little battle with the whole area each side of the Ponte Buriano swarming with troops. So the four of them were forced to hide in the long grass hoping fervently that a passing German soldier did not trip over them.

Their situation was extremely serious. They could not go back to the house, they had been extremely lucky not to bump into soldiers as they left it, it would be suicidal to return now. It would be equally dangerous to go on to the river, which had become a battle field. The last option was to stay where they would be sitting ducks when dawn broke.

'I'll go and have a look see,' Cowan said suddenly, and before Lynne could stop him, he had disappeared into the night.

'Coraggioso,' Mario muttered generously.

'If they get him, they will guess there are more than one of us,' Lynne said quietly.

John knew that she was right, and as he lay face downwards on the wet grass with the damp seeping up into his body, he realised that they would be found easily enough if a search was mounted. So what was the point of pressing his nose into the mud? He seemed to have spent so much of the war hugging the ground. Gingerly he sat up. Mario and Lynne had done the same and were whispering urgently together, this time it was not the big seduction scene any more. There was a lull in the fighting, although the noise of sporadic small-arms fire continued all along the river, some of it seemed to be coming straight in front of them.

'Johnnie.'

'Yes?'

Lynne came and sat by his side. 'I'm sorry.'

'What for?'

'All this.'

'It is not your fault.'

'Yes it is. I never liked the plan, but Gonshaw-Bliss talked me into it. I wanted to go straight to Florence, it is my city, we would have been safe there.'

'Do you think Cowan will come back?' John desperately sought reassurance.

'I don't know, do I?'

'But he might.'

'Oh yes he might, but even if he should we are not out of the wood.' She touched his hand lightly. 'Johnnie listen, this is important.'

'Yes?'

'Mario and I do not intend to be taken. So he will shoot me and then himself.'

'Lynne.' John swung round and tried to take her into his arms.

'No,' she snapped at him. 'No. I don't think I can bear it if you come over all sentimental.'

'But —'

'Shut up and listen. You should be all right, an escaped British officer on the run. You would be very unlucky if they link you with the death of the German Captain. They know all about Parcel Post, you are just one of the parcels, that's all. It is different for us.'

'How?'

'They would give Mario the full treatment as an Italian bandit and I am a spy if you like, it doesn't matter what you call it. They would give me the treatment too.'

'I will protect you, I won't let them take you, I won't.'

He couldn't talk any more, tears of shame stifled his words. Cowan had gone off on what might well turn out to be a suicide mission, Mario was going to kill Lynne and then himself to avoid capture, yet he himself was to be saved. The parcel diverted to a P.O.W. camp.

'No, no, no.' He caught hold of her and held her tight. Her resistance weakened, but only for a moment. She allowed him to kiss her and then pushed him away and sat up.

'We must be sensible. Mario and I will carry out our plan, it is up to you,' she paused and looked away, 'afterwards.'

'Carla,' Mario said softly. 'Ti e Giovanni, siete amorosi?'

'Si,' Lynne replied.

'In Positano,' John added.

'A Positano! Per forsa' Mario chuckled. 'Fortunato Giovanni. I come matrimonio a Londra dopo la guerra.'

'Buono idea!' Lynne said in English, 'You know what, Johnnie, if we do survive all this, I think I had better marry you.'

Under normal circumstances John would have been transported, for just a moment he allowed himself the luxury of imagining the party given by Sholto, of showing Lynne off to his mother and sister, and getting married in Florence with Mario as best man, but this twopence coloured daydream expired almost as soon as it was born, killed off by the stark reality of the present.

He couldn't find the words to answer Lynne because he did not believe her. She had made the offer of marriage because she was sure she was going to die and she wanted to leave John with something, a spectral engagement, to remember her by.

Finally he said 'I love you Lynne, more than words can express.'

'Did you hear what I said?' She turned to look at him again. 'Did you?'

'Yes, I heard.'

'And that is all you have to say?'

'Yes, that is all.'

Then the appalling screech of a *nebelwerfer*, the six-barrelled German mortar opened up at that moment from just behind them, the missiles seemed to be almost scraping the tops of their heads before they exploded in or just beyond the river.

Funnily enough, it was John who first realised that this was their opportunity. There would certainly not be any Germans within range on this barrage, they ran a chance of being hit certainly, but with any luck they might get across the river unscathed.

'Now!' John shouted. 'Run!'

He seized Lynne by one hand and Mario by the other and charged forward. The ground was uneven and marshy in places so progress was slow, also the rain, which had mercifully abated, started to fall again in stair-rods accompanied by thunder and lightening. One fork came down seemingly on the bridge itself and for a fraction of a second they saw men running back. A part of John's brain registered the fact that this meant the mortars were covering the enemy withdrawal and that they would go on blasting away until all the patrol was safely back onto the south side of the river.

All three sensed that the best thing to do was to separate themselves from the battle, so instead of trying to cross the river where the mortars were exploding and chucking fountains of water into the air, they began running downstream away from the bridge.

John hit the barbed wire first, it was in coils about five feet high. His hands and knees collided with it simultaneously. The pain shot up to his thighs, he heard the tearing of his trousers and his hands were covered with blood. By throwing an arm out sideways he was able to stop Lynne and Mario just in time. Obviously, though, they could go no further in that direction.

Meanwhile there was no sign of the mortar-fire ceasing, in fact it was worse, for now most of the missiles were falling short of the river. One exploded right on the wire only a few yards away, chucking the little pieces of sharp metal like confetti. John and the others fell flat almost under the fence and waited.

The stonking ended at last, slowly they stood up. Both John's knees were bleeding and he began to feel the pain in his hands. The great thing was that the mortar-fire had stopped, but as they started to make their way to the river the staccato rattle of machine guns started up from the other side. The partisans sensing victory had begun to spray the whole area with rapid fire to make the German withdrawal as uncomfortable as possible.

It was Mario who noticed the hole in the wire, the mortar had blown a neat passage about four feet wide.

'Ecco!' he shouted.

They stumbled through it. John was conscious again of

strands cutting into his legs but he hardly felt anything. They ran and ran across the splodgy ground. Often it was like trying to walk through treacle, but they did not stop until they reached the river, a good half mile from the wire.

Here they felt comparatively safe, but a German patrol could still come across them, so although exhausted and almost at the end of their tether, they plunged into the water. The rains had swollen the river and the gentle pace of the current at this point of the Arno had changed into a minor torrent. It was easy to begin with, they were in their depth and waded happily across breasting the spray as it burst over them, but in the middle the bottom shelved sharply without much warning and Mario was in difficulties. John remembered he could not swim, so he shouted to Lynne to carry on and tried the familiar life-saving operation that he had practised with great success on Lynne in Positano. Easy enough in just bathing trunks to turn over on one's back and cradle the other man's head in both hands and kick off for the shore. But they were both fully clothed and the water had made them twice as heavy and the dead weight of their boots dragged them down. 'What a bloody fool I was' John thought, 'we could easily have taken off our boots and carried them.'

Once out of their depth the current took over, swirling along centre stream. The river must have widened at this point, for they could no longer see the far bank or Lynne. They began to sink, the weight of Mario's body bore down on John who was so exhausted by this time that he could no longer fight the current.

'We are going to drown.' John's head was quite clear of the fatigue, the coolness of the water had revived him. 'We were nearly over but it is not the Germans who are going to get us, but the Arno, the famous Florentine river is going to kill us both.'

As he went under John let go of Mario and straightened up. He came to the surface within seconds, and then treading water in an upright position and gasping for breath, he seized Mario under his arms and tried to propel him forward. Not at all orthodox life-saving procedure, but it seemed to do the trick. Mario with his head just above the water rather like the figurehead on the prow of a ship, with his legs kicking and his boots hammering against John's bleeding knees, led the procession.

And then it became obvious why this manoeuvre was working. Mario was treading water. He had of necessity learned to swim or at any rate dog-paddle, to keep afloat.

They struck the shallows so suddenly that both pitched forward onto a small beach of stones on the far bank. They lay sprawled out, too exhausted to move. John managed to lift himself a little so he could vomit all the water out of his lungs and stomach. They heard Lynne's voice though they could not move to greet her.

'I watched you both from the bank. I nearly dived in to help, but I thought I might make matters worse,' she paused to catch her breath. 'At any rate I knew you were rather good at life saving, Johnnie. Stay there, both of you. Don't move until I get back. I will go and make contact.'

Mario was the first to recover. He knelt by John.

'Grazie, Giovanni, molto grazie. Ti "strong man" adesso, not myself.'

'Your English, bène.' John managed to whisper, though his throat was still like a wet sponge.

Gently, Mario turned John over so that he was lying on his back, gathered him in his arms and tried to lift him to his feet. The blood had dried on his hands, but he buckled at the knees, the hammering from Mario's boots had been like a steam roller. Every movement was agonising, so Mario helped him to the soft mud of the bank.

John was conscious of Lynne's return with a few shadowy figures but he couldn't speak. They half carried him across the marshy land to the car waiting on the road. Lynne kissed him lightly on the forehead.

'I'll see you at the other end, Johnnie,' she said. 'I'm just going back to find Roger Cowan.'

'No.' John found the strength to seize her hand, and grip it hard. 'No. You are not going back.'

'Let go Johnnie,' she said sharply. 'He is my responsibility.'

'No! He went off on his own without orders, sod him. We have not come so far together for me to let you go. Mario help!' he croaked.

The Italian took in the situation at once. He picked

Lynne up and deposited her in the back of the car next to John.

"No. Cowan bastardo.' he said, as he climbed into the front seat by the driver. 'Avanti!'

They drove fast to San Giustino where they were taken into a doctor's surgery. John was given a large Cognac and his wounds treated, apparently there was no serious damage to his legs, just cuts and bad bruising. Mario and Lynne seemed to have fared much better, their injuries were superficial.

The effect of the alcohol on John's exhausted state was predictable. He could not stop crying and laughing together in relief. They had made it. He was in the Pratomagno with Lynne and Mario and he could not find it in his heart to care a damn about Roger Cowan.

They spent twelve hours in the doctor's house. John slept most of the day though every time he turned over and his knees came into contact with the hard mattress he woke with a stab of pain. His hands too were throbbing under the heavy bandages. But his exhaustion combined with the sheer happiness of their deliverance conditioned him to sleep and he did not really awake until about four the following afternoon when Mario came into the room.

'Where is Lynne?' John asked immediately.

'Di sotto. Descendi adesso, è l'ora di mangiare.'

Mario helped him wash, John could not stand so it involved holding him up with one hand and splashing water on his face with the other.

At the supper table Lynne sat at one end and the doctor at the other. There were lumps of meat in spaghetti, the red wine was from the doctor's own cellars. It was delicious and deadened John's various aches and pains with increasing success as glass followed glass. This time there was no reproof from Lynne.

'They had a drop yesterday,' she said. 'The first after months of asking. Apparently they still think the Germans might defend Florence, so the partisans up here warrant some supplies. They were meant to drop on a plateau near Castelfranco, in fact they came down all over the place. But now they also have a good supply of petrol, otherwise we might have had to walk yesterday. All the food disappeared somewhere or other.'

'Si.' The doctor talked too fast for John to understand, but Mario roared with laughter.

'You understand?' Lynne asked John.

'No.'

'This village was bombed with tins of M. & V. They did a certain amount of damage too. The doctor's garden received two crates of it, hence your supper.'

After dusk they were on their way again in the same car to Loro Ciuffenna. When they arrived Cowan was there to greet them. 'What on earth happened to you?' he asked. 'I went back but you had all scarpered.'

'After you had just wandered off,' John replied hotly, 'we went through the barbed wire and crossed the river.'

'I didn't just wander off. I went to find a path to the Arno. There was one, too, in a hollow out of sight. Then I went back to find you and as you had all gone I just waited until the fireworks were over, swam across, found a bloke with a motorbike and came up here on his pillion.'

'You left us without orders,' Lynne snapped.

'Just as well really, wasn't it? At least I haven't got bandages all over my hands. Incidentally, that wasn't very bright going through the wire, there is a minefield there. You all made very heavy weather of the whole operation if you ask me. It was simple enough if one kept one's head. A piece of cake.'

9

'How did he know that it was a minefield beyond the wire?'

It was some weeks later when Lynne put the question.

Nervous breakdowns are a peace-time luxury, all the same once John had settled into the little room in Loro Ciuffenna, he collapsed both physically and mentally. Both legs had swollen up like balloons and his hands obstinately refused to heal. Iodine was the only disinfectant available and when the doctor applied it John almost passed out with the pain. There was no aspirin or analgesics so relief came from Italian brandy, distilled locally, or in gin. The latter was particularly obnoxious, guaranteeing nausea after the second glass.

The nighmares were ghastly and during the day he began to suffer from hallucinations. The theme throughout was constant, though the details would vary. He would see the Germans coming on motor cycles over the little bridge below his window. He would try to escape, but the door would not open, to scream but no sound would come, then the officer would appear in the room, his face becoming bigger and bigger until the spectacles that he was wearing resembled the headlights of a car, and through them he saw instead of eyes two neat holes ringed with blood.

During the day John became obsessional about the bridge. Below it was a deep gorge, and even by going out on the little balcony and leaning out he could not see the bottom. He could keep an eye on the bridge for any sign of activity, but if he concentrated his gaze there, he was missing out on the gorge; and from there, in his nightmare, fat little soldiers with piggy eyes came swarming up the banks, their flies wide open and out of them thrust bayonets dripping with blood.

He was in danger of going out of his mind. The trouble was that Mario left on the first day to join the partisans training on the hills behind the village. He had hugged John long and hard.

'Il mio più grando amico.' He had said. 'Gentile, coraggioso Giovanni.'

Lynne disappeared too. She was much in demand in keeping some sort of peace between the locals and the various nationalities of the Parcel Post spread out all over the area. This was not always easy. Yugoslavs took against the Italians, as did the Greeks; the Americans and British were becoming bored and wanted some action, the Poles likewise, the few Russians who turned up were morose, frightened and silent. There were only two other British officers whom John never saw, to try and sort out the chaos and the administrative nightmare of trying to feed them, keep them happy, and contain them.

During the first day John virtually lost the power of speech. The Italian doctor who came to dress his wounds was a little puzzled by his silence, but he put it down to unfamiliarity with the language. In fact John now spoke and understood Italian up to a point, and he longed to communicate with the doctor. But the words stuck at the back of his throat, exactly as in the nightmare, all that came out was a rasping sound, like a death rattle.

His landlady brought him food which he hardly touched, he could not bring himself to move away from the window. He sat there immobile, his forehead damp with cold fear, his eyes blurring as, through exhaustion, he fell asleep. But the nightmares came at once so he forced himself to keep awake, the woman came again as dusk was settling to give him food which he waved away. In the half light he saw the grey men again, over the bridge and up from the gorge.

He decided to end it all. The pain all over his body and the hammer blows in his head were more than he could endure. A jagged triangle of gold light began to move across his eyes, open or shut, it was there. He had always had a terror of going blind, and now it was happening to him. He rose to his feet, there was a grinding pain in his knees as they were forced to function once more. He staggered to the little balcony, the flimsy looking railings were only about three feet high, and leaned out. The road was fifteen feet below, the span of the bridge two yards away, the wall at the edge of the gorge was low.

John wondered if he dived whether he could miss the road and the bridge walls and end up down the gorge, but there was a small triangle between the road and the cliff where someone had cultivated a tiny garden. He was sufficiently in command of his senses to realise that he would end up either on the road or the soft earth of the garden, in either case he would probably cripple himself, but live.

As he stood on the balcony the rain started again in a torrent. He remained, allowing the fresh water to douse him like a warm shower. It cleared his head, the golden triangle over his eyes melted away as did the little men in field grey on the road below. He struck a match and lit a paraffin lamp, conditioned by years of blackout he pulled the shutters to, and locked them. He noticed that his landlady had left a loaf of bread, a hunk of cheese and some small pastries on a tray by his bed, together with a carafe of red wine. The closing of the shutters and lighting the lamp were symbolic. The outside, full of demons, was blotted out. He still felt weak with fear, but the food and drink gradually eased his tortured mind and he fell asleep in his chair.

The devils returned when he awoke at first light, half in his sleeping nightmare he tried in vain to scream, then ran and opened the shutters. The soft colours of morning bathed the village in iridescent hues, and a mist billowed in the gorge, not gentle like the dawn, but turbulent and angry, swirling and menacing. Again John was transfixed in the window, mesmerised by the scene below. But mercifully again like the night before, the cool air acted like a tonic, bringing him back to sanity. With the return to normality, though, came the realisation that he was losing his reason, he was going mad.

All his props were gone, he was now completely alone. Although terrified by war, when with the regiment he had friends around him, he was sustained by the greater fear of being thought a coward, of letting down those who depended on him. Then after his capture and rescue he had Mario, with enough strength for two, and later Lynne whom he loved. Now they were no longer there, he did not know where Mario and Lynne were, he could not call on them for help, he could not call on anyone for help.

It was nearly dusk on the second day when he heard a loud knock on the front door, followed by heavy footsteps on the stairs. He had been dozing on the bed, but he was wide awake within seconds. He looked around for a weapon, the heaviest was the paraffin lamp by his bedside, as yet unlit. He bitterly regretted leaving his vigil by the window but he needed to stretch out his legs. He stood well back, as soon as the door opened he would throw the lamp at the first person who entered the room, they would certainly be armed so they would shoot, but he had the advantage, the element of surprise if he was quick enough.

'Carla, which room is it? I can't see a bloody thing.' A very English, rather bad-tempered voice sounded clearly from the passage outside.

Lynne opened the door and came in first, John was rooted to the spot. He remained like a statue with the lamp held a few inches above his head.

'Advance friend, and be recognised,' Gonshaw-Bliss said, sheltering behind Lynne. 'Don't chuck that at us old man, you might do someone an injury.'

'Johnnie, give it to me,' Lynne said quietly. John slowly lowered his arm, all the strength seemed to have drained out of his body so he dropped the lamp. Lynne caught it neatly and replaced it on the small table.

'God, you are in a bad way, Crabbe,' Gonshaw-Bliss said. 'I had better go and fetch the bloody quack.'

'No,' Lynne said. 'I will look after him. I'll move in here tonight.'

'Good idea. Oh by the way, Crabbe, one bit of news which I think will cheer you up no end. Cowan has got jaundice quite badly, he is holed up in a house at the top of the hill, been there from the moment he arrived.'

Lynne was tough with John from the start. She told him that it was all self-indulgence and that he could talk perfectly well if he tried. She said that he was malingering, playing for sympathy, and who was he trying to impress anyway? Mario who called in on the fourth day was angry with her for treating his Giovanni this way, but in a volley of quick-firing Italian she put him in his place. Even Gonshaw-Bliss thought she was treating young Crabbe rather badly, but she ignored them both.

She slept in the same bed with John, but never touched him. She took away the brandy bottle and only allowed him one glass of wine with his meals. Morning and evening when she was in the room she made him walk, and gradually the pain in his knees began to ease. While Lynne was out John had to translate an Italian play, *Gioconda* by D'Annunzio, which she had brought him.

During this time John went right back to childhood. Lynne was the mother he never had. The terror of being caught by the enemy began to fade, and the nightmares stopped. While Lynne was out during the day he toiled at his work trying to please her, but still his speech was strangled some way at the back of his throat, gasps and rattles came out of his mouth, but no words.

One night she came back earlier than usual, about four o'clock in the afternoon.

'Rome has fallen, Johnnie,' she said, taking him in her arms for the first time. 'The Allies are advancing towards Florence, it may not be long now.'

He opened his eyes wide but did not know how to express his joy. He just nodded his head furiously. It was then that she started to shake him.

'I have had enough,' she cried. 'Today a Pole called me a fascist which made me very angry. I am fed up with this bloody war and I am fed up with you. You just follow me around like a snotty-nosed little boy and you are getting on my nerves. I want a man, not a snivelling little brat. You saved my life and Mario's, so be the man you ought to be.' She slapped him hard across the face. 'Wake up, Johnnie! For Christ's sake, wake up!'

John cried out, 'Stop it, stop it, stop it!' Words had come at last.

Lynne rubbed his crimson cheeks with both hands gently, and her eyes were full of tears.

'Oh Johnnie, you have come back to us,' she said.

☆ ☆ ☆

The little room above the bridge soon took on an appearance of cheerful domesticity. A slip folded over the foot of the bed, a pair of stockings on a chair, jars and a dusting of powder on the small table in the window. Lynne had taken over, as she slowly coaxed John back to normality. After his speech returned, the fits of trembling stopped and the screaming in the night became less frequent. The trouble was that he could not overcome the shame he felt at being so feeble, and this made him impotent. Lynne was sure that only when he could exercise his manhood again would he really be himself. It was a vicious circle, the inability to consummate the love that John felt for Lynne only served to increase his feeling of inadequacy, he had dreamed of this moment for months, and now that she was in his arms, he failed her.

Lynne tried everything she knew to try and arouse him and after a time her patience began to wear thin. In Positano she had become attracted to a slightly awkward young man who refreshingly was quite unaware of his appeal, and who was different from the British officers like Thomas she had met at G.H.Q. John had probably saved her life, or at any rate extricated her from a nasty situation in the water, and done the same with Mario, who loved him with a dogged devotion which was all the more potent for being entirely asexual. But hers was sexual, and full of Italian passion, and she was fed up to the teeth with her passive lover.

One afternoon when she returned early John was lying naked on the bed reading. The shutters were closed to keep out the heat but a sharp blade of bright sunlight cut a thin yellow stripe across his buttocks.

'Stay there,' Lynne said as he began to get up. 'Stay where you are.'

Then she took a leather belt and thrashed him across the bottom. Everything else had failed, perhaps this might work. It did, triumphantly.

Afterwards Lynne went to the window and threw open the shutters, letting the sun stream into the room. She wanted to shout to all the village of her happiness. Her hair fell over her face as she returned and kissed John gently on the lips.

'You won't be able to sit down for a week,' she said, laughing and crying at the same time. 'Mario would murder me if he knew what I had done to you. But Johnnie, listen.'

'Yes,' he replied, pulling her down on top of him.

'This is not to become a habit.' She kissed his ear and began to nibble it gently. 'I want a lover, not a naughty little boy. I spanked you because I had run out of ideas —' she found herself giggling. 'It worked a treat though, didn't it?'

It was a little later after they had had coffee, that Lynne put the question.

'How did he know it was a minefield?'

'Who?'

'Cowan.'

'I don't know, why?'

'Johnnie this is important. What do you think about him?'

'He is an arrogant, nasty twit.'

'Apart from that. Do you think he is genuine?'

'Oh Lord, yes. My God, you don't think he is a spy or something, do you?'

'I don't think anything at the moment. All we know is that someone has been betraying the Parcel Post, and I have a nasty suspicious mind.'

'But he is too bloody-minded! I mean if he was a German in disguise or something, he would try to ingratiate himself, wouldn't he? He would not go out of his way to behave like a complete shit. At all events he is so English, isn't he? A typical swollen-headed fighter-pilot who has become too big for his boots.'

'In my experience fliers are not like that. Have you met any RAF pilots who were?'

'I haven't met many, but no, I don't think I have.'

'So behaving badly could be a subtle double bluff.'

'Lynne darling, isn't that rather far-fetched?'

'Perhaps. All I know is that we are looking for a traitor, and we might as well start with him.'

'O.K. What do you suggest we do?'

'Think back.' Lynne began to dress and as she pulled her stockings over her thighs, John felt an irrepressible urge to pull them down again. She looked at him seriously.

'Mind on the job, Johnnie. Our lives may depend on this. Think hard. Anything odd about Cowan?'

'Just one thing.' John paused. 'At our first meeting, he said he began medical training at St Bartholomew's. Everyone calls it Bart's.'

'Anything else?'

'I don't think so.'

'Try and remember.'

'Well, he talked to the Kraut officer at Sulmona station, but then he speaks the language, and we were not arrested or anything afterwards.'

'He would have wanted to infiltrate much further up our line before he handed you and Mario in.'

'Darling,' John began to look alarmed, 'do you really think he is a German?'

'I have an open mind. But to continue. He leaves us the night of the river crossing, and turns up the next day unscathed. He could have talked to a German patrol using a password, and told them to leave us alone. He would have wanted to find out our position on the Pratomagno before alerting the Germans, but he made a mistake. He could not have known about the minefield or seen any sign at night. Now he is laid up with jaundice and has not left his room, that I know, so at the moment he cannot do any damage. Assuming he is our fifth columnist of course, and I may be wrong.'

Johnny felt a lump in his throat. 'Who has been betrayed? Not the Bartolinis at Subiaco?'

'We don't know, but all at Avezzano were, and Cowan started off there. You have forgotten Johnnie, but two of the partisans left Subiaco after you and Mario, and when they arrived they found the Trattoria Firenze at Avezzano bust wide open, but they were wily enough not to get caught and sent a message to us. The Teds hanged Giuseppe in the Piazza.'

'Oh no.'

'I didn't tell you while you were ill, but you need to know, Johnnie. Gonshaw-Bliss only got away from the farm by Perugia just in time.'

'How on earth did he get here so quickly?'

'Train from Arezzo to Florence and then bus to Vallombrosa. No one stopped him. Our little river crossing was probably a waste of time and energy. G-B thought you were hot because of the shooting of the Captain when you were rescued, so we should not risk a direct approach. I wish we had, but there you are.'

'Oh my God, Gussy.'

'Don't forget we are behind enemy lines, it is comparatively safe here because the partisans are all around us, but the Germans could break through if they really wanted to know exactly where our H.Q. was. Cowan's jaundice is an act of God, if he is the one.'

'And if he isn't?'

'Our situation is even worse, because we do not know what to expect or when.'

'Lynne darling, before the river crossing, you and Mario said that you would kill yourselves to avoid capture,' John reminded her.

'Yes.'

'I couldn't stay alive if you do that.'

'Oh John don't be silly.'

'I'm not. You don't understand how I feel, I have never before in my life loved anyone like you. How could I see you die, and then go off calmly to a P.O.W. camp —' his voice faltered.

'Anyway, I don't intend to die if I can help it.' She smiled at him. 'We just have to be careful, that's all. I will be a lot happier when we know about Cowan. The trouble is I don't know where to start.'

Mario turned up the next day and he and John went on a walk together in the hills. The Italian had changed. No longer the peasant, but now every inch the guerrilla soldier with tales of training and various skills in shooting and unarmed combat. He wore a gun in a holster on his side and demonstrated the draw to John, like Gary Cooper in a Western. He had become indoctrinated by the communists and tried to convert John with no success.

'Kings non buono. We 'ave, you 'ave. Non buono. All the mens uguale.'

'Your English has improved, Mario,' John chuckled. 'But you 'ave Musso.'

'Si, ma egli è finito.' He made the sign of cutting his throat.

'Giovanni.' He saluted smartly. 'Soldato Italiano.'

He began to laugh and put his arm round John's shoulder. As they looked down on the houses below, he burst out into Puccini's *Madame Butterfly*. The clear tenor rang out, though the only audience was a flock of indifferent goats. John had once asked Mario how he had learned the arias, for obviously he had never been an operagoer. It was from the old *grammofono* and a pile of scratchy records that his father had collected. The sad thing was that Mario had a beautiful voice, untrained, but very sweet. John wondered how many potential Carusos lived among the olive trees and vines of Italy.

In full throat he had forgotten all about Karl Marx and the Communists. He persuaded John to provide the backing, hums, whistles and pom-de-poms. Again, as in the lorry above Subiaco, John was struck with the incongruity of it all, there they were in enemy occupied territory blasting the countryside with Puccini, for even the goats had packed up and gone.

Mario had to leave for his village up the hill, and when John returned to Loro Ciuffenna, Gonshaw-Bliss and Lynne were waiting for him.

'That prick Cowan,' G-B said in his usual morose way, 'is belly-aching about not seeing a proper doctor. Actually, he is on the mend. The jaundice cures itself if you keep off the booze and avoid fats, but he is threatening us with an Air Vice-Marshal relative, so we had better humour him. Carla has a liver specialist friend in Florence and Cowan has condescended to agree to see him. It will take a week or two to organise the trip. There is a mobile ambulance unit that calls here, the Hun accepts it, and we can get in on the act. Carla will go but she wants you, Crabbe, as a bodyguard. Unofficial medical orderly. O.K. by me. I will let you know when it is laid on.'

After G-B had departed Lynne said, 'We will watch Cowan like hawks Johnnie, you and I. If he gets away from us I believe we have had it.'

☆ ☆ ☆

Lynne did not tell her suspicions to anyone except John, not even G-B. She told the local telephone exchange not to put through any call from Cowan, and to alert her if he tried to make one. She also had him watched when he went for a walk in the village, which was not difficult as he was too weak to go very far.

It took over a week before they were able to make the trip to Florence. These operations were becoming easier as the Allies advanced from Rome, because the local police now wished to earn the approval of their new masters down the road.

An officer of the Carabinieri drove the ambulance. Cowan was meant to be one of their number, wounded fighting the bandits in the hills, John his nurse, Lynne his sister. They had a special pass signed by the Medical Section of the German H.Q. in Florence. Forged, but excellently done. The ambulance was to drop the patient and the others at a doctor's house in the Lungarno Della Zecca near the Ponte Alle Grazie and pick them up two hours later. Even G-B conceded that the whole plan was excellent.

'Well, I suppose you will be all right,' he added gloomily, 'If the Italian policeman does not betray you.'

The journey took all morning. They were stopped on a couple of occasions. The first at S. Ellero, where they joined the main Florence-Arezzo road, this was the edge of partisan country and two German Military Police, after speaking with the police officer, insisted on inspecting the back of the ambulance. Lynne turned on the charm and chatted up the soldiers in German. She kept going, not allowing anyone to get a word in edgeways. Cowan played his part too, dressed in police uniform from the waist down and covered with bandages, he turned and groaned on the stretcher, displaying excellent acting skills.

After the ambulance started again they all relaxed. Lynne had a Luger pistol and John a heavy Service revolver, but if Cowan had betrayed them there was little they could have done except kill Cowan and themselves, but all had gone smoothly, and they began to feel that the worst was over.

John's natural good nature overcame his personal dislike of Cowan, so he made an effort to be friendly.

'That was a jolly good performance, Roger,' he said.

'Go jump in the lake,' the other man said, and gave John a look of contempt.

The second stop was at Pontassieve. There the Germans were not all that interested and let them through. Now they were on the north side of the Arno within half an hour of their destination.

John had been most impressed by Cowan during the stop at S. Ellero. But 'Go jump in the lake' did not ring true. An RAF fighter pilot who had come across a "Brown Job", (here Cowan had the correct phrase), whom he disliked would have said 'Piss off' or even 'Fuck off', the kind of casual obscenity so current in the British Forces, but whose essential importance a German could well miss. From that moment, remembering St Bartholomew's, John was convinced beyond doubt that this prickly bastard was a German giving a very clever performance.

They arrived at the doctor's house just before two o'clock during siesta time, and there were few people about. It was a small, rather pretty house with three floors and the shutters had recently had a coat of green paint. Dr Antonio Lelli met them at the door, and took them to his sitting room on the first floor. He was a plump rather jolly man, not at all like the self-important consultants that John had met back in England.

'Welcome to Florence,' he said in excellent English. 'I will examine this officer in due course, there is plenty of time. First we will have coffee, it is real, a present from a grateful patient, German naturally. They also arranged for my house to be painted as you will have seen, very chic. There is much jaundice in the German army so I am kept busy. This has many advantages. I am above suspicion, and so I can meet Lynne's friends, oh sorry, Carla, I cannot get used to all the cloak and dagger. And I get supplies for my own patients, so it is often desirable to dine with the devil, is that not the phrase?'

'Sup, actually,' John said.

'I correct myself, have supper with the devil.' He turned

to Cowan. 'You should of course be in hospital, but I can prescribe some tablets and a regime. I can also tell you how serious is your illness, but the yellow has nearly gone, so I hope you are not too bad now.'

'Thank you sir,' Cowan said respectfully.

'Not at all, I am pleased to help you if I can. Not coffee for you so we will go downstairs to the nurse, who is totally trustworthy, and who will remove all those ridiculous bandages.'

After he had gone John and Lynne looked out of the window. The glare of the sun on the water of the Arno dazzled, but by shading their eyes they could see across the river.

'That church is San Nicolo, and beyond you can just make out the old wall. It is too misty to see San Miniato, but it is up there on the hill,' Lynne said.

'Not a good view,' Dr Lelli observed when he returned. 'You can never see San Miniato because of the trees, and the Ponte Vecchio and the Pitti Palace are round the corner.'

After the maid had brought the coffee he continued, 'I like this house because when I am tired I can watch the water passing my window. It is always gentle at this time of the year, though in winter it can flood. I love it though, even when it is angry.' He turned to look at John suddenly. 'Is your army going to destroy my beautiful city?'

There was no time for an answer. A click of the front door closing alerted John, who ran to the window in time to see Cowan making off down the road. John was out of the room and down the stairs in a question of seconds, Lynne was not far behind.

There was no sign of Cowan, so John ran hell-for-leather in the direction he had taken. The first turning on the left was the Via Delle Casine and John stopped and looked down it. There was still no sign of him, nor straight on up the side of the river. He had completely vanished. Without stopping John ran on and then pulled himself up suddenly. There was a narrow pathway on the right leading off the Delle Casine, it was an avenue of maple trees interspersed with palms and cypresses, it was quite extraordinary, a country lane in the middle of Florence. Cowan was there, leaning against one of the maple trees in a state of exhaustion, he must have heard the footsteps so he turned round.

John felt a throbbing in his temple and his hand shook so hard that he nearly dropped the revolver.

'You must come with me now, or I will shoot.'

'You won't use that, you are too bloody feeble. I am going to take it off you.'

Cowan came towards John unsteadily, his face was the colour of uncooked suet and the sweat bubbled on his face, the cold sweat of the sick man.

John pulled the trigger twice in quick succession, he had forgotten the recoil of a 45 revolver, also the noise of the report. The first bullet struck Cowan in the stomach and stopped him, his hands instinctively went to his belly and were soon covered in blood. The close range of the shot split open the flesh and entrails began to spill over the top of the blue serge trousers. The second went through his neck and as the blood of the torn artery began to spout, John threw the revolver away and ran back to the road.

Lynne arrived at the same time. 'Where is the revolver?' was the first thing she said.

'I threw it away.'

'It will have your prints on it if they ever find us.' She took him by the arm. 'Don't run. We are two lovers smooching about, stay close to me.'

The empty streets at siesta time were a mixed blessing. True, there were not many people about, but also there was no crowd to hide in. A woman did come out of her house at the corner of the Via Tripoli but Lynne persuaded her without much difficulty that the bangs had been a car backfiring.

They made their way arm-in-arm to the Piazza S. Croce. One of the cafes that border the square was still open and a few German soldiers were sipping drinks, Lynne and John curled up on the steps of the S. Croce church in the shade. At least two other couples were doing the same. The sounds of heavy breathing came from the pair just below them, and out of the corner of his eye John caught a stockinged leg twitching in pleasure.

'Couldn't we go inside?' John asked.

'No,' Lynne whispered. 'The first place they would look for you. Necking on the steps is a Florentine pastime, we will be cleared off when they open the church at three, but if the police start combing this area, they will ignore us. Go on, Johnnie.' She could not help giggling slightly in spite of their predicament, 'Show some Italian passion, we must look convincing.'

She lay across his lap as he bent and kissed her, she allowed her skirt to ride right up so she was displaying a great deal to all and sundry.

Shortly after three, just as the doors of the church were opened, a police car arrived and three officers ran out. They concentrated on the cafes and ignored the couples snogging on the steps of the Santa Croce church. The authorities did not bother to eject them as the visitors to the church were so few, the heat had put off the German sightseers.

At three-thirty John and Lynne left. They dragged along, closely enveloped in each other, seemingly oblivious of the world outside, and went down the Via De Benci back to the Ponte Alle Grazie, and arrived without incident at the doctor's house at the same time as the ambulance drew up by the front door.

☆ ☆ ☆

'You are out of your minds, both of you.' Gonshaw-Bliss was puce with anger. 'I sent you to Florence to escort a sick RAF officer to see a specialist and you, Crabbe, shot him down in cold blood.'

'Listen a moment, G-B —' Lynne began.

'Shut up. Crabbe you are under house arrest until our forces arrive and then you will be handed over for Court Martial.'

When in trouble John usually remained rooted to the spot and tongue-tied. But he had been the one to confront Cowan between the avenue of maple trees, and felt sure of his ground.

'I killed a German spy,' he said, choosing his words carefully, 'because he would not come with me.'

'Balls! I don't know where you got that idea from, but I have news for you. He was in the clear. Giuseppe checked with Bari before you left Avezzano. A Flight-Lieutenant Roger Cowan had been reported shot down and missing over Italy. He was aged twenty-four with fair curly hair. A perfectly adequate description of our Cowan, wouldn't you say?'

'They could still have planted an agent using a dead man's papers,' Lynne said.

'Oh don't be so bloody stupid, Carla. How very convenient that when an RAF pilot is shot down and presumably killed, the Germans have his double waiting in the wings to take over.' He turned to John. 'You have made an appalling mistake, Crabbe, and killed a fellow officer. That's all there is to it.' G-B exploded again and it seemed as though he was about to burst a blood vessel. 'And all you say to me is that Cowan said "take a running jump" or something instead of piss off.'

'Sir,' Lynne said trying to defuse the situation, 'we have a great deal of evidence, may I go through it with you?'

'Oh please do, I am only your commanding officer. But it had better be good, bloody good.'

Lynne recounted the whole story starting with Cowan's contact with the Germans at Sulmona station and ending with his flight from the doctor's house in Florence.

Gonshaw-Bliss had calmed down but his anger had not abated.

'So you did not see fit to tell me anything about this?'

'No sir, I am sorry,' Lynne replied.

'Why?'

'Because I thought you would stop the trip to Florence.'

'I bloody well would have done.'

'I know. I just felt that he would make a break if we took him there, and he did.'

G-B looked at her coldly. 'If you are wrong I will get you thrown out of the Army and Crabbe Court Martialled. By not taking me into your confidence, you have betrayed any trust between us. I have no intention of sacrificing my career to save you two.'

'But sir,' John felt compelled to speak, 'he ran away from the doctor's surgery, he told the nurse he wanted the lavatory and then escaped.'

'Perhaps he just wanted a walk.'

'G-B really —' Lynne started, but John interrupted her.

'It was I who found him. When I took out the revolver he showed no surprise at all. He knew we had rumbled him. He taunted me by saying that I had not the guts to pull the trigger, he was coming to take it off me, before I fired.'

G-B paused 'He thought you were a pain in the arse, Crabbe, and showed it, so you settled the score.'

'No!' John shouted.

'The fact remains,' G-B rapped out the words, 'that even if Cowan was a German officer, which has not been proved, you shot and killed an unarmed man, who was so sick that he could hardly stand up, I hope you are proud of yourself.' He went out and slammed the door.

For just a few moments John was numb with shock, but as the full import of G-B's words went home he ran towards the door of their room. Lynne barred the way.

'Don't go after him, Johnnie,' she said quietly.

'He — he — he can't talk to me like that, how dare he?' John hated the fact that his voice always became shrill when he was angry.

'He said a lot of stupid things which, when he simmers down, he will regret —'

'Regret?' John managed to control the tremor in his voice 'That man accused me of murdering Cowan because I disliked him. Did you know Giuseppe at Avezzano, Lynne?' He did not wait for a reply. 'He was a charming bloke, rather like a gentle school-master. Cowan was quite affectionate with him really, called him Gussy. Afterwards the fucking bastard had him hanged in the Piazza, I know it. I saw it in Cowan's face. He looked at me as though to say, "you stupid prick I dare you to pull the trigger!" so I shot him dead.' He took a deep breath to keep the sobs at bay. 'It is the best thing I ever did in all my life.'

Lynne put her hands on his shoulders and said 'We must prove it, Johnnie, now. We will go and search his room before the idea occurs to G-B.' She smiled at him, 'You are meant to be under house arrest, but I am allowing you out under escort of Commander Gardener A.T.S., that's me, in case you didn't know.'

John was very impressed by Lynne's search, all he did was keep out of the way. The meticulous manner in which she went about the operation was a testimonial to her training. She looked in all the unobvious places, like the lining of the curtains, the spine of every book, the hinges of the shutters, even the lock on the door. It was only after she had drawn a blank with these that she started on the obvious places, and in one of the drawers in the dressing table she pulled out an unfinished letter. It read:-

To:- Mr and Mrs T.E. Cowan,
The Grange,
Little Upton,
Ipswich,
Suffolk.

Dearest M & D,

I am hoping at long last to get this letter to you. You will not have heard for some time and must have given me up. Well I am alive and have so much to tell you. Writing makes you feel close somehow, and I think of you both so much and of Rusty and Cleo. Actually I have been ill with jaundice but am a good deal better now. Tomorrow I am seeing a specialist and so will continue the letter when I get back.

☆ ☆ ☆

The series of battles starting around the shores of Lake Trasimeno in late June and continuing further north between Arezzo and Siena throughout most of July do not warrant much in the history books. If they appear at all they are described as skirmishes or rear guard actions by the Germans to give them time to prepare their main defences in the massive Appenine range north of Florence. This was the famous Gothic line which was to deny the Allies a breakthrough to the Po Valley before winter set in and fighting ground to a halt.

To the soldier who actually does the fighting though, the importance of any engagement is conditioned solely by how it affects him personally, his platoon, regiment or in this case, 622 Battery of the 321 Field Regiment R.A. the Home

Counties Yeomanry. And the advance from Civitella over rough hilly ground was described afterwards by Sholto as an absolute sod. The objective was Montevarchi on the Arezzo-Florence road, known as Route 69. This attractive old town was in fact only about ten miles as the crow flies from G-B's H.Q. at Loro Ciuffenna. But the Germans were on the high ground the other side of the road from the Pratomagno, known sometimes as the Chianti Mountains. Here they overlooked not only Route 69, but also the Arezzo-Siena highway, and the hilly road across to Poggibonsi in the west.

The battery had been told that speed was essential, so it was close on the heels of the Ross and Cromarty Highlanders and the tanks of the Cumbrian Yeomanry, both old friends from previous battles. All went well until they reached La Torre about three miles short of Montevarchi, then something happened which every artillery man dreads. The Battery was caught on the road. There was the inevitable traffic-jam ahead, so all eight guns, spread out at regular intervals, came under intense enemy shelling. Charles Pilling leading in his O.P. tank was also subjected to machine-gun fire. The infantry went to ground, wherever it was possible the Cumbrian tanks tried to manoeuvre off the road to be in a position to engage the Germans, thus presenting their flanks to enemy fire with disastrous results. The trouble was that for most of the route the land on each side fell away sharply, so the majority of the vehicles were stuck on the track.

As luck would have it "C" Troop had halted by a small field, Taffy jumped out and led the guns off the road oblivious to the metal flying around him. What followed was not at all according to the rule book. The guns were usually given fire orders over the wireless by the O.P. officer on carefully chosen targets. However Charles was in no position even to poke his head out of his tank, so the British talent for improvisation took over.

Taffy ran to each gun in turn. 'Open sights, boyo!' He yelled at No. 4. 'Hammer the bastards to the left of that wood and keep going, give them merry hell, boyo.' He gave similar instructions to the others so that the whole field of vision in front of them was covered. Priests are guns surrounded by an armoured chassis, so although a shell can hit a track, and the gun not be able to move, it can still keep firing, but it only needs a shell to fall right on top of the gunners to cause horrible casualties. This happened to a "C" Troop gun.

Seargeant-Major Cobber was with No. 2, helping load up the ammunition and was killed instantly with the others. There was nothing that anyone could do for them. No wounded, only what had been a group of men were now blood-soaked bits of khaki and lumps of raw flesh distributed over a wide area, and the disgusting stench of cordite and roasted meat permeated the whole position. Taffy and the others still alive had no time for remorse and horror, that came later.

With the barrage belting away, the Ross and Cormarty Highlanders came to life and stormed up the ridge. It must have been much the same when the Highland clans in support of the Young Pretender routed a superior force at Prestonpans, they looked like a swarm of bees sweeping ahead over the rocky land. Soon one or two of the Cumbrian tanks managed to get off the road and roared alongside.

By dusk it was all over and the Jocks entered Montevarchi with the sound of the pipes loud and clear from across the valley.

Meanwhile, as soon as the war came to the neighbourhood of Arezzo the command of the Parcel Post decided to vacate the villages of the Pratomagno and spread out on the slopes of Poggio Masserecci, the highest mountain of the range, nearly 5000 feet. Not only was the German army too close for comfort, but everyone wished to save the *Contadini* from reprisals. The partisans had been training up here but had gone, Mario with them, to carry out raids on Route 69.

John and Lynne had been badly shaken by the discovery of Cowan's letter. It seemed to have demolished all their theories. John began to realise with growing horror that he may have killed an innocent man. But, and there were many buts, so many things did not tie up, chiefly, why did he run away in Florence? They showed G-B the letter, they had to. It would have been criminal to conceal evidence of this kind, particularly from one's C.O. in time of war.

Possibly because he had simmered down, and also this time John and Lynne had been open with him, G-B's reaction was less explosive.

He looked at them lugubriously. 'None of this would have happened if you had been frank with me from the start, I blame you for that, Lynne.' It was the first time he had used her real name.

'I'm sorry,' she replied quietly.

'Bit late for that. You landed young Crabbe in it, but it was he that pulled the trigger. It is a complete bloody mess. I will have to inform Bari on the radio call tomorrow. Gives me no pleasure, still it won't be long now before the Krauts are clear of this area, and then it will all come out in the wash.'

The three of them moved at first light to the sound of gunfire in the valley below. It was a long arduous climb, invigorating in the crisp morning air, but by eleven the sun had risen above the peak of Poggio Masserecci and the increasing heat slowed them down as they stumbled over the rocky terrain.

G-B stopped and handed the wireless to John.

'Your turn Crabbe. We had better leap-frog from now on. The rendezvous with the others should be only another thousand feet. I have a map reference but it is only a piece of mountain, and God knows whether all the parcels will ever come together. I would put my money on the Poles and our chaps, but whether the Russians, Yuogoslavs and Albanians — did you know we had Albanians? — will turn up, God only knows. Anyway, what does it matter? This is the end of the war as far as we are concerned. He paused for a moment and added 'I will push on, you can rest for half an hour and then follow. O.K.?'

'Yes sir,' John said.

They watched the bulky frame of G-B lumber slowly up the hillside.

'He has got a big behind,' Lynne said. 'He looks like an elephant from the back.' She chuckled and then added, 'That was mean. He has had a good war, G-B. Hundreds of soldiers of many nationalities owe their lives to him, and he cared very much for the *Contadini* who helped us. But he won't get a medal, he isn't the type to attract attention.'

She turned round and sat up. 'Look Johnnie, Firenze!'

'My God, yes,' John replied, peering at the layer of heat haze studded with the thousands of red roofs which seemed to produce a glow of pink fire. They were too far away to pick out the *Duomo*, but tiny diamonds of light flickered here and there where the sun caught one of the many pinnacles of the city.

'It must have been rather an ordeal for you going back?'

'Yes.'

'I am sorry, I never asked you how you felt.'

'We had other things on our minds.'

'Yes. Where did you live exactly?'

'We had a villa in San Martino, it was on a slope just beyond the suburbs of Scandicci, there was a big drawing room with French windows going out on to the garden. I used to love to sit there and look at the city spread out on the plain only five miles away.'

'Did your father do his restoration of paintings there?'

'No, he had a studio on the top floor of a house on the Via Verdi which leads off the Piazza S. Croce. When we were necking on the steps, the house was just round the corner.'

'Perhaps you will be able to show it to me soon.'

'Why not? If we are not both under arrest somewhere.'

'Oh God, Lynne, I wish we could put the clock back, I wish we had never been in Florence.'

'Come on.' She pulled him to his feet and helped him load the radio on his back. 'I will tell you one thing though, we were never bothered at Ciuffenna were we? As far as I know none of the positions on the Pratomagno were betrayed.'

'Darling, you don't think —' John started with a new eagerness in his voice.

'I don't think anything, Johnnie, I have no ideas at all, the whole business of Cowan makes no sense to me.'

When they began their climb a jet-black cloud shaped like a giant soup plate appeared on the summit.

'We had better hurry,' Lynne said 'or we shall get very wet indeed, and that won't do the radio much good.'

They pushed on as fast as they could and were within sight of some rough wooden huts that the partisans had built when the rain came. It roared like a waterfall as the fork lightning struck the rocks around them making a sharp hissing noise as it pierced the pools of water that had already formed. John put the radio under his body and lay on it, pulling Lynne close to him.

In five minutes it was over, the black mass was heading off towards the hills to the west. John took hold of Lynne and hugged her hard. She was shaking and so was he, her wet dress clung to her body and her hair to the sides of her face. He was reminded of her coming out of the sea that night in Positano only a few months ago.

'We seem to make a point of getting wet, you and I,' she smiled at him.

'I was terrified,' John said frankly 'they are very nasty these hill storms, they come on without warning and are very vicious, if we had been on the summit, we might have had it.'

There was another rumble and John jumped like a startled rabbit.

Lynne looked up at a bright blue sky puzzled and then pointed down the valley to the south.

'Those bangs are man-made,' she said. 'Look!'

They could see, over the houses of Montevarchi, the balls of black smoke and flashes, followed seconds later by the sickening cracks that John knew so well. They watched for a while as the sun began to dry them both, steam rising from their clothes and bodies.

'It could be my regiment down there,' John said at just about the time that his friend Cobber was being plastered all over No. 2 "C" Troop gun.

The Parcels and their minders remained on the heights for a few days and then received instructions on the radio to return to their respective villages. When John entered his little room over the bridge in Loro Ciuffenna there was an army Major sitting on his bed.

'Crabbe?' The officer stood up and shook hands. His battle dress was immaculate and he had the kind of voice one associates with Eton and Sandhurst.

John's throat had dried up and he did not reply.

'Smythe. Field Security. Home Counties Yeomanry?'

'Yes sir,' John mumbled.

'Your mob were in that little party down the road. Did damn well. Colonel Alex should get a medal out of it. Expect you are keen to get back to them.'

'Yes sir.'

'De-briefing here. It will take a few days, I have a team with me. Then we will see that you rejoin your unit. First we have to go through all the Parcels with a fine tooth comb. Never know what you might find in that polyglot mob.'

'No sir.'

'Food and drink coming up, so the waiting should not be too bad.' He walked over to the window. 'Pretty little village. Lovely country, don't you think?'

'Yes sir.'

'Why did you shoot Cowan?' the Major asked without turning round. 'Take your time, there are some cigarettes on the table by your bed.'

John did not smoke much but he took a Senior Service and inhaled it greedily. In a low voice he gave an account of how the suspicions about Cowan gradually built up, without mentioning Lynne.

'It was Commander Gardener's idea,' Smythe said, as a fact not a question. 'I gather from your C.O. that the letter unnerved you both somewhat.'

'It was written to his parents.' John's voice became faint.

'That's right, an only son. Cleo and Rusty were cats. What made you pull the trigger?' the Major turned round.

'I was sure at the time that he was a German, his manner, his attitude, he knew I had found him out.'

'But he wasn't a German. He was as English as you or I.'

'Yes,' John mumbled.

'Do you know when he was shot down?'

'About May I think.'

'July actually, over Sicily. '43, he had been in German hands for over a year. They turned him.'

'I beg your pardon.'

'Granted Mr Crabbe. He had been keen on the blackshirts before the war, Mosley's gang. They threw him out of Bart's so he joined the RAF and then found his true vocation as a Nazi agent. He did a great deal of damage, you must have known our man in Avezzano?'

'Gussy, yes.'

'You know they hanged him.'

'Yes.'

'It all started from the time Cowan showed up. He never learned about the Bartolinis, so they are O.K. in Bari now, but from Avezzano up the line he created havoc. Lynne Gardener kept us up to date on the blower. Then we all had some luck, he got jaundice which immobilised him until you put a bullet in his throat.' He went to the door. 'You shot a man dead on a hunch didn't you?'

'Yes sir, I suppose I did.'

'Lucky for you the hunch was kosher wasn't it?'

10

By the time John rejoined the Regiment, the Germans had retired from Florence and the unit was stationed in or around Pontassieve about ten miles east of the city. After the excitement of the first few days with the Battery John began to experience a feeling of anti-climax. He had looked forward to showing Lynne off to them all, but she had been ordered to Rome before he had left Loro Ciuffenna. And everybody in the unit was tired out. They had suffered the worst casualties of the campaign at Montevarchi. John himself was sick at heart over Cobber's death. In his daydreams of eventual reunion with his friends, Sergeant-Major Cobber had always had a pride of place. 'What have you been up to, sir?' he had asked so often in John's imaginings. Now he would never speak to him again. Sergeant Price had been promoted in his place from No. 1 gun, a square tough little man, without any of Cobber's charm. Taffy was just the same, and Sholto, but Charles Pilling had retired into his shell and John found him remote. Everybody was talking about Taffy's exploits at Montevarchi so John was shy about mentioning his own adventures and kept quiet about Cowan in case it looked as though he was shooting a line.

He missed Lynne dreadfully and their little room above the bridge and also he had had no news of Mario since he had taken part in ambushes against the retreating Germans. John tried to get information from the British Military Government in Florence, but they were not the least interested in the fate of an Italian peasant from the south.

One day John had a summons to see Colonel Alex.

'You have a knack of getting yourself into unusual situations, haven't you Crabbe?' The blue eyes were like two laser beams.

'Yes sir.'

'I have here a report from a fellow called Gonshaw-Bliss, bloody silly name, but apparently he did a pretty good job. He says you shot and killed a renegade.'

'Well, yes sir.'

'Well don't be ashamed of it. No other officer in the Regiment has that distinction.' He paused. 'However, all is not sweetness and light because some cocky bastard at Brigade has it in for you, suggesting that after escape from the enemy you consistently went backwards not forwards and took three months to rejoin this unit. What have you to say to that?'

'That it is very unfair, sir.'

'Taking into account all the circumstances I am inclined to agree. I have spoken to the Brigadier and suggested a Court of Inquiry here. I told him I don't like my officers subjected to rumour and innuendo, so the Court can bring everything out into the open. Sholto will be with you to see fair play. It will convene next Monday. Oh, you can call any witnesses that you want, the Brigade Major will fix that.'

'I can call Lynne.' John decided as he saluted smartly, and this thought dispelled all other worries from his mind.

☆ ☆ ☆

The windows were wide open, even so the room was hot and stuffy. Dust particles danced in the shaft of sunlight which beamed on to the square wooden table, like the projection of a film in a cinema. Sounds of the town, vehicles grunting in low gear only partially obscuring the chatter of the locals, gave a clear indication that Pontassieve had come back to life.

The house, once elegant, now looted of all valuables by either German or Allied troops, probably both, was the Regimental HQ of the Home Counties Yeomanry. Out of the window behind the table one could see the meeting of two rivers, the Arno and the Sieve, and through the door blue mountains flecked with green nudged their way close to the large casement at the top of the stairs, or so it seemed. The smell of Italy also came through the window, rising heat brought a whiff of olive oil, vino, drains and strong tobacco.

Behind the table sat three men, a major in the middle with a staff captain on his right and a lieutenant on his left. John and Sholto sat on two chairs facing them.

The Major did not seem at all fierce. He wore rather thick glasses and his hair sprouted out each side from a bald head giving him the appearance of a university professor. The Staff Captain was rather good-looking, wavy hair and a little moustache rather like Robert Donat in "The Thirty-Nine Steps'. The Lieutenant was almost an Albino, very light hair was brushed back off his forehead, and the skin on his face had the fragile look of the very fair.

'It is damned hot but we'd better shut the door,' the Major said. The Lieutenant did so, moving silently across the room. John felt that if he had done it, he would probably have fallen over a chair. Sholto gave him a smile of reasurrance.

The Major spread out a map on the table and the other two peered at it. The silence in the upstairs room was pervasive, so when a dog barked suddenly just below the window, John jumped out of his skin.

'And then it started like a guilty thing,' Horatio's words from *Hamlet* came to him, and he felt himself blushing.

Whether the major noticed John's discomfort or not, he chose that moment to begin the proceedings.

'This is a Court of Inquiry, Crabbe,' he said 'not a Court Martial. Brigade have ordered us to find out certain facts, this is not unusual when an officer, or any rank for that matter, is away from his regiment for some time. In a Court Martial the prosecution thinks that it has a case against the accused, otherwise it would not have been convened, but in a Court of Inquiry we assume nothing. You are not in the dock, Crabbe. We have to find out what happened, that's all. You understand?'

'Yes sir.'

'We are meeting in the RHQ of your regiment for your convenience, so that you can feel free to call on anyone to give evidence and Major Sholto, your Battery Commander, is here in support, so to speak. Let me introduce the Court. Captain Cox is from Brigade and represents the Brigadier, Lieutenant Chase of the Indian Army was captured on the Rapido crossing at Cassino, but managed to escape, so he understands the problems, and I myself, Major Hetherington, was a lawyer before the war but am now an Infantry Battalion Commander.' He turned to the others. 'Are we ready, Gentlemen?' There was a murmur of assent, so Major Hetherington pushed the map to one side and picked up a sheaf of papers from the table.

'We have been reading, Mr Crabbe, a deposition based on your debriefing and also studying the relevant maps, so we have a good idea of the events that transpired after you were taken prisoner, but we would like to hear your account please; take your time, there is no hurry.'

John started hesitatingly at first, but soon began to get into his stride; he had made notes of the salient points, but it was all so vivid in his mind that he hardly referred to them.

'Would you say that you were rescued or kidnapped by the partisans?' the Lieutenant asked suddenly.

Sholto intervened.

'Mr Crabbe,' he said, 'is in the middle of a lengthy account of his story, it is very distracting for him to be interrupted; can we please leave any questions to the end?'

'Of course,' the Major said. 'Continue, Mr Crabbe.' The Lieutenant, though, did not appear the least put out by the implied reprimand, instead he pulled an envelope out of his pocket and started to scribble on the back.

John found it difficult to pick up the threads, the Lieutenant's interjection had thrown him, as was clearly the intention. When he finally came to the end, he felt, like in the aftermath of so many auditions in the theatre, that he had not done himself justice.

'Rescue or kidnap by the partisans, which was it?' the Lieutenant came in sharply as soon as John sat down.

'Rescue, they shot the German captain and may well have saved my life.'

'So you were under no duress from them.'

'No I wasn't.'

'Mr Crabbe,' Captain Cox's voice was so smooth that John found it intimidating, 'can we establish exactly where you were rescued?'

'A few miles away from Route 6.'

'You could not possibly have known exactly how far our troops were behind you, but did you have any idea?'

'No sir,' John replied 'I never knew exactly where the village was, but not more than a few miles from Route 6.'

'Where you were saved by the partisans?'

'Yes sir.'

'I see. Thank you.'

'You must have known, though,' the Lieutenant continued, 'that this village was not very far from the front line, what would you say ten to fifteen miles?'

'Twenty at least I would think.'

'All right, twenty, not very far from the 8th Army advancing up the Liri Valley, why did you not just stay in the crypt and wait for our troops to arrive?'

'Mario said the Germans were just down the road and likely to arrive before the Allies.'

'Mario?' the Major queried.

'The leader of the partisans, sir.'

'Oh yes. He was your constant companion for nearly three months?'

'Yes sir.'

'What sort of a chap is he?'

'He knew the country and was an excellent leader. He was also very brave. He taught me that all Italians are not cowards.'

'So you thought very highly of him.'

'Yes sir.'

'It was this Mario was it,' Captain Cox asked, 'who, each time you stopped at a stage in the Parcel Post, persuaded you to keep going north instead of staying put?'

'Because a British officer who was willing to be led away from the front was a very useful asset, whichever way the war went,' the Lieutenant remarked.

'It was not like that at all.' John blushed as he realised that his voice was becoming shrill again.

'I do not care for this line of questioning,' Sholto snapped, 'and I care even less for the attitude of the very junior member of the Court.'

'I think,' the Major replied gently, 'that Mr Chase's questions were quite in order. We are here to arrive at the facts.'

'Quite so,' Sholto glared at the Lieutenant, 'Well, the facts are that Mr Crabbe was taken to a village about twenty miles from the Allied Armies and advised by the partisans to get the hell out of it as the Germans were just down the road. As they were on the spot and in a position to know what was going on, I would certainly have taken their advice in similar circumstances. Wouldn't you, Major President?'

'I don't think that is really relevant, Major Sholto.'

'I do. You are a fighting soldier like myself, like Mr Crabbe. I suggest to you that all of us here might well have come to the same decision.'

There was an almost imperceptible grunt from the Lieutenant, not loud enough to constitute an impertinence to the Court, but loud enough to be heard.

'Very well, Major Sholto,' the President replied, 'let us continue to discuss the later developments.'

Captain Cox spoke next.

'You haven't been with your regiment very long, have you Mr Crabbe?'

'About eight months, sir.'

'Three of which you spent with your partisan friends.'

'No sir, with the Parcel Post.'

'An organisation to help escaped prisoners of war to become repatriated.'

'Yes sir.'

'How long ago did you do your basic training as an officer cadet?'

'Just over a year, sir.'

'Did they teach you, during that training, that if you were captured by the enemy, it was your duty to try and escape and rejoin the Army as soon as possible?'

'I think so, yes sir.'

'Well you must know. Did they teach you that or didn't they?'

'Yes sir.'

'And yet, having escaped within twenty-four hours of

your capture, it took you nearly twelve weeks to catch up with us, several hundred miles to the north.'

'It was how things worked out, sir.'

'Very convenient,' the Lieutenant muttered.

Sholto was on his feet. 'I am not having that,' he barked.

Major Hetherington turned to the Lieutenant. 'Any more remarks, Mr Chase, and you will leave the room. Understand?'

'Yes sir.' His face was expressionless.

'And in future you will only give an opinion when asked.'

'O.K. sir.' He had made his point.

John felt a cold feeling in the pit of his stomach, with a growing belief that he was losing control of the situation.

The President continued, 'So the next stop was Subiaco, which was not very far from Rome, was it?'

'No sir.'

'Did the Italian officer who was working for us,' he looked down at the deposition, 'a Captain Bartolini, did he inform you that Rome was full of escaped P.O.W.s, and that there were plenty of safe houses, even the Vatican was a possible source of asylum?'

'Yes sir.'

'Then why did you not make for there instead of shinning over the mountains in the opposite direction to Avezzano?'

'Because there was a rumour that the Germans were looking for me, as I was with the Captain when Mario shot him.'

'Rumour?'

'I think Captain Bartolini must have heard it on the phone or radio,' John concluded lamely.

Captain Cox now put in his oar, his voice like plush velvet.

'You left Avezzano, I understand, after about twelve hours, because you were told that the Germans might decide to defend it.'

'Yes sir.'

'So it would in that case become the front line.'

'That is what Giuseppe said.'

'The Italian at the safe house?'

'Yes sir. Actually he had the status of a British officer, the Germans hanged him.' John looked down, fighting back the tears.

'I'm sorry to hear that. The Tedeschi are not very gentle with those Italians who came over to us.' Having expressed his regrets without much conviction, Cox continued, 'You see, Mr Crabbe, I cannot understand why on earth you did not find yourself a hiding-hole and wait for the Allies to catch up. Instead you shot off again north to Perugia.'

The President intervened, 'After you came under the command of Captain Gonshaw-Bliss, I accept that you had no option but to obey orders, but before Perugia, three times in three different locations I feel that the opportunity was there to try and reach our lines if you had shown some personal initiative.'

'Major President,' Sholto said, 'we have a witness, an Intelligence Officer, who is in the building, who we might call at this point.'

'Of course, Major Sholto. I must add, however, that the Court is not interested in events after the arrival in Perugia, so will his testimony be relevant?'

'I am sure it will.'

'Fine. The Court would appreciate a discussion in private, so when you have collected your witness perhaps you would be kind enough to wait outside.'

'We will be in the trattoria opposite, Major President,' Sholto indicated Lieutenant Chase, 'so send your boy over to fetch us when you are ready.'

☆ ☆ ☆

The court had been expecting a man, so Lynne's entrance caused a minor sensation. The Lieutenant was no longer there, but had been replaced by a corporal clerk. Lynne was in uniform but she did not look like an A.T.S. officer. Her hair was not at all regulation, but swung jauntily on and off her shoulders. The cap which was tilted at a raffish angle gave the impression that it had been borrowed for a joke. She contrived, in this strange get-up, to appear both innocent and erotic at the same time.

Major Hetherington reopened the proceedings.

'Major Sholto,' he said, 'I formed the opinion that you were not very happy with having Lieutenant Chase on this court so I have dismissed him.'

'Thank you,' Sholto replied.

'Corporal Rogers here will take down the rest of the proceedings in shorthand, as the testimony is new and will not appear on the deposition.'

'A good idea, Major President.'

Major Hetherington turned to Lynne.

'Good morning. Company Commander is your rank, isn't it?'

'Just Commander, sir. The full rank was abolished some time ago. Commander Gardener,' Lynne added.

'Major Sholto has explained to you the remit of this Inquiry?'

'Yes sir.'

'Good.' For a moment he looked flustered, and then pulled himself together.

'You are an Intelligence Officer.'

'I am, sir, yes.'

'Please tell us as much as you can about your work. I appreciate that you have to be discreet.'

'I was part of an organisation known as the Parcel Post, which looks after Allied P.O.W.s behind enemy lines. There is no secret about this, the enemy knows all about us.'

'Is there a particular area that you covered?'

'Yes, for the last few months it has been between Perugia and Florence.'

Major Hetherington leaned back in his chair. 'I rather thought that might be your answer and therefore I doubt that you can help us, Commander. You see we acknowledge that once Mr Crabbe reached Perugia, he was bound to follow your orders, it is his movements prior to meeting up with you in which we are interested.'

'But I know all about them, sir.'

'How?'

'You don't imagine that we work in a vacuum, sir? We have to know all that is going on down the line. We were a large organisation ranging from Milan to south of Rome.' She smiled. 'The Fascists and the Germans know of our H.Q. in Milan, but they cannot find it.' She paused, 'From the time that Mr Crabbe arrived at Torrice, he was in our hands and under our orders. The priest in the crypt of the church was one of ours.'

'Torrice?' Cox asked.

'Yes that was the village near Route 6.'

Lynne was doing very well, for a moment Major Hetherington hesitated, uncertain exactly how to proceed.

Captain Cox, however, felt that he should have a go. His voice was even more black velvet.

'My,' he had contemplated saying 'my dear' but thought better of it, 'Commander Gardener, we are fascinated by your description of all the cloak and dagger stuff, but there are one or two stumbling blocks. First Mr Crabbe made no mention of the priest in the crypt being our agent, he inferred that the decision to go to Subiaco was Mario's.'

'Captain Cox,' Lynne raised her eyebrows, 'do you imagine that the priest would have said that he was a British agent with the crypt full of peasants and the Germans just down the road?'

Cox was conscious of the fact that Lynne was getting the better of the conversation, so he continued a little testily, 'Commander, is it not the object of your organisation to repatriate P.O.W.s?'

'Of course.'

'Well it took you a long time to achieve that with Crabbe, three months.'

'Because he was important to us.'

'I don't understand.'

'Then I will explain,' Lynne replied calmly. 'When the front was static, as at Cassino, we were able to channel our Parcels back to the Allied Armies, but when the war is mobile, the priority is to keep them safe. Our organisation is then stretched to the limit. As regards Mr Crabbe, we needed British officers badly to assist us. My area was run by one Army Captain and myself, so Mr Crabbc was moved back to the Pratomagno hills.'

'But —'

She interrupted him. 'Where he killed a German agent who had already started to undermine the whole organisation, we had a good bargain in this officer.'

Cox was having his nose put out of joint by a young girl and so the black velvet began to disappear.

'We have heard all about the Lieutenant shooting a spy

in Florence, very commendable I am sure, but it is not the brief of this Inquiry.' He paused, his cheeks becoming a little pink. 'The fact remains, and you cannot get away from this, that Second-Lieutenant Crabbe was lucky enough to escape during an air raid and then allowed himself to be led by a lot of "Ities" away from the Allied armies. We were fighting the Italians up to a few months ago, for God's sake, and they were always past masters at running away.'

Almost anyone could have intervened at this point. The President, though, was embarrassed that his second-in-command had lost his temper; Sholto and John felt that Lynne was entirely in control so kept silent. The Corporal clerk, sensing a bit of drama, looked up from his writing pad.

Lynne's eyes opened rather wide as they always did when she was angry. 'I am an "Itie", Captain Cox,' she said. 'My home is about fifteen miles from here at S. Martino. I am one of many Italians in the Parcel Post service. If you yourself were unlucky enough to be taken prisoner, your fate would be a P.O.W. camp in Germany, our fate would be death. As for the Italians like Mario, Captain Bartolini, the priest and many others, their families would die also.'

She then spoke directly to Major Hetherington. 'I will not complain, sir, about Captain Cox's offensive remarks because they are based on the ignorance of an officer who has not been in the field. My evidence is quite simple. Lieutenant Crabbe was under our orders from his arrival in Torrice. If you wish to have all this corroborated, the Brigadier N. Section will confirm everything I say. As a matter of fact, sir, I believe the Brigadier was rather angry when he heard about this Court of Inquiry. You see Mr Crabbe is rather a blue-eyed boy at Bari.'

Five hours later a lunch party was still in progress at the Trattoria Fortuna, Charles Pilling and Taffy had joined the three who were celebrating.

'I would love to have been a fly on the wall and seen Lynne puncturing the pomposity of the Staff Captain,' Taffy chuckled.

'She is one hell of a girl you have there, you lucky old sod,' Sholto observed, 'I hope you realise it.'

'I do.' John's happiness was complete. Major Hetherinton had advised them that he would report that in their view there was no irregularity in John's conduct after capture, which meant vindication. Captain Cox sulked but did not feel able to contest this opinion. After which Lynne gave both Sholto and his junior officer a hug and a kiss, not conduct entirely becoming for an officer in the A.T.S. And then after formal salutes all round, the three of them repaired to the trattoria across the road.

After several bottles of vino and an excellent lunch, during which time John and Lynne were asked to tell them their story from start to finish, John asked suddenly, 'Lynne, was the priest in the crypt one of our agents?'

'No. Obviously he was eager to help, but he was not one of the Parcel Post officers.'

'So what you said was not entirely accurate.' Sholto smiled at her.

'No. I don't even know that the village was Torrice, though by John's description I expect it was the one.'

'Your Brigadier will back you?' Charles asked.

'Yes.'

'You are sure?'

'Absolutely. What was completely true is that John is considered to be a blue-eyed boy at Bari. When I told the Brigadier I was called to this Inquiry, he said, "Bloody cheek. Tell them to keep their hands off that boy, or they will get a kick up the arse from me." '

'You delivered the kick yourself all right.' Sholto rubbed his hands together in glee. 'Right on the target, in the most ladylike way, of course.'

'Of course.'

'Well, they were splitting hairs in holding the Inquiry at all, we were quite right to retaliate with all our guns firing.' Taffy was becoming just a little drunk.

'To split hairs?' Charles asked.

'Oh, don't make fun of me, Charles, you know what I mean.'

'I love you, Taffy.' Lynne pressed his hand. 'Not as much as I love John, but quite a lot. Incidentally, I was worried that they might have used that, I expected Cox to bring it up, but I wouldn't let him get a word in.'

'Used what?' Sholto asked.

'The fact that John and I are lovers,' she said simply. John found himself blushing furiously. Lynne added, 'They might have said that my evidence was suspect.'

'But how on earth could they have known?' Pilling asked.

'Because I think Thomas was behind the whole thing.' She reminded them of the snubs which he had received in Positano and his fury at being shown up as a homosexual in front of John.

'He was posted to this Brigade after the fall of Rome. John's debriefing papers would be seen by him as a matter of course, he must have thought this was a Heaven-sent opportunity for revenge. You can imagine the whole scene can't you? Letting it be known about John's running away from school, allowing the poison to sink in, then suggesting this Court. Cox is probably a chum and I would guess that Chase was probably a boyfriend.'

'He must have worked pretty fast,' Sholto said.

'He is a very efficient staff officer, but he misread the signals. He underestimated the importance of Cowan's death, the whole incident was rather played down in the deposition; we had the whole weight of Bari H.Q. on our side, but he didn't realise that.'

'But all this is supposition, isn't it?' Pilling said.

'It is as good an explanation as any.' Sholto lit a cigar. 'We will never know for certain. Cheer up, though Johnnie, if it was Thomas, he has fallen flat on his face.'

'The bastard,' John mumbled.

'Oh yes, and as I said before and I will say it again, Thomas is a Welsh name, but I accept no responsibility (Taffy had difficulty with that word) for that abominable creep, he is a disgrace to the land of his fathers.'

'Hear, hear.' Lynne leaned over and kissed him. 'Major Sholto,' she said rather formally.

'Yes, Commander Gardener.'

'I have seven days leave starting on Monday. Could you wangle the same for Johnnie?'

'Done. But I expect a kiss first.'

☆ ☆ ☆

There was a carabinière on the gate of the villa at S. Martino. He saluted smartly as Lynne approached and when she began to talk to him, the tricorn hat tilted forwards as his eyes settled on her legs. John could hardly blame him, she was wearing a simple cotton dress and looked charming.

'Hi, you.' a Military Government Lieutenant came out. 'All Ities queue at the back.'

The army despised Mil.Gov., as it was called, looking upon them as a bunch of civilians who lorded it over the Italians and made a killing on the black market. It was an unfair generalisation, of course, but John shared this prejudice so he looked upon the fat little man with the toothbrush moustache disdainfully.

'Does she speak any English?' the man asked.

'A little,' John replied innocently.

'Hi, Signora, out the back, join the queue in the garden to see the small claims officer. Capito.'

Lynne ignored him, she and the carabinière were enjoying a huge joke.

'Look here,' the Lieutenant had become pink in the face, 'I am a British officer, do you know this girl?' he turned and glared at John.

'Johnnie,' Lynne turned round, 'hold this policeman's rifle, he wants to kiss my hand.'

It was quite an elaborate ritual. John took the rifle, the carabinière then bowed and kissed her hand, John handed back the rifle and the policeman presented arms. The face of the plump Lieutenant was a study.

Lynne turned to him and took her security pass out of her handbag.

'Take this officer and myself to your C.O. will you,' she said.

The Lieutenant was clearly impressed by the pass, but felt he ought to make some move to regain his dignity.

'I am not at all sure that the Colonel is free.'

'Then perhaps you could go and find out, please.' She underlined the last word.

A few moments later they were in a small study looking out on the garden. Behind a desk sat a white-haired colonel

with a row of First World War medals on his chest.
John saluted smartly while the colonel looked at the pass.
'Thank you for seeing me, sir,' Lynne said. There was a new respect in her voice, at last a proper soldier.
'Not at all. Who is this officer?'
'My fiancé, sir, may he stay?'
'He may.' He looked at John for a moment, he had gentle humorous eyes. 'You are an extraordinarily lucky young man.'
'Yes sir, I know.' John felt a mounting excitement, he had never dared mention her promise made by the Ponte Buriano, even now he could not be sure.
'What can I do for you, Commander Gardener?' He handed Lynne back her pass.
'This is my father's study sir.'
'I beg your pardon.'
'This is my house.' She explained the situation briefly.
'Good God. Your parents were able to depart for England before the war?'
'Yes sir, just.'
He was silent for a moment and then said. 'The ownership of this house will be made known to the proper authorities and you say there is a studio in Florence?'
'Yes, 46 Via Verdi.'
'You can leave everything to me. I suppose you would like to be taken round.'
'I would appreciate that sir, thank you.'
'You will find it painful?'
'Yes sir, I expect I will.'
'There was considerable looting and your garden has been churned up by tanks. We have cleaned the downstairs, where our officers are. My God, that explains it.'
'What sir?'
'All the English novels in the drawing room. Evelyn Waugh, Howard Spring, Aldous Huxley. I will keep them safe for you.'
'You are very kind sir, I am most grateful.'
'How old are you, Commander?'
'Twenty-three sir.'
My goodness, the Colonel thought, 'how the young grow up in a war, she has the poise and intelligence of a

woman twice her age.' "Come on," he said.

Upstairs everything of value had been taken and there was a deal of wanton damage, the duvets had been ripped open and even the bath and lavatory basins smashed. Below, the rooms looked shabby but tidy, army furniture had replaced the family's. They went to the drawing room last. It was exactly as Lynne had described it. A long, rather narrow room running the length of the house with three sets of French windows opening on to the garden. The front wall and the ceiling were decorated in *trompe l'œil*, cupids fired their arrows, cherubs blew their trumpets, while flowers and serpents coiled around slender pillars, all in grey and white, colour enough in the strong Italian light. The bookcase on the east wall was nearly full, having escaped the vandal's hand, mostly of English titles. Grass and weeds two feet high had taken over the garden and tanks had completed the ravages of time and war. But over the far hedge Florence rose like a phoenix, the orange pink of the *Duomo* glowing against a bright blue sky.

Lynne stood silent looking out towards the city, while the queue of Italians snaked across the terrace.

'What are the people waiting for, sir?' John asked the Colonel.

'To see us about small claims. They have had German and now Allied occupation, so it is all a shambles. We just try to unravel the mess, but it is a mammoth task. See yourselves out will you, I must go.'

Lynne turned round 'Thank you again, sir, for everything.'

'Not at all. Goodbye.'

They went back to the city in silence and stopped the car outside 46 Via Verdi. The whole house was boarded up and looked dismal and forlorn. They only stayed a minute and then Lynne drove down to the river and turned left for the doctor's house. Someone had painted a swastika on the wall between the windows of the first floor; they must have climbed up to one of the little balconies to do so.

Dr Lelli had lost weight and looked tired and drawn. After a warm welcome, John and Lynne followed him to the self same first floor room overlooking the river. She explained about the events and Cowan's death, while coffee was served.

'I was surprised, of course, when you all departed before you had drunk your coffee,' the doctor said 'but I am accustomed to very strange happenings during the war.' He looked at John. 'You must not feel bad because you shot this man, he was a traitor. Some of my compatriots think I am such a man. You saw the decoration outside the window?'

'Yes,' Lynne replied. 'Why for God's sake? Have you not had a letter from my C.O., he promised me he would send it as soon as the Germans had left.'

'Oh yes, I have had it. A kind letter signed by a Brigadier-General. Is that correct?'

'Just Brigadier now.'

'Ah I see. But my enemies say, and I have a few, that I worked for the Germans also, so what does it matter that I worked for the English.'

'What can I do to help?' Lynne asked.

'Nothing, Cara Mia, I have lost a few patients, but not many. The British also have jaundice in their army, so I help them as I helped the Tedeschi. So I am busy enough. But,' he took Lynne's hand, 'I am at the end of my road. I have a cancer in the stomach, in a year's time I will be dead. I would like to go to Lucca, I am not married as you know, but I have a *nipote*?'

'Niece.'

'Yes. Niece who lives there, I like her very much. It is near the sea at Viareggio.' He turned to John, 'Your Shelley drowned there and his body was burned on the sands. Puccini lived by a lake not far away. I do not wish to die in Florence, a city I love very much, while the worms come from the ground and paint my home with dirt.'

'When do you wish to go?' Lynne asked.

'I could leave in a month perhaps. I must of course hand over my patients first.'

'Give me a date and I will arrange for a truck to take you and your valuables to Lucca.'

'You can bring about such a miracle?'

'Yes.'

'The last day of next month.'

'I will arrange it.'

'Lynne, I have known you since you were six years. You were determined then and you always persuaded others to attend your wishes.'

'I must have been a horrible little brat.'

'No, never. Because you were ever charming and kind.'

They left the car at the house and walked along the river.

'Listen, Johnnie,' Lynne said, 'we must go back to the lane, to lay our ghosts.'

He followed her reluctantly down the drive off the Via Delle Casine and stopped abruptly when the avenue of maple trees began. There was still blood on the ground, no longer red but a chocolate brown, it had spread out over a wide area in patches, some of it almost worn away by passing feet.

He shuddered.

'Can we go to the S. Croce church?'

'It is closed — a shell landed behind the high altar.'

'Nowhere is sacred in war.'

'No.' She gently took his arm. 'You have to kill in war, many innocents die, but Cowan deserved your bullet. He would have handed us over to the Gestapo without a second thought, as he did with Giuseppe. He was a doctor's son from East Anglia who chose to fight for the Nazis. You were an actor, Johnnie, but this was not make-believe, you had the guts to pull the trigger. You ought to be proud of yourself.'

She kissed him. Then they strolled back to the car.

'Have you laid your ghost?'

'Yes.'

'Sure?'

'Quite sure.' It was true, John felt an extraordinary peace, as though a heavy load had been taken off his back.

Florence was now once again vibrating with life. Lynne and John booked in a hotel near the Palazzo Vecchio and then went out. It was late afternoom but the Palazzo was still open. They walked around like two tourists past the copy of Michelangelo's David and climbed to the upper rooms. Here they looked across the red roofs of the city to the Pratomagno hills, and John thought he could just see the Ponte Buriano where they had made the night crossing, but could not be sure.

The Uffizi Palace and gallery had not yet been re-opened, so they went to shop on the Ponte Vecchio.

John bought Lynne a bracelet. Six hearts with mosaic inlay strung out between little red stars. He really wanted to buy a ring, but had not yet the courage to discuss their future together, so decided that must wait. They crossed the river, visited the Pitti Palace and the San Miniato church on the hill. They were tired by the time they returned to the Piazza Vecchio, but Lynne wanted to make one more call. She took him to the Medici-Riccardi Palace near the *Duomo*. It was closed but the concierge, who she had known before the war, lived on the premises. After an Italian reunion accompanied by a torrent of language, many and intricate gestures and a deal of kissing, John was taken to the little chapel to see the frescoes. The biggest was *Voyage of the Three Kings* by Benozzo Gozzoli. He could not tear himself away from it, in this magnificent tableau of colour Renaissance Italy came alive again.

They found a restaurant near the Duomo and sat outside on the pavement. Inside, a girl was singing popular Italian songs including the now famous *Sorrento*, it wasn't hackneyed then, and her voice was clear and sweet. After two cognacs John plucked up courage to speak. The food was due to arrive any moment and it is difficult to propose whilst drinking soup.

'You called me your fiance at S. Martino,' he said.

'So I did.' She smiled at him.

'Don't tease me, Lynne, it is not fair.'

'I'm not. Like you I have been thinking long and hard about us. I meant what I said at the river crossing, and since then I have become used to you, Johnnie darling.'

'So you will.' John's voice was shaky.

'Let's get engaged anyway. But the war isn't over yet. When you and I meet at home, if we both feel the same way, we will marry. I am not refusing you Johnnie, just asking you to wait, that's all.' She took his hand. 'If this was a novel called "The Villa at S. Martino", we would marry in Florence and live happily ever after, but it is real life. There will be many difficulties after the war, your job and mine, where are we to live? I might wish to stay in Italy, and you might be off on tour, perhaps to

America. Anything could happen. The war could be over next year, it is not so long to wait.'

'You are right, of course, you always are. But I have dreamed ever since the river crossing. In my heart I knew it was a fantasy, but —'

'I have punctured your dream.'

'Yes.'

The waiter came and smiled indulgently. John remembered the lunch on Capri when the Padrone had been so fatherly with a young couple in love.

After he had gone, Lynne said, 'We have six more days on leave, Johnnie, and I will not be recalled this time. I have made sure of that.'

'How?'

'G-B has a conscience about you. He thinks he misjudged you and the situation, which he did. So I asked two favours. One to be left alone for my leave and secondly for him to arrange Dr Lelli's transport to Lucca. He agreed and doesn't break his word.'

The sun had almost set as they walked to their hotel. The *Duomo* had lost its orange glow and appeared navy blue against the evening sky. Night clubs and bars were just coming to life, but John and Lynne had been a long way together and on this their first day of leave, they wanted an early night.

By common consent the next day they decided to go back to Loro Ciuffenna. They crossed the Ponte Buriano, parked the car and strolled towards the river bank where they had crouched in the marshland a few months before. There was a party of sappers clearing the minefield upstream and a few trucks dotted around.

A sergeant came up to them. 'This is a restricted area, sir,' he said. 'You should not really have left the road. If my C.O. catches you, he will blow his top.'

'I am sorry, Sergeant,' John replied, 'we crossed this river some time ago when it was in German hands. This lady is an A.T.S. officer.'

'Be that as it may, sir, it is dangerous here. We borrowed an Itie, one of those so-called partisans. He was able to tell us where the mines started, but Jerry remembered to take away his "Achtung Minen" notices, so I must ask you to keep your distance.'

Then two things happened simultaneously. From the direction of the Ponte Buriano a Jeep came along the track, driven by an irate red-faced major and, from the minefield, a lone figure with a big black beard came dancing towards them.

'Carla, Giovanni, Carla, Giovanni,' he shouted at the top of his voice. Mario lifted both of them in turn right off their feet and there were kisses and hugs all round.

'I speak Inglése, buono, my work finito, I show them the mines, now we must be briaco, molto briaco.'

The Jeep pulled up sharply. 'What the hell do you think you are doing?' the Major shouted at John.

'About to get very drunk sir,' John replied.

'Si molto briaco, Maggiore,' said Mario.

'I think they may well be right sir,' said Lynne, as they linked arms and ran back to the car.

Appendix

'You must not do anything, keep silent, you nearly got us shot back at Campo Staffi. Leave everything to me. We spend the night here and leave in the morning at dawn. Capistrello is just below us, and from there there are a number of small roads over flat lands leading to Avezzano. If we are lucky we should not meet the Tedeschi, they will use the main route. The Trattoria Firenze is near the railway station, the padrone there will tell us what to do. Understand?'